GRIEVOUS BODILY HARM

A TONI DAY MYSTERY

Jane Bennett Munro

GRIEVOUS BODILY HARM
A TONI DAY MYSTERY

iUniverse books may be ordered through booksellers or by contacting:

iUniverse
1663 Liberty Drive
Bloomington, IN 47403
www.iuniverse.com
1-800-Authors (1-800-288-4677)

ISBN: 978-1-5320-2756-7 (sc)
ISBN: 978-1-5320-2757-4 (e)

Library of Congress Control Number: 2017911926

Print information available on the last page.

iUniverse rev. date: 09/21/2017

Also by Jane Bennett Munro

Murder under the Microscope
Too Much Blood
Death by Autopsy
The Body on the Lido Deck

For my friend Banu—

may she never again have to deal with this nonsense

CHAPTER I

With devotion's visage
And pious action we do sugar o'er
The devil himself.

—*William Shakespeare,* **Hamlet**

Marcus Manning entered my life innocuously enough.

The entire medical staff knew we were getting a third administrator. We'd heard all about him at previous staff meetings.

He'd received his bachelor's degree at Brigham Young University and his MBA at UCLA, after which he'd served in a variety of administrative positions at various hospitals in the LA area and Orange County, my old stomping grounds. But that wasn't what impressed my colleagues the most, oh no. Marcus Manning was homegrown. He was descended from one of the earliest and most prominent Mormon families to settle in Idaho. He'd been raised right here in Twin Falls. People knew him.

In particular, Jack Allen, our chief of staff, knew him. Or rather, Jack's brother did. Jack's brother, also a hospital administrator, had worked with Marcus at a hospital in Orange County. As Jack was telling his brother all about our hospital's growing pains, Marcus was expressing a desire to return to his roots. I guess it was inevitable that Marcus should end up here. A match made in heaven? Time would tell.

His references described him as "up and coming," a "ball of fire," a "mover and a shaker," and a "force to be reckoned with." They stated further that Marcus had accomplished "great things" at all the hospitals where he'd worked, bringing them into the twenty-first century, implementing computer systems, and the like. Jack's brother described him as a "really great guy" and a "breath of fresh air."

In short, Marcus seemed to be exactly what Perrine Memorial needed. We'd had enough trouble dragging ourselves out of the nineteenth and into the twentieth century, let alone the twenty-first. To me, he sounded too good to be true. And you know what they say about that.

The breath of fresh air first made his appearance at the June medical staff meeting. At first glance, I thought that JFK had been resurrected from the dead. The resemblance was uncanny. Marcus Manning was tall, at least six two, and built like an athlete. He wore his blond-streaked, light brown hair slightly long, with that Kennedyesque sweep across the forehead. His deeply tanned face had just the right degree of cragginess to keep it from looking too boyish, with deep-set, bright blue eyes in which one could see the Pacific Ocean and the California sun. If he'd been twenty years younger, he'd have looked right at home on a surfboard. He smiled with a mouthful of straight white teeth that gave the impression that he possessed more than the requisite number of them and caused the crinkles around his eyes to become even more appealing.

There he stood, in the middle of a group of male doctors that kept increasing in number. As more arrived, he shook hands with the newcomers and flashed that smile. I predicted that our predominantly female workforce would be talking about him for some time to come. The cubicles would be buzzing big-time.

Jeannie Tracy from internal medicine had already helped herself to the buffet lunch and found a seat near the end of the long table that ran the length of the conference room. Jeannie, a petite platinum blonde who looked deceptively like Tinker Bell but took no shit from anyone, seemed singularly unimpressed. I caught her eye, and she gave me an eye roll. I decided to forgo the locker room huddle in the center of the room and collected my own lunch at the buffet before joining Jeannie at the table.

She jerked a derisive thumb in their direction. "Jeez Louise, would you look at them? They're practically *drooling* over him. Anyone would think he's Brad Pitt."

I shrugged. "He's either a good ole boy or a hell of an actor. And he looks good too. What more could they possibly want in an administrator?"

She shook her head. "'Handsome is as handsome does,' as my mother used to say. Personally, I wouldn't trust him as far as I could throw him."

"I know what you mean," I said. "Beauty is only skin deep, but asshole goes all the way to the bone."

I'd barely gotten that out of my mouth before the others began to join us at the table, and to my dismay, I found myself directly across from our guest. I hoped he hadn't heard what I'd said.

Marcus Manning favored me with his bright white smile and stuck his hand out. "Marcus Manning," he said. "And you are?"

With that, the Kennedyesque aura vanished. He clearly didn't pahk his cah in the Hahvahd yahd.

I shook his hand. "Toni Day," I said. "Pathology. And this is Jeannie Tracy, internal medicine." My partner, Mike Leonard, was busy doing frozen sections. He might make it later, but I knew better than to count on it.

He shook Jeannie's hand too. Jack Allen took his place at the head of the table, with our current administrator, Bruce Montgomery, known to nearly everybody as Monty, and assistant administrator, Charlie Nelson, on his right and left, respectively.

Monty and Charlie were the Mutt and Jeff of administration. Monty, tall, spare, gray haired, and severe, always stood and sat ramrod straight. Charlie, on the other hand, was relaxed, plump, and jolly and favored three-piece suits with a watch on a chain. Unaccountably, a space had been left vacant on Marcus's right. Mitzi Okamoto, from radiology, took it and introduced herself to him.

When she turned back to face me, her normally impassive

countenance wore an expression of severe distaste. Anyone who didn't know her well probably wouldn't have noticed it, but I'd known Mitzi long enough to recognize what her barely perceptible expressions meant. A diminutive second-generation Japanese American, Mitzi was the personification of inscrutable.

As her eyes met mine, I gave her a slight nod. I knew what it was that she had seen. One glance at Jeannie told me that she'd seen it too.

The smile, seen head-on, did not reach to those Pacific-blue eyes. They remained as cold as the Humboldt Current.

This guy was trouble.

CHAPTER 2

Man is the only animal that blushes. Or needs to.

—Mark Twain

After giving everyone a chance to eat lunch, Jack Allen, a short, wiry, terrier type with dark hair and eyes, stood up and called the meeting to order. Jack was a born leader; maybe that was why he was chief of staff so often. He introduced our new junior administrator and asked all the doctors to introduce themselves in turn, which we did, even though Marcus had already met nearly all of us. Then, in an effort to lighten the mood and relieve tension, Jack got off one of his usual sexist and politically incorrect comments by remarking that Marcus was starting off true to form, surrounded by girls.

"Bullshit," said Jeannie sotto voce. "We were here first."

Jack didn't notice. He continued on. "As you all know, the recession that began in 2008 had a severe adverse effect on our bottom line. More patients can't pay their bills, third-party payers aren't paying as much or as soon, and complying with all these new government regulations is costing us a fortune. We've taken on ten more physicians, and we've got more than enough patients to go around, but we don't have any place to put them! We need more office space, more emergency room space, more bed space, more operating rooms—"

"More lab space," I contributed. Jack glared at me. I glared back.

The medical staff tended to gloss over the lab's needs, but that didn't make those needs any less real, and I had no intention of letting them get away with it. Therefore, I had earned a reputation as somewhat of a pest at medical staff meetings.

"Because of our space constraints," Jack continued, "we are in danger of losing our JCAHO accreditation, and you know what that will do to our Medicare and Medicaid reimbursement."

I didn't back down. "Our lack of lab space is considered not only hazardous but an impediment to patient care, and we stand to fail our next inspection over it. Losing CAP accreditation would also lose us Medicare and Medicaid reimbursement."

Jack sighed. "Toni, nobody asked for your two cents' worth."

Jack tended to be intolerant of interruptions. When God was passing out patience, Jack must have been in the bathroom.

I folded my arms and gave him my best impassive face. "You never do. You're getting it anyway."

Monty spoke up. "Doctor, you're out of order."

"I know. I'm sorry. Just don't overlook the lab. That's all I ask."

Jack appeared rattled. "Toni, we have no intention of overlooking—"

"Don't overlook diagnostic imaging either," Mitzi said. "We're in the same boat."

Jack cast his gaze at the ceiling. "Could we please have no more comments from the peanut gallery?"

"Objection!" Jeannie said. "Disrespectful and sexist. Our respective heights are irrelevant."

At five three, I was taller than both my female colleagues and nearly as tall as Jack.

"Pot calling kettle black here," I murmured to nobody in particular.

Jack either didn't hear me or purposely ignored my comment. "If you girls are finished, could we get on with this?"

"*Girls?*" Jeannie asked in mock outrage. "Do you suppose you could bring yourself to address us as 'ladies'? Or better yet, 'doctors'?"

"Take it easy, Jeannie," Mitzi said. "It's better than when he used to call us 'broads.'"

"No way!" Jeannie gasped in mock astonishment.

"Ladies," Monty said severely, "I can't allow you to continue to disrupt this meeting. We only have so much time and a great deal to cover."

Marcus's gaze moved back and forth between us as if he were watching a tennis match. Jack's face had taken on a delicate shade of puce. I decided to put him out of his misery. "We're done," I said graciously. "Please continue."

Jack took a moment to collect himself. The other doctors had begun to shift restlessly in their seats and talk among themselves. "Gentlemen," he began.

I raised a finger.

"And *ladies*," he added. "In case you've forgotten, I was addressing our severe space constraints. We can't expand in our present location, because we're landlocked. We can't go up, because the foundation and walls won't support the added weight. We can't afford to build in another location. Something has to give, or we'll be forced to close."

A collective gasp ran around the room.

"However, salvation may be at hand. We've received an offer from Cascade Medical Enterprises, out of Washington State, to buy our hospital and build us a brand-new one at a new location where there would be plenty of room to expand. They propose to purchase a forty-acre tract of farmland northwest of town, and if construction begins right away, the new hospital, which would be called Cascade Perrine Regional Medical Center, should be ready for occupancy two years from this summer."

Cascade Perrine Regional. CPR Medical Center. *How appropriate,* I thought, *because that is essentially what Cascade Medical Enterprises would be doing for us: resuscitation.*

"However," Jack continued, "the matter has to be put to a vote of the medical staff, and before we do that, everyone should be aware of the financial ramifications. Monty, would you mind?"

"Not at all, Doctor." Monty rose and began distributing sealed envelopes. The one he handed me had my name on it. Mitzi's and Jeannie's bore their names as well.

"The envelopes Monty's passing around contain each physician's individual financial information—your buyouts, your equity in any partnerships you may have made capital contributions to, and your equity in the building. Cascade has agreed to pay off our mortgage and buy all of you out of your partnerships and pension plans. These documents show what each of you stands to gain monetarily if we accept Cascade's proposal and the tax consequences thereof."

An excited murmuring ensued as each of us looked at our documents. I gasped. Under Cascade's proposal, I stood to receive nearly a million dollars. Unfortunately, I wouldn't get to keep much of it after taxes.

There's always a catch, I thought.

"What's the downside?" asked Dave Martin, from family practice, as if he'd read my mind.

"We won't be independent anymore," Jack said. "We'll be part of a system. Cascade has hospitals all over the Pacific Northwest, including Boise. Our policies will have to be consistent with those of the system. The equipment we buy will be from the same vendors used by the rest of the system, in order to take advantage of the volume discount. We won't be able to pick and choose like we could before."

"What about our offices?" asked Jeff Sorensen, a general surgeon.

"Those of you who have offices here in the hospital will have offices in the new hospital," Jack said. "The others will be given the opportunity to have offices there if they want them. These are things to be dealt with down the road. All of us will be involved in the plans for the new hospital, as will the department heads. There will be a lot of meetings with the architects if we accept this offer."

"So how long do we have to dink around about this before we vote?" George Marshall, our curmudgeonly gastroenterologist, asked, pulling at his moustache.

"We can vote today," Jack replied, "as long as nobody has a problem with the offer."

"I call for the question," George growled.

Apparently everyone in the room was tired of dinking around. The vote was unanimous in favor.

That had to be some kind of a record. Usually getting a bunch of doctors to agree on anything was like herding cats.

Jack had to raise his voice over the cacophony of hoots, whistles, and high fives to get our attention. "Please, everyone, settle down. We're not done."

The room slowly quieted. Jack continued, "So in keeping with our move into the future, with a new hospital and our new medical staff, it seems appropriate that our administration should also undergo a face-lift, and Monty will tell you all about that. Monty?" Jack sat down.

Monty stood up. "As you know, I've been administrator here at Perrine Memorial for the last thirty years, and even with all that I've experienced along the way, I feel singularly unprepared to tackle a new hospital. Changes are coming at me so fast it's like a tsunami. I'm sixty-two years old, gentlemen, and I'm tired. I'm drowning, and all I want to do is get my ass off the beach."

Titters ensued. Monty was a Mormon bishop and usually proper to the point of stuffiness, so his remark took everyone by surprise. He must have been really tired to let his guard down that much.

"I want to retire," he went on. "I want to spend time with my grandchildren. I want to go on a mission with my wife. But I'm willing to continue, at least for a while, as long as I have help. My plan is to step down and let someone else step up."

Charlie Nelson, our present assistant administrator, shifted uncomfortably in his seat as everyone turned and looked at him. Charlie was in his early fifties, somewhat computer literate, and had great people skills (i.e., everybody liked him). But hospital administration wasn't a popularity contest. Sometimes unpopular decisions had to be made, and Charlie usually passed the buck on those right back to Monty, whose austere personality was much better suited to delivering bad news. Someone had to step up, and that person clearly wasn't going to be Charlie.

"So this is the plan," Monty continued. "We've created the position of chief operating officer, who will be in charge of ancillary services, and that position will be held by Marcus. I will continue to hold the position of chief executive officer for one more year. Charlie will continue as chief financial officer for the next six months. At the end of six months, Charlie and Marcus will switch positions. That way, Marcus will become familiar with both positions.

"At the end of the year, Marcus will become CEO, Charlie will go back to CFO, and I will be COO. In the meantime, we'll start looking for another COO. When we find one, I'll retire, but until then, I'll be around to provide guidance, if Marcus should need it. Any questions?"

I looked around. My colleagues were all nodding sagely, as if it were a no-brainer. I had to agree. Theoretically, it should work. It all made sense.

There was only one thing wrong with it. The COO was directly in charge of ancillary services, otherwise known as lab and radiology— sorry, diagnostic imaging. I guessed that if I was going to keep up with the modern terminology, I'd have to give the lab a fancy new name too, like clinical pathology, not to be confused with anatomic pathology, the body parts division. As a general pathologist, I was board certified in both. So was Mike.

But fancy names aside, if Marcus lived up to my suspicions of him, it meant that Mitzi and I were in deep doo-doo, at least for the next six months. After that, Charlie would be COO and Marcus CFO, which put Marcus in a position to approve or disapprove any capital expenditures for lab or x-ray equipment.

Mitzi and I would still be in deep doo-doo.

Then, if all went well, Marcus would become CEO and be in charge of everybody and everything.

Then the deep doo-doo would hit the fan.

I knew that when I went home and told my husband, Hal, about all this, he would tell me that (a) I had a shitty outlook on the situation and (b) I was probably getting all upset for nothing, because I always imagined the worst-case scenario, and he would be right about that, because I always did. Most of the time it never happened.

But sometimes face-lifts just don't accomplish what they're intended to. Sometimes they just make things worse. This felt like one of those times.

I also knew that if I didn't start paying attention, I'd miss out on the rest of the grand scheme.

Jack said, "If the new hospital is to remain viable in the community, we need to improve our public relations. Therefore, we've also hired a public relations officer, who will be in charge of outreach—that is, forming relationships within the community and encouraging their business. I'd like to introduce you all to Debra Carpentier, who will give us an overview of her plan. Debra?"

An attractive but unfamiliar blonde at the opposite end of the table stood and came forward to the head of the table. I couldn't imagine why I hadn't noticed her before; she had to be at least six feet tall. She had very long, shapely legs and wore four-inch heels.

As a five-foot-three woman in Birkenstocks, I really hate six-foot women in spike heels on principle. The last one of those I'd encountered had damn near gotten me killed. So I was prepared to dislike Debra Carpentier on sight, but as she spoke, I feared that I'd have to revise my assessment. She had a nice smile, complete with smile lines. Her dark blonde hair escaped in curly tendrils from her slightly messy ponytail. Her long legs ended in generous hips. Her shirttail had come partially untucked, and she unselfconsciously tucked it in as she spoke. In other words, she was human.

She also had a rather ambitious agenda, about which she spoke fluently without referring to notes.

"Dr. Allen is right," she told us. "It's time for hospitals to become part of the community, and to that end, I propose that the hospital become a member of the chamber of commerce and take part in Business After Hours, in which members entertain the community with after-work cocktail parties on Thursday nights."

I imagined that all of us had heard about the Twin Falls Chamber of Commerce Business After Hours. It had been in the paper and on TV. The first business to host it, six months ago, had been a local car dealership.

"These are open to the public but also serve as a venue at which business owners can deal and network. I also propose that we prepare a series of new commercials to air on local radio and TV stations; some of these would consist of short interviews with various doctors. We could also have some of the doctors interviewed in more depth on the morning news. This would familiarize our public with our medical staff and make us look more human."

I looked at Mitzi. She shrugged. We both knew that diagnostic imaging and pathology had an exactly zero percent chance of being asked to give one of those interviews.

"We'll hold health fairs," Debra continued, "for certain groups of people, like the college, city, and county employees and employees of various large local industries. Department heads could conduct tours of their departments for junior high and high school students, and some of us could give presentations at the schools. In fact, one of the surgeons has already volunteered to coordinate that program, and now I'll turn the meeting over to him. Dr. Jensen?"

As Debra Carpentier went back to her seat, Russ Jensen replaced her at the head of the table.

Russ, a general surgeon, was exactly what everybody would want their doctors to look like when they grew up and got old. He had a generous head of wavy salt-and-pepper hair and heavy eyebrows that shaded his deep-set eyes but didn't hide the twinkle in them. He also had that slightly plump and rumpled appearance that made him look comfortable, like the good ole family doc of yesteryear. His bedside manner was comfortable too. Russ was deeply involved in serving the community, and this was just another way to do it besides giving smoking cessation classes, doing athletic physicals, and having students shadow him at work.

"Thank you, Debra," he said. "I've arranged to teach a class at the high school called Health Occupations. Every week we'll have a different specialty represented. Not just doctors either. Representatives from all departments will be part of this, from transcription to information technology. I'll be teaching two days a week, and I'll be calling upon all the doctors and many of the other employees to teach the other three days—a different specialty or department each week. How you divide up that time is up to you. I'll be coming around later to set those up individually, depending on your schedules."

Oh, goody. Teaching high school. My heart sank. If I'd wanted to teach, I'd have gone to a big university hospital with a medical school affiliation. Or skipped medical school altogether.

I left the conference room immediately after the meeting adjourned, eager to get back to my department and tell Mike all about it, as I suspected Russ would waste no time in lining us up for his Health Occupations class. But I didn't get the chance.

I might have known. Pathologists are pretty easy to locate during the workday, unlike surgeons. We're usually either in our offices or our labs, right there in the hospital.

Russ Jensen was practically right on my heels as I walked into Mike's office to bring him up to date. "Wonderful!" he said. "You're both here. I need to schedule you guys for my Health Occupations class at the high school."

"Health Occupations class?" Mike asked.

"Russ is going to teach this class," I told him, "and he's going to have all the doctors and the various department heads and some of the other employees come and talk about their specialties and their jobs to the students."

"Wait a minute," Mike begged. "You mean us too? We've gotta get up in front of a bunch of smart-ass high school kids and tell them what we do for an entire class period?"

"Absolutely," Russ said. "How does the third week of September grab you?"

"Week?" Mike yelped.

"Not the whole week," I said. "Just three days of it."

"You can divide it up any way you want," Russ encouraged.

"Right," I said. "One day each for us, histology, and the lab."

"Oh, no," Russ said. "The lab gets its own week. You and histology divide up the three days any way you want."

"So we'll do two days, and histology can do the third," I said. "The third week of September is fine. I suppose you want the lab the week before or the week after?"

"The week after," Russ said.

"Do you want to tell Margo, or shall I?" I asked.

"Would you mind doing that?" Russ asked. "It would sure save time."

I consented, and Russ left in search of his next victim.

Mike looked as if he'd been punched in the stomach. "Jesus," he moaned. "Two days? How the hell did we ever get into this? I hope you didn't volunteer us, I tell you what—"

"Don't tell me you've got stage fright," I teased.

Mike put both hands over his face and groaned heartrendingly. Lucille, my senior histotech, poked her bleached-blonde head around the door. "You guys okay in here?" she asked. "Sounds like somebody's dying."

"Somebody is," Mike mumbled through his hands. "Me."

"He's okay," I told her. "He's just clowning around. Go back to work." She'd find out soon enough, I figured.

Lucille vanished, and I turned back to Mike. "Chill," I told him. "This is June. We've got until September. Now all we have to do is talk people into participating."

Mike Leonard had come to Perrine five years before. His father-in-law had been doing a locum tenens—that is, filling in for me during a time when I was fighting a murder charge and couldn't work. The poor man had been so overworked that he'd browbeaten administration into recruiting a second pathologist, and Mike just happened to be finishing up his residency without a job offer in sight.

Mike was from Texas, from a family of five brothers and a pathologist father. His perpetually sunny disposition made my work situation much more pleasant than it had been before. But sometimes the most gregarious people turn to jelly at the thought of public speaking, especially in front of a class of smart-ass high school students.

Poor Mike. For his sake I'd tried to sound more confident than I actually felt. I'd worked my way through medical school as a medical technologist and had some training in histology, so I could have done the whole thing myself, but I didn't really want to. Things had changed since I was in school, and my techs knew that better than I. On the other hand, I couldn't think of anyone in the lab whose forte was teaching or public speaking, and I couldn't really see either of my histotechs wanting to do it either.

But I didn't have a chance to worry about it, because my next visitor was the illustrious Marcus Manning himself, the smile firmly plastered in place.

What he had to tell me, however, was nothing to smile about.

CHAPTER 3

There is less in this than meets the eye.

—Tallulah Bankhead

"I took a chance that you'd have some time to talk to me now, because this is a fairly urgent matter," he said, and before I had a chance to object, he had planted his butt firmly in my visitor's chair.

Uh-oh. I had no idea what urgent matter he was talking about, which was worrisome, but the urgent matter to which he referred was the farthest thing from my mind.

"Are you planning to retire anytime soon?"

"Retire? Are you serious? I'm only forty-five."

The smile remained firmly fixed in place. "Serious as a heart attack," he said. "I've heard a number of complaints about you, and before we take any kind of action, I thought I'd just check and see if there might be a painless way to replace you. For instance, if you could retire or voluntarily resign …"

Painless for whom?

I sank into my chair, feeling as if I'd been poleaxed.

I couldn't believe my ears. What complaints? My colleagues had never been reticent when they had problems with me or the lab; it was compliments they seemed to have trouble with. Besides, Marcus Manning had only been here for one day. Not even one day; only part of a day. When had he had time to collect a "number" of complaints? Had he spent the morning going around quizzing the other docs about me and the lab? If so, why? Who told him to do that? Or had it been his idea?

As my head buzzed with questions, my mouth remained open, and no words came out. At least not until he reached out and idly picked up the picture of Hal and me, taken on our tenth anniversary, that sat on my bookcase. "Is this your husband?" he asked. "No children?"

That did it. My marriage and my lack of fecundity were none of his damned business. "Put that down," I snapped.

Startled, he did so. Now it was his turn to stare at me with his mouth open while I attacked. "Now you tell me about these complaints. What are they? Who complained?"

Marcus recovered quickly. "I'm not at liberty to say," he said smugly, the smile back in place.

"Bullshit," I told him and then called for backup. "Mike! Could you come here, please? Now?"

That wasn't usually the way I summoned my partner, but these weren't usual circumstances. Mike appeared in the connecting doorway between our offices. "You bellowed?" he asked.

"Have you heard any complaints about me?" I demanded, without bothering to introduce Marcus. The son of a bitch was on his own.

"No," Mike said. "Why?"

Before I had a chance to answer, Marcus stood and smoothly interjected, "I'm Marcus Manning, the new COO." He extended a hand. "And you are?"

This tactic was intended to put Mike on the defensive, but it didn't. "Mike Leonard. Glad to meet y'all. Now what's all this crap about complaints? And what the hell's a COO?"

Attaboy. That put Marcus on the defensive. "Chief operations officer," he answered. "I'm in charge of ancillary services, which includes the laboratory and pathology, as you know. I've received a number of complaints about these services in general, and Dr. Day in particular. They need to be dealt with before things get any worse." He calmly resumed his seat.

"Apparently things are so bad that I'm supposed to either retire or voluntarily resign," I told my partner.

Mike burst out laughing. Marcus looked nonplussed.

"You gotta be kidding," Mike said. "You don't know what you're talking about. Everybody loves Toni. It's me they've got issues with, because I don't mollycoddle 'em like she does."

Now I had to suppress laughter, because this was pure bullshit on Mike's part. I didn't mollycoddle anybody either. Mike was a good ole boy. He spent a lot more time chatting with the other docs than I did, so if there'd been any complaints of the severity that Marcus had implied, Mike would certainly know about them.

And since Mike was such a good bullshit artist himself, his bullshit-o-meter was in excellent working order, which gave me courage. "So Mike hasn't heard anything about these so-called complaints either," I said. "And you're not willing to tell me what they are or whose they are, so I can't deal with them. So I can't help but think that you're making the whole thing up to intimidate me and get me to resign. Now why would you do that?"

Marcus opened his mouth, but I didn't give him a chance to speak, because the reason had just occurred to me. "Aha! I know—it's because you've got somebody in mind to replace me. That's it, isn't it?"

Mike didn't give Marcus a chance either. "Now that's just plumb crazy. Didn't anybody tell you that Toni started this department from scratch, right out of residency? It's her damn department, for Chrissakes. What makes you think she's gonna just lie down and let you walk all over her?"

Marcus stiffened. "There are ways to make that happen," he said, reminding me of something out of a bad World War II movie, or perhaps Colonel Klink from the old *Hogan's Heroes* series.

Mike wasn't through. "You don't say. Well, I'm here to tell you, this lady is tough. Did you know that since she's been here she's solved two murders and survived two attempts on her life? If she can do that, she sure as hell can survive you. Who the hell do you think you're gonna replace her with?"

Marcus didn't get a chance to answer that either, because a surgical tech in scrubs appeared in my doorway with a specimen for frozen section. I rose from my chair to accept it, looking upon it as a means of escape and totally forgetting that Mike was on call, not me.

"We're not done with this conversation," Marcus said.

"Oh yes we are," I retorted. "You're not going to stay here and harass me while I do this."

"I'm not harassing you," he said. "That's a woman's argument." The smile was long gone.

"This isn't about gender," I said. "It's about patient care. You can call it whatever you want, but I'm not doing anything with this specimen until you leave, and when surgery calls to find out what's taking so long, I'm going to tell them. No, why wait? Why don't I just tell them now and save time?" I picked up the phone.

"Hang on," Mike said. "Toni, I'll take care of that frozen. I'm the one on call, not you." He held out his hand. I gave him the specimen, and he left.

Marcus, unfortunately, didn't. "There *is* another way to handle this, Doctor."

Yes, there is. How about you get the hell out of here and leave me alone? I put down the phone and narrowed my eyes at him. "And what would that be?"

"I could be induced to forget the whole thing."

"Really. And what would that entail exactly?"

"Nothing much. All you need to do is just be nice to me." He smirked.

Be nice to him? Did that mean what I thought it meant? I felt my blood pressure rise at the very thought, but I held on to my temper and continued to play dumb. "Well, then these complaints can't be very significant, can they, if that's all I've got to do. So why bring them up in the first place?"

"I don't think you understand, Doctor," Marcus said smoothly. "Surely you know what I'm referring to when I say 'be nice to me'?"

Suddenly I'd had more than enough of this conversation. "Yes, I suspect I do," I said, equally smoothly, "and I must say I'm appalled. In fact, I'd advise you to get out of my office while you're still in one piece."

Mike came back into my office just in time to hear that last remark. "What the hell's going on here?" he demanded.

"I'm not sure," I said, "but I think I've just been sexually harassed."

CHAPTER 4

Conceit in weakest bodies strongest works.

—*William Shakespeare, **Hamlet***

Marcus smiled and held up both hands. "I think Dr. Day misunderstood me. I was merely suggesting that she assist me in getting to know more about this department, since I'm COO and in charge of ancillary services."

The hell you were, you oily bastard. "I'm sure Mike would be glad to do that," I said sweetly. "Since I'm about to be fired and all."

I waited, curious to see how Marcus would handle this. Apparently he'd decided to run away and fight again another day, because he nodded in Mike's direction, said merely, "Sounds good," and left.

"What the hell was that all about?" Mike asked as soon as Marcus was out the door.

"He said all this business about me having to resign could all go away if I would just 'be nice to him,'" I said, making air quotes. "Now how would you interpret that?"

"Probably just about the same way you did," he said. "And if I were you, I'd tell Monty about it."

Tell Monty about it. Sure. I knew Mike was right, but right then I was more anxious to know if there was any substance to Marcus's claim that there were complaints about me than I was about being sexually harassed. Sexual harassment was old hat to me—there'd been so much of it in medical school. I sank into my chair and put my head in my hands. What the hell was really going on here? Supposedly there were complaints serious enough for me to be fired but not so serious that a little dalliance on my part wouldn't make them go away.

What I needed to do was talk to some of the doctors most likely to have complained, because I suspected the complaints didn't exist. I was pretty sure they were just a way for Marcus to have his way with me and then use it to ruin me professionally. The very thought made me cringe. What a slime. And this guy was going to be our CEO? Not if I could help it.

The physician who'd held the record for the most complaining about the lab was the late Tyler Cabot, an internist. But Tyler was no longer with us, having passed on five years ago in ignominious circumstances.

Now George Marshall, the Grumpy Old Man of the medical staff, filled that role. The learning curve obviously had not gone up. George Marshall was a gastroenterologist and almost as impatient as Jack Allen. His tall, stooping figure; scruffy rim of gray hair around a bald head; and Gnarly Finger were familiar sights in my department. George liked to look at his own biopsies, and he knew what he was looking at because he'd done a fellowship at the Armed Forces Institute of Pathology. The arrangement worked well for me because if I knew what George wanted from me, I could put it in my path reports. It kept the Gnarly Finger out of my face most of the time.

If George didn't know what Marcus Manning was referring to, nobody did.

George didn't. "Toni, what the devil are you talking about? You must have heard him wrong."

"I didn't hear him wrong," I said. "And he wouldn't tell me who complained or what they complained about. He said he wasn't at liberty to tell me."

George snorted. "That sounds like bullshit to me."

I considered telling George about the sexual harassment but decided not to. As long as I didn't give Marcus what he wanted, he would continue to threaten me with these complaints, and since I had no intention of giving Marcus what he wanted, the complaints were what I needed to deal with at this point.

"Maybe he just doesn't like women doctors," I said half-jokingly.

"If the asshole's agenda is to get rid of women doctors," George growled, "he'll probably talk to Mitzi Okamoto and Jeannie Tracy next. Maybe you'd better warn them."

Maybe so, but the whole idea of sex discrimination seemed far-fetched, even way out here in the Wild West. I mean, medical school classes were over 50 percent women now. Even so, it hadn't been that long ago that George had wagged his infamous Gnarly Finger in my face and told me it was a lucky thing that Mitzi and I had gotten onto the medical staff when we had, because after the tenure of the late surgeon Sally Shore, whose murder was the one I'd been accused of five years ago, it would be a cold day in hell before another female physician would even be considered.

And then of course the cold day in hell had arrived two years ago with the acceptance of pretty, blue-eyed Jeannie Tracy, who had charmed even crusty old George.

I got similar reactions from Dave Martin and Russ Jensen, docs with whom I had a much more congenial working relationship than I did with George.

So I talked to Mitzi next, and it was a darn good thing I did.

Mitzi was outraged. I could tell because her almond eyes flashed fire. Otherwise, her facial expression looked as serene as ever.

"He must have come here right after he talked to you," she said. "He said all the same things to me that he did to you, pretty much."

"What did you say?" I asked.

"Well, I asked him what the complaints were and who complained, just as you did, and he wouldn't tell me. So I asked Dean if he'd heard any of these complaints, and he hadn't." Dean Maxwell was Mitzi's partner.

"Did he suggest that you should retire?" I asked.

"He did. Is he kidding? I'm only forty-seven, for God's sake."

"Did he also say that he could make the whole thing go away if you were 'nice to him'?"

Mitzi's eyes widened fractionally. "How did you know?"

"He said the same thing to me."

"What did you do?"

"I told him to get out of my office while he was still in one piece."

"Did it work?"

"I don't know. Mike came in just then." I told her about what Marcus had said.

"Oh, well weaseled," Mitzi said.

"Yeah, that's what I thought. Do you suppose he's trying to get rid of us?"

"Whatever for?"

"To replace us with men. What else? I'm pretty sure all those complaints are just a product of Marcus's imagination."

That made Mitzi mad. Her eyes became slits; her full lips compressed. But she said nothing. I wished I had her self-control. My face was an open book, with an open mouth. When I got mad, the world knew it. *When Toni ain't happy, ain't nobody happy.*

"Did you talk to anybody else to see if they know about these complaints?" I asked.

"No, not yet."

"Maybe you should," I said, and I told her about my conversations with the other doctors. "They didn't know what I was talking about."

"Did they say anything about me?" she asked. "Or Jeannie?"

"I did mention the possibility of sex discrimination," I told her, "and they scoffed. But George suggested that I talk to you and Jeannie, just in case. Remember what he said about Sally Shore? He said back then that there were still a lot of chauvinists on this medical staff. So it's not impossible that that's Marcus's motivation."

"Don't forget," Mitzi said, "that he's in charge of ancillary services. Maybe it's just you and me he wants to get rid of."

"Well, let's go talk to Jeannie and find out," I suggested.

Jeannie told us that Marcus hadn't visited her yet, but after hearing what we had to say, she'd be ready for him when he did. She was as outraged as Mitzi had been, if not more so.

"Retire, my ass," she growled. "I've got news for him. Whoever heard of anybody retiring at thirty-seven? Who the hell does he think he is? Who the fuck died and made *him* king?"

"Calm down," I said. "Don't waste it on me; save it for him."

"Okay, but I can tell you this," she said. "To my knowledge, nobody's been complaining about you or Mitzi. I certainly don't have any complaints. I'd say that if George doesn't know, there aren't any."

"I suspect that's true," I said, "because Marcus told both Mitzi and me that all we had to do is 'be nice to him' and the whole thing would go away."

Jeannie's face twisted with distaste. "Does that mean what I think it means? That's sexual harassment!"

"I know."

"What are you going to do about it? Did you tell the guys you talked to?"

"No," I said. "I plan to take it up with Monty at some point."

"So what's his problem?" Mitzi asked. "Who's next on his list?"

"Besides me, you mean?" Jeannie asked. "If he's making the whole thing up, hoping we'll just slink away like good little girls, he's got another think coming."

"Maybe he thinks that if he can get us in the sack, he can use it for blackmail and get rid of us that way," I said.

"Ugh," Jeannie said. "I certainly don't plan to do that. Nobody needs sex *that* bad. You know, if we go around asking all the other docs about these so-called complaints and nobody knows anything, it'll show that he's making the whole thing up. And besides, it'll get everybody else wondering about his truthfulness."

"Perhaps," Mitzi said quietly, "unless they're all in on it."

CHAPTER 5

In skating over thin ice our safety is in our speed.

—Ralph Waldo Emerson

Whoa. Now there was a scary thought.

Jeannie's normally rosy cheeks paled. "Holy shit," she said. "What a horrible thought. What do you think we should do?"

"Surely they can't all be involved in the sexual harassment. I think Mitzi and I should go report that to Monty straightaway."

But as so frequently happens, life interfered. Monty wasn't in his office. Marcus intercepted us at the door and told us that Monty and Charlie had both left for the day. "Is there anything I can do to help you, ladies?" he asked with a smile that again didn't reach his eyes.

Yes, please drop dead. "No, thank you," I said. Mitzi merely shook her head.

We both turned to go, but Marcus's voice stopped us. "Have either of you considered my offer?"

Mitzi turned a look upon Marcus that should have disemboweled him on the spot. I was a little more civilized. "In your dreams," I told him.

Mike was in his office when I got back, so I sounded him out on Mitzi's conspiracy theory.

"She's kidding, right?" was his response.

"Maybe. We don't have any idea what goes on in executive committee meetings, do we? I mean, all that stuff about CEO and CFO and COO was presented to us as a fait accompli, and Marcus and Debra Carpentier had already been hired before they were introduced to us at the staff meeting."

"Who's Debra Carpentier?"

"Oh, that's right; you weren't there. She's the new public relations officer. She's going to do all kinds of outreach to the community, like Business After Hours and health fairs for the major businesses and commercials and stuff like that. But getting back to this conspiracy—if there is one, who's in on it and why? What's the reason for it? If this harebrained idea of Marcus Manning's is to get rid of female doctors and replace them with men, is it just his, or was it somebody else's and he was hired to put it into effect? And if it was somebody else's, whose?"

"Wait a minute," Mike said. "You don't know for sure that it's female doctors he's after. Just because he started with you and Mitzi doesn't mean he isn't going after one of the male docs next. After all, he hasn't talked to Jeannie yet. Not that he won't."

"I wish I knew," I said. "I wish I knew if there actually *was* a conspiracy. All I actually know is that Marcus Manning wants me and Mitzi gone and is willing to lie to get rid of us."

"He's also willing to sexually harass y'all," Mike said. "I hope you're planning to report that."

"I am," I said. "Mitzi and I already tried, but Marcus told us that Monty was gone for the day. I'll try again tomorrow."

"Good," Mike said. "How about I go with you when you do, since I heard him too, more or less?"

I was touched. "Thanks," I said, feeling embarrassed and then angry at myself for it. Why should I be embarrassed? I didn't do anything wrong.

Mike removed his glasses and rubbed his eyes. "This whole thing is like tryin' to grab a handful of fog, I tell you what," he complained. "If they want a male-only medical staff, why'd they hire Jeannie? And what about administration? Why'd they hire this Debra person? They could've hired a man for that position too; why didn't they? And are they planning to extend this male-only thing to the department heads? Are they gonna go after Margo? And Jackie in radiology? Barbara in billing? Dixie in surgery? The director of nursing? Where does it stop?"

"It's worse than fog," I said. "It's pea soup. We don't know who he's after, besides Mitzi and me. We don't know if it's gender based or not."

"Hold it," Mike said. "As COO, Marcus is in charge of ancillary services. Jeannie's not an ancillary service; she's a primary care provider. Maybe he's not planning to talk to her at all."

But Mitzi and I were ancillary services, and here we sat, in deep doo-doo, just as I had predicted. A lot sooner than I'd predicted.

How deep remained to be seen.

Hal was out on the back deck when I got home, having drinks with his daughter, Bambi; her husband, Pete; and our next-door neighbors, Jodi and Elliott Maynard.

My husband, Hal Shapiro, was a doctor in his own right, a PhD, and taught chemistry at our local community college. However, at this time of year, he taught summer school, which was out by noon, so he had afternoons off. Towering over me by twelve inches and outweighing me by almost a hundred pounds, he looked like a big blond Norwegian, with bright-blue eyes that missed nothing.

Up until two years ago, he hadn't even known he had a daughter. He'd hired Bambi as his lab assistant and had only found out who she was when his ex-wife had shown up with her husband and two other children for Hanukkah.

Then Bambi had almost immediately fallen in love with police detective sergeant Pete Vincent, whom Hal and I had known since his college days.

Now Hal listened to my account of the day with mounting disbelief and then asked, "Are you shitting me?"

I sipped my scotch and shook my head. "I shit you not."

"Did he actually expect you and Mitzi to just quietly leave?"

"Either that or have sex with him."

Hal choked on his scotch.

Jodi said, "You're not serious." Jodi owned a beauty salon, apparently styled her red hair with an eggbeater, and was given to wearing psychedelic clothing and big, chunky jewelry. "In this day and age?"

"That really sucks," Bambi said, her blue eyes flashing. The Beach Boys must have written the song "Surfer Girl" for someone who looked just like her—long blonde hair, blue eyes, creamy tan, long legs, standing six feet in flip-flops. Bambi had already encountered more than her share of sex discrimination and was all ready to do battle on my behalf.

"He can't do that," Elliott said. "It's against the freakin' law." Elliott should know; he was a lawyer. As tall and thin as Jodi was short and chunky, he favored three-piece suits and looked like a rabbi with his bushy black hair and beard.

Hal asked, "What exactly did he say?"

"He said he could make the whole thing go away if I was 'nice to him.'"

"You have to report him," Hal said. "They'll fire him."

"He didn't seem too concerned about that," I said. "He said the same thing to Mitzi."

"How the hell does he think he's gonna get away with it?" Pete asked, slouching in his chair and stretching his long legs out. Pete was nearly as tall as Hal, with sandy hair and ruddy cheeks.

Hal snorted. "Just who the hell does he think he's gonna replace you with?" He sounded like Mike.

"I have no idea. Maybe he has a brother who's a pathologist. After all, it was Jack's brother who steered him our way in the first place. Maybe he intends to replace everybody with someone he's related to. Kind of like Saddam Hussein."

"Is he LDS?" Jodi asked.

"Probably," I said. "At least his family is, and he went to BYU."

"That would explain it," Hal said. "He was probably raised to believe that women are supposed to stay home and have babies while the menfolk go out and do the important stuff."

I knew that was an exaggeration. Many Mormon women held jobs, as well as raising huge families and serving in various ways within their churches, such as running the relief society. Superwomen, I sometimes thought, with hardly a minute to themselves. When did they fit in things like eating and sleeping and going to the bathroom?

"Yeah," Bambi agreed. "I mean, whoever heard of a female Mormon bishop?"

Not I, but to be fair, I'd never heard of a female Catholic bishop either or an Episcopal one, although there were female Episcopal priests, like the fictional Clare Fergusson, who also wore combat boots and flew helicopters.

"If he's got a big enough family," I remarked, "he could conceivably replace everybody."

"Sure," Jodi added. "Then he could call it Marcus Manning Memorial Hospital. No, wait—that won't work. He'd have to be dead first."

"Any volunteers?" Bambi quipped.

"Besides, you can't just take Ira Burton Perrine's name off the hospital and put someone else's name on," Elliott objected. "The man founded Twin Falls. That's why they named the bridge over the Snake River Canyon after him."

"Hey," Bambi said, "do you suppose if we threw Marcus off the bridge into the river, they'd rename the bridge?"

Hal went into the kitchen and came back with two more beers for himself and Pete. "So did you have a chance to check around and find out what these complaints were supposed to be?"

I told him about my conversations with George, Dave, and Russ. "George suggested I talk to Mitzi and Jeannie. If I hadn't done that, I'd still be thinking it was just me. But now I think it's either sex discrimination or ancillary services or both, since that's the only place Marcus has any authority. Maybe that's why he hasn't talked to Jeannie."

"That makes absolutely no sense," Pete said. "I'm not sure it's even legal."

"Especially since we're supposed to be 'dragging ourselves into the twenty-first century,' as Jack Allen says," I said.

Elliott poured more wine into his glass. "Seems to me the one who needs to drag himself into the freakin' twenty-first century is your new COO," he declared. "Forcing female doctors to resign so that he can replace them with male ones? He's opening himself up to a hell of a sex discrimination suit. Even if he doesn't succeed, he's still guilty of sexual harassment. Are you sure you heard him right, Toni?"

I thought back. "Actually, he didn't mention replacing me with a man. He just intimated that I should resign because there were so many serious complaints about me, and then he refused to tell me who complained or what they complained about. I'm the one who accused him of having somebody in mind to replace me. He didn't have a chance to deny it, because a frozen section came. Mike took it away from me and left me alone with His Sleaziness. Once we were alone, he said the whole thing would go away if I hopped into the sack with him. Not in those exact words, of course."

"So you just put that all together and came up with a conspiracy to replace all women in key positions with men," Elliott said sarcastically.

Gosh, it was so nice to have a lawyer right next door to bounce things off before making a complete ass of myself at work. "I just got a sense of it from the way he said it. He never actually came right out and said he wanted to replace me with a man."

"Tell him what Mitzi said," Hal suggested.

"He told her the same thing he told me, that she should resign because of serious complaints, and wouldn't tell her what they were, and he made her the same offer he did me."

"And whose idea was the conspiracy?" Elliott asked.

"Mitzi's," I said and explained.

"So to sum it all up, you really don't know anything for sure. It's all conjecture."

Resentfully, I had to agree, at least in part. "I do know, from my own knowledge, that he wants to replace me unless I have sex with him," I argued.

"So what do you want me to do? Sue him? Sue the hospital?"

"Oh, heavens, no," I said. "I just wanted to know what you thought. Now I do. We can talk about something else now."

"Good," said Elliott.

"Oh no you don't," Jodi objected. "This is just getting interesting."

Elliott groaned and did an eye roll. Jodi paid no attention. "So after he talked to you, you talked to Mitzi because she's female too?"

"That's right, and then we both talked to Jeannie Tracy for the same reason. But he hadn't talked to her yet, and now I don't think he will."

"You don't? Why?"

"Because she's not an ancillary service."

"You could just bring the conspiracy idea out in the open and see what happens," Jodi suggested.

I thought that was a terrible idea. Mention conspiracy and everybody thinks you're crazy. Any credibility I had would go right out the window if I did that. I mean, I'd been all ready to vote for Hillary Clinton in the last election until she'd mentioned the "vast right-wing conspiracy." That had turned me right off.

And that was me, whose paranoia was legend among my friends and family. I could find the dark side to almost anything without even trying. To say that I could think the worst of people was throwing roses at it. How well would it sit with all those men? Hal and Elliott weren't looking our way, but I could practically *hear* the eye rolls we were getting. "No, I don't think so; it's much too soon. I need more information."

Jodi wouldn't give up. "Sure, and if there really is a conspiracy, any information you get will probably be lies. Then what?" Jodi wasn't too far behind me in the suspiciousness department. Maybe that was why we were such good friends.

Jeez Louise, I thought. *There's probably nobody in that place I can trust.* As Chester A. Riley used to say, "What a revoltin' development this is!"

As far as the sexual harassment thing was concerned, I just wanted to talk to Monty and get it over with. Maybe that would be the end of Marcus as well, and the whole thing really would go away. It never occurred to me that Monty might not believe me and would do nothing.

"Oh well," Hal remarked. "Maybe somebody will murder him and get him out of everyone's hair."

"Ooh, that would be so cool!" Bambi said. She was studying criminalistics at our local community college. Her goal was to become a forensic technician and work at the police lab, and she was simply (you should excuse the expression) dying to help me with another murder mystery.

Having been there, done that, I didn't exactly share her enthusiasm. However, Hal gave me an idea.

"Why don't you go straight to the horse's mouth?" he asked. "Wasn't it Jack's brother who started all this? Why don't you talk to Jack?"

CHAPTER 6

These are the times that try men's souls.

—Thomas Paine

So the next morning, I went to talk to Jack. It wasn't pretty, but it seldom was when I talked to Jack.

"Make it fast, Toni," he greeted me. "I've got a bronchoscopy in ten minutes."

I got right to the point. "Do you have any complaints about me or the lab?"

"Not really," he said. "Well, I did have to call the lab about a serum potassium this morning, but nothing really earthshaking. Why?"

"Nothing so serious that our new COO would come to me and suggest that I retire or voluntarily resign?"

Jack looked startled. "Jesus Christ, no! Toni, what are you getting at?"

"Marcus Manning came to me right after the meeting and told me that there was a situation that needed to be dealt with right away concerning the lab and me and that I should resign to make it easier to deal with."

Jack shook his head. "No, no, you must have misunderstood him."

"If I did, then Mitzi did too," I said evenly. "He said the same thing to her."

Jack stood up and reached for his lab coat. "We'll have to continue this some other time, Toni. I gotta go." And without further ado, he was gone.

Humph. That was convenient, I thought, and it didn't relieve my mind in the slightest. Just the opposite, in fact. I felt pretty sure that Jack was hiding something. But what?

Mike, when I recounted that conversation to him, had no idea. "Leezie and I talked about it last night," he said. "She couldn't believe it either. I mean, whoever heard of an administrator trying to get rid of female doctors in this day and age?"

"Well, yesterday when we were talking," I reminded him, "you were wondering whether he was going after female department heads as well."

"But then, if you remember," he said, "I suggested that he might limit his firing spree to ancillary services, since that's what he's supposed to be in charge of."

"In that case, he's probably going to go after our respective chief techs," I said.

"If he hasn't already," Mike said. "We'd better warn them."

But Margo already knew.

"I overheard that conversation," she told me. "So did Jackie. We were just coming back from break and were talking in the hall, and when we heard you raise your voice, we both just stopped talking and listened." She chuckled. "Dr. Mike certainly did a number on him, didn't he? Of course, Jackie and I had to split when you guys came out in the hall, so we missed some of it."

Jackie Romero was Mitzi's chief tech. Looking back, I could vaguely remember seeing both Margo and Jackie in the hall, but it hadn't registered at the time. Now I was grappling with the fact that my chief tech had eavesdropped on me. "Do you two make a habit of eavesdropping on people?" I asked, not knowing what else to say.

"Of course," Margo said. "How do you think I manage to know everything that goes on around here?"

It was true. Margo had worked at Perrine Memorial for nearly thirty years, and what she didn't know about the goings-on around the hospital really wasn't worth knowing. And instead of chiding her for eavesdropping, I decided that maybe I could put her and Jackie to better use as spies.

Why, I thought, rubbing my hands together fiendishly, *maybe we can get a whole spy network going, between my techs and Mitzi's.* We could even drop morsels of disinformation at strategic points as needed, if it came to that. This could rival the CIA. Or the KGB.

"Doctor?" Margo's voice brought me back to reality. "What's the matter?"

I told her.

She grinned. "You know, I'm going to be sixty-five in December. I've been thinking of retiring anyway, even without that jerk forcing the issue. But now I get to go out with a bang. This is going to be fun. Don't worry, Doctor. Just leave it to me. I'll tell Jackie."

Sheesh. That was almost too easy. Now I needed to warn Mitzi, not to mention my own partner.

"Anything new on the western front?" Hal asked while we were having lunch in the hospital cafeteria.

I looked around to see who else might be listening. Our hospital cafeteria was a veritable hotbed of HIPAA violations, with doctors discussing patients in booths right next to where the very patient under discussion might be dining with his or her family. Maybe the new hospital would have a separate dining room for doctors, but as it was, I sincerely hoped no government agents dropped in to have lunch in the meantime, or we'd all end up in federal prison.

I saw nobody sitting close to us who'd care about our conversation, but I leaned in close to Hal anyway so that I could keep my voice down. "Well," I said conspiratorially, "when Mike and I were talking this morning, it occurred to us that if he wanted to replace Mitzi and me, he might also want to replace Margo and Jackie, our respective chief techs."

"And you don't want that."

"Well, no, of course I don't. I'm probably going to have to replace Margo sometime soon anyway, because she's thinking of retiring, but Jackie isn't; she's much younger and has small children, and her husband works construction and was laid up for several months last winter for an injury. She needs that job."

"So what's your next step?" Hal asked. "Beard the lion in his den?"

"Counterintelligence," I said, and Hal looked mystified. "It seems I have a ready-made spy network right in my own lab," I told him. "I've put them to work, and I may have reinforcements from radiology as well. If anything's cooking, we should hear about it well before anything official happens."

Hal looked worried. "You shouldn't take everything you hear that way as gospel," he warned me. "It might come back to bite you in the butt."

"Don't worry," I said airily. "I'll check it out first."

"With whom?" he said. "If you're right about a conspiracy, they'll just lie."

I had just begun telling Mitzi about my conversation with Margo when Jackie, a stocky, fortyish Hispanic woman with curly black hair to her shoulders, appeared in Mitzi's doorway. "Could you come down to room twelve for a minute, Doctor? There's something I think you should see."

Mitzi gave me a tiny shrug and followed Jackie out the door. I started back to my own office, but I'd no sooner stepped out of Mitzi's office than Marcus Manning intercepted me, the smile firmly in place. "There you are, Doctor. I've been looking for you. I need to talk to you."

"So talk," I said.

"Not here," he said. "In my office."

"You mean right now?"

He gave me a quizzical look. "If you can."

"Sure," I said. "Give me five minutes, okay?"

I knocked on Marcus's office door five minutes later to the second. He admitted me graciously, the smile back in place. "Welcome, Doctor, please have a seat," he said and started to close the door.

Uh-oh. The door had to stay open if my hastily hatched plan was to work.

"Oh no you don't," I objected loudly. "Leave that open. I'm not going to be in here with you behind closed doors. What would people think?"

Marcus frowned slightly, and the smile diminished somewhat, but he left the door open. "Perhaps they'd think we were having a private conversation," he said mildly, looking at me oddly. "Why are you talking so loud? I'm not deaf."

"Oh, I don't know. I must be coming down with a cold. Or maybe it's allergies. Anyway, my ears are all plugged up. So you're going to have to speak up. I can't hear a damn thing with my ears all plugged up like this."

"I said they might think we're having a private conversation," he repeated, raising his voice slightly.

"Private conversation? Whatta we got to have a private conversation about?" I asked with a volume worthy of a rock band in concert.

Marcus shifted uncomfortably in his chair and glanced out at the office beyond his open door, where staring eyes were quickly averted. When he turned back to me, the smile was gone, and his Pacific-blue eyes were icy. He had obviously decided not to let his discomfort show. "First of all, I'm quite aware that you called me an asshole the other day at the staff meeting. I heard you."

Shit, I thought. He'd heard me? The man must have ears like a bat.

"*Asshole?* You say I called you an *asshole*? Is that what you said? I still can't hear you very well."

"I distinctly heard you say the word *asshole*, Doctor."

"And you thought I was talking about you? Well, for your information, there are plenty of other *assholes* in my life for me to talk about besides you. You've got to realize everything's not always all about *you*, you know."

The sound of muffled giggles came wafting through Marcus's open door. He reddened. "Let's move on," he said. "Let's talk about the matter we were discussing the other day, before we were so rudely interrupted."

"You mean before I got a frozen section? You're all pissy because I got a frozen section? Hey, it wasn't my idea. You got a problem with frozens, talk to the surgeons."

Marcus sighed. The poor man must have felt as if he were slogging through quicksand. One could almost feel sorry for him. Not me, though. I was having too much fun.

"Doctor, if you're doing this on purpose to embarrass me, I don't appreciate it," he said. "I'm warning you: it will only hurt you in the long run."

Gee whiz, the man was scolding me. I felt the urge to apologize but squelched it quickly. This was not the confessional, after all.

Forgive me, Father, for I have yelled.

"Doing what on purpose? I'm not doing anything, and will you please speak up? I don't want to have to ask you again."

Marcus's face had turned a lovely shade of puce. "I said," he shouted back at me, "if you're putting on this deaf act to embarrass me, I don't appreciate it!"

In a show of mock outrage, I stood and shook a finger at him. "*Deaf act?* Did you say *deaf act?* Don't you know it's not nice to make fun of people with handicaps? You are in violation of the Americans with Disabilities Act. You'll be lucky if I don't report you. Now can we stop screwing around and get to whatever it was you wanted to talk to me about? I haven't got all day, you know."

After this megadecibel diatribe, Marcus's face deepened to magenta. A vein throbbed in his right temple. His neck veins were distended too. Would he, I wondered, stroke out before he managed to speak his piece? One could only hope so.

But no such luck. He leaned forward on his elbows, hands clasped in a white-knuckle death grip. "Doctor, there is something we must discuss, and it is a confidential matter. I must insist that you close the door."

Here it comes, I thought. *The rubber hits the road right here.* Much as I'd rather not have it made public that Marcus had propositioned me yesterday, I might be better off if as many people knew about it as possible. Since I had no intention of going along with it, the more people who knew that, the better.

"No way," I said, in the same deafening tone. "Not after you dropped that little bombshell on me yesterday. For your information—and I can't believe you don't know this already—that was sexual harassment, and it's against hospital policy, if not the law. So if that's the confidential matter you wish to discuss, then no way. I'm not closing that door, and that's final." I folded my arms defensively across my chest.

Faces out in the front office were all turned our way, eyes widened in shock.

Marcus didn't notice. "Doctor, you had better be careful," he said grittily. "I didn't sexually harass you; you simply misunderstood me. If you persist with this silly accusation, I can make it very difficult here for you. I can make sure you never practice medicine anywhere in the United States, if need be. You will be very sorry you ever decided to tangle with me."

CHAPTER 7

Great blunders are often made, like large ropes,
of a multitude of fibers.

—*Victor Hugo,* **Les Miserables**

My blood ran cold. He sounded like Don Corleone, making me an offer I couldn't refuse. Could he actually do that, make sure I never practiced again anywhere in the country? How?

My knees trembled, but I remained standing, placing my hands on my hips and cocking my head quizzically. The show must go on. "*Tango* with you? I can't do that, you silly man—I'm married. Is that all? Because I still have work to do, you know. I can't just stand around chewing the fat all day like some people."

"*Out!*" Marcus shouted, in apparent desperation. "*Just get out!*"

I got out. Just outside the door, I threw my hands up in mock despair and said, "*Now* he speaks up! Go figure!"

Everyone in the outer office burst into laughter. Just outside Marcus's door, Margo signaled me with a wink and held up her cell phone. *Got it!*

On wobbly legs, I detoured past Monty's office on my way back to my office, but again he wasn't there. *Oh well,* I thought. Maybe after what had just transpired in Marcus's office in full hearing of the entire front-office staff, I no longer needed to report it. The gossip mill would do that for me. Besides, it was recorded on Margo's cell phone for posterity, or at least until she recorded something over it.

I stopped off in the ladies' room to recover my composure and sat on the toilet until my knees stopped shaking, blotting my face and pits with toilet paper until they stopped dripping. Damn, I wasn't cut out for this. Mum had raised me to be respectful and polite to a fault. But she had also advised me never to back away from a fight if the outcome was important. In other words, pick my battles.

Had I been right or wrong to pick this one?

Only time would tell.

At home I treated Jodi and Elliott to the recorded rendition of the Marcus-and-Toni Show. Margo had sent it from her cell phone to my computer at work, and I had e-mailed it to my laptop so that Hal and Jodi and Elliott could listen to it and I could save it into a file to use in my defense later if I needed to. Isn't technology wonderful?

Jodi clapped her hands with delight. "Oh my God, I wish I'd been there. That is just priceless! Toni, I swear, you've missed your calling. You should have been an actress."

Hal wiped tears of laughter from his eyes. "He'll know better than to try to 'tango' with you again!"

Elliott squelched the hilarity, however, with a cold splash of lawyerly reality. "Maybe, but I think it's more likely that you've inadvertently made it worse for yourself, Toni. You made him mad, and moreover, you made him a figure of fun in front of the entire freakin' front-office staff. You undermined his authority. You humiliated him. You probably got him into a whole lot of trouble. Most guys react poorly to that, even if they're not narcissistic and egotistical, and it sounds like this guy has had it all his own way up till now. I suspect he's really gonna be on your case now, more than ever."

"Well, aren't you just a freakin' little ray of sunshine," I retorted. "Who propositioned whom here?"

"Elliott may be right, though," said Hal. "Marcus did threaten you."

"Yes," I agreed, "and Margo got it all on her cell phone. Tomorrow I can make sure that Mike and Monty and a few more of the doctors hear it."

"But, Toni," Jodi said, "aren't you worried about what he can do to you? About making sure you never practice medicine again anywhere in the country? Can he really do that?"

"I don't see how," Hal said. "What can he actually do?"

"Well, one thing he can do is report me to the state board of medicine," I said. "All he needs to do is make up a fake patient chart and put in an erroneous, fake pathology report. Then they'd have to investigate me, and I'd have to prove I didn't do anything wrong."

"So you'd be vindicated," said Hal. "What's wrong with that? You'd come out on top, and he'd look bad."

"Nobody would know the complaint came from him," I said. "The state board is all about protecting the patient, not the doctor. They wouldn't divulge the name of the complainant to the public. They wouldn't divulge *anything* to the public until the whole thing was settled, and then it would just be a brief blurb in the quarterly newsletter, that Dr. So-and-So was disciplined for such and such a violation of the Medical Practice Act. So I'd look bad, not him."

"Not if you weren't disciplined," said Elliott.

"Well, that's true," I said, "but how the hell would I defend myself against a complaint from a fictitious patient?"

"Couldn't you show that the patient wasn't in the hospital database?" Hal asked.

"Marcus could always get somebody with registrar privileges to register a fictitious patient in the computer," I said. I was probably mentally mass insulting all employees who registered patients, including those in the lab, but I had no doubt that Marcus could find out something embarrassing about an employee and then blackmail him or her into doing whatever he wanted. There would be nothing I could do about that.

"But who's gonna create the fictitious path report?" Hal demanded. "Even if Marcus could blackmail a lab employee to create one, who's got the knowledge or vocabulary to create a legitimate-sounding pathology report other than you and Mike?"

Hal was absolutely right. Unless Marcus actually had a pathologist in his family who would go along with his nefarious plan, the only way that scenario would occur was if one of us actually did issue an erroneous report. A misinterpretation of a frozen section resulting in unnecessary surgery, for example, or a misdiagnosis resulting in failure to treat a potentially serious condition. Perhaps a case sent out for a second opinion at the request of the patient or the physician, in which the consultant's diagnosis differed significantly from ours. No, not ours—mine. Marcus wasn't after Mike; he was after me.

Mike could err with impunity, theoretically, though of course he wouldn't. But I had to be pure as the driven snow and constantly on guard. Damn it. Just thinking about it made me tired. I sighed.

"Earth to Toni," I heard Hal say.

"What?"

"Where were you, darling?" asked Jodi. "You seemed to be a million miles away."

"No, I was right here," I said. "I was thinking about all the ways that Marcus could get me into trouble."

"Well, first you'd have to do something wrong," Hal said. "And you don't. You've never been sued. You've never had a patient complaint of any kind. You've actually saved patients' lives. How about that one with chronic lymphocytic leukemia and iron-deficiency anemia a few years back who you thought might have colon cancer, and she did? And how about that guy with esophageal cancer that the University of Washington just blew off?"

That wasn't exactly true; the University of Washington hadn't blown anybody off. I had diagnosed Barrett's esophagus, a condition in which intestinal mucosa replaces the normal squamous mucosa of the esophagus, caused by gastroesophageal reflux. I had also diagnosed high-grade dysplasia—a premalignant change, not quite cancer, but close—and couldn't rule out cancer. I'd sent my results to the University of Washington for a second opinion, and the expert had called it Barrett's esophagus with possible dysplasia and had recommended rebiopsy. But before that could happen, the patient had developed an obstruction and had to have surgery. At surgery he'd been found to have full-blown adenocarcinoma of the esophagus that had metastasized to a lymph node.

Well, that sort of thing can happen. The original biopsy hadn't included diagnostic cancer tissue, and neither the University of Washington nor I had actually called it cancer. But that hadn't prevented the patient's wife from telling everybody she talked to that Dr. Toni Day had diagnosed her husband's cancer "while the University of Washington was just twiddling their thumbs!"

Great for me; bad for U-Dub.

But none of my past accomplishments would help me now if Marcus Manning really put his mind to ruining me.

"And how about the time Ken Resnick told Dave Martin he thought you were the best GI pathologist in the Pacific Northwest?" Hal continued. Ken Resnick was the new gastroenterologist, George's new partner.

"Well, however overblown and untrue that comment is," I said, "it might come in handy if Ken could be induced to repeat it to Marcus in front of witnesses."

I should be making a list, I thought.

"Just because I haven't made a serious mistake up until now doesn't mean it can't happen," I argued. "No matter how cautious I am. Shit happens."

"You could have your partner check you when you read out surgicals," Jodi suggested.

"We already do that," I said. "Mike and I review each other's cases from the day before and reconcile any differences. If we have to, we send out corrected reports and call the surgeon about it. If we can't agree, we send it to an expert. If one of us has a difficult case, we consult with each other, and if we can't make a diagnosis, we send it to an expert. We do the same thing with Pap smears. That's all part of our quality assurance program, which is required by CAP, the College of American Pathologists. We keep records. CAP provides us with national benchmarks for acceptable levels of error, and we stay below them. We can prove it. We prove it every time we have a CAP inspection."

"What about the lab?" asked Hal.

"They do the same thing. They have a quality assurance plan of their own and keep their own records, which we review and sign off on."

"So what if one of the doctors makes a comment about not believing the lab's results on a certain test and your white-haired boy gets wind of it?" asked Elliott.

"We validate every new test method by running it in parallel with the old method. We test it for linearity, reproducibility, and precision before we put it into use for patients. Plus, we run preassayed controls at two or three levels every day that we run the test, and we test the instruments every shift by rerunning certain patient samples as well as controls. If the controls are out of range, we don't run patients until we find the cause and fix it."

These words rolled off my tongue easily because I heard them every day from my techs, and they made perfect sense to me, having been a med tech myself back in the day. But whenever I had to use them on my nonpathologist physician colleagues, their eyes tended to glaze over. I could see that Elliott was struggling with them too, but he made a nice recovery.

"And you can prove it?"

"Of course we can prove it. We keep records of everything."

"Everything? Even the daily stuff? Every test, two or three levels, every shift?"

"Everything," I said firmly.

"That sounds like an awful lot of paper," Elliott said doubtfully.

"You have no idea," Hal put in. "I've seen the reams of stuff she signs off on every day. And it was worse before everything was computerized."

"That's for sure," I said. "Now I don't have to decipher everybody's handwriting."

"So what happens if you can't find the cause of a control being out of range?" asked Elliott.

"We always find the cause," I told him, "but we can't always fix it. If there's an instrument problem that we can't fix, we have to call for service, and if we can't run the test on another instrument, we have to send it out to a reference lab."

"Then don't the other doctors complain?" Jodi asked.

"Of course they do, but what choice do they have?"

"But suppose they complain to Marcus Manning?" asked Jodi.

"Then we explain the problem to him. What's he gonna do? Report me to the board of medicine for *not* giving out erroneous lab results? Come on."

They all laughed and allowed as how I had a point, but deep down I suspected that Marcus Manning could actually pull that off, especially if he could talk a relative into posing as the injured party.

I might be vindicated in the end, but in the process I'd have to waste a great deal of time and effort, which would interfere with my ability to pull my weight in the pathology department, and Mike would have to do my work as well as his. If that were to result in path reports being delayed, it might be construed as interfering with patient care.

And Marcus could report me for that too.

CHAPTER 8

The motions of his spirit are dull as night,
And his affections dark as Erebus.
Let no such man be trusted.

—*William Shakespeare,* ***The Merchant of Venice***

In short, I was damned if I did and damned if I didn't, and I would be damned if I was just going to sit back and let it happen.

First thing tomorrow, I vowed, I'd figure out how to be proactive about this. I'd get rid of Marcus if I had to hog-tie him with baling wire and duct tape and throw him into the back of a pickup like a trussed elk.

My first priority at work the next morning was to bring Mike up to date on what we'd all discussed the night before, since if Mike was going to help me, he'd have to know what we could be up against.

The first thing I did was e-mail the cell phone record to his computer, hoping that Marcus hadn't already found a way to hack into either of our computers. I was sure he had a relative who could do that and would soon, if he hadn't already, replace someone in IT (information technology, a.k.a. the computer geeks) with that relative. All our computers were part of a system, and all our records were backed up nightly on a server common to all the computers in the building. Come to think of it, it might be safer to burn the recording onto a CD for safekeeping. Marcus could have it removed from the server if he found out it was there.

I suggested that Mike should listen to the conversation first thing, behind a closed door so that it wouldn't be overheard, especially by Marcus, but he just laughed. "You're kidding, right? The whole front office heard it. You had Margo record it, and it's still on her cell phone. You don't think she's already shared it with everybody in the lab? Not to mention Jackie and all the x-ray techs? Hell, she might have already put it on YouTube. Nobody, no matter how good a hacker he is, can get it deleted from YouTube. It'll be out there for friggin' ever. Marcus can't do a thing about it."

"But, boy, is he gonna be pissed, I tell you what!" I said, mimicking Mike.

He laughed. "What we oughta do," he suggested, "is to make a party out of it. Pretend it's somebody's birthday, order pizza, tell everybody in lab and radiology—excuse me, *diagnostic imaging*—and anyone else who comes by. I'll put the conversation on continuous loop as background."

The recording sounded great on Mike's computer; we could even hear the muted guffaws of the outer-office staff.

So we did as Mike suggested, and it wasn't long before Marcus began noticing that various front-office personnel were disappearing and followed them to check out why. His entrance to Mike's office was blocked by a crowd of people out in the hall talking and laughing and eating pizza. Furious, he shouldered his way through the door, no doubt expecting to find me, but I wasn't there. I watched from behind the door into histology. He raised his voice in anger over all the chatter, and I caught the words "have you all fired" before he burst out of Mike's office and charged into mine. He then charged back out, slamming the door behind him.

I stepped out into the hall to intercept him. "What were you doing in my office?" I demanded, using the most accusatorial tone I could come up with.

Marcus wasn't cowed. "Just exactly what the hell do you think you're doing?" he demanded, his face even more purple than it had been the day before.

"I was doing a frozen section," I informed him. "I'm on call. Now, why were you in my office?"

"You recorded our conversation yesterday," he accused, "and you're using it as an attack on me. I don't appreciate it."

"*I* didn't record anything," I told him, "and I can't be held responsible if someone else did, and I don't appreciate your baseless accusations. That's an attack on *me*. Not to mention that little lot you dumped on me yesterday. In what universe was *that* not an attack?"

As I spoke, I surreptitiously moved closer to the crowd in the hall, and Marcus had to move too if he didn't want to yell at me from a distance. They had fallen silent and were watching us avidly. As we moved closer, they gathered around us. Marcus tried to ignore them, but I saw him swivel his eyes toward them and then back to me more than once.

"I want the person who recorded this fired," he informed me in a low, threatening tone.

I stared back directly into his eyes and folded my arms defiantly over my chest. "Knock yourself out," I said.

Marcus moved closer, until his face was mere inches from mine. "Now you listen to me," he said, and I swear I could hear his teeth grinding—all forty-six of them. "If someone doesn't own up to that recording, I will have everyone in the lab and diagnostic imaging fired."

I stepped back and spread my arms to include everyone in the hall, who were clustering ever closer to us. "Did you all get that?"

"I did," Mike said, emerging from his office. "Right here on my cell phone."

"What's going on here?"

Monty came striding down the hall toward us, and he didn't look happy. However, his demeanor was nothing compared to Marcus's. Marcus took one look at Monty's forbidding expression and seemed to swell visibly. He folded his arms defiantly across his chest. He opened his mouth to speak, but I forestalled him. "Mr. Manning was just telling us that he was going to fire everybody in the lab and diagnostic imaging, right, guys?"

Everyone in the hall, including Mike, nodded. "That's what he said, I tell you what," Mike added for good measure. "I got it right here on my phone."

"So do I," I said, producing my open phone from my lab coat pocket. I pushed a button, and Marcus's voice came through loud and clear. *"I will have everyone in the lab and diagnostic imaging fired."*

Mike and several other employees held up their cell phones and played back the same phrase in a ragged and dissonant chorus.

Monty held up his hands for silence. "Would you all get back to work now, please? We do have a hospital to run." Then he took Marcus by the arm and drew him aside as people slowly dispersed. Mike and I stayed within earshot.

"Manning, what the hell do you think you're doing? Your first act as COO in charge of ancillary services is to fire them all? Are you nuts? Do you have any idea what that would do to this hospital? We'd have to close! Is that what you want? Four hundred people out of jobs in this economy?"

"Oh, this wasn't his *first* act as COO," I observed to nobody in particular. "Or even his second."

Monty turned his head slightly. "Doctor, please, this is a private conversation."

"So was this one," I countered. "Mikey, if you please?"

Mike went into his office, and shortly Marcus's voice boomed out into the now-silent hallway.

"I can make it very difficult here for you. I can make sure you never practice medicine anywhere in the United States, if need be. You will be very sorry you ever decided to tangle with me."

Monty frowned. "You said that to Dr. Day? Why?"

"I didn't—" Marcus began, but I interrupted.

"That was his third act as COO: to threaten me. His first was to suggest that I retire or resign. His second was to sexually harass me."

Now Monty just looked bewildered. "Whatever for?"

"I told her that we had received a number of serious complaints about her," Marcus replied, puffing out his chest even more.

"But we haven't," Monty said. "Have we? I haven't heard anything about any complaints."

"That's because there aren't any," I said. "And if there are, he won't tell me what they are or who made them. So if you can get him to tell you and let me know, Monty, maybe I can do something about them, assuming they actually exist." *Preferably something involving thumbscrews and bamboo shoots under the fingernails.*

"What about the sexual harassment accusation, Doctor?" Monty asked.

"After he threatened me, he said he could make the whole thing go away if I had sex with him."

Monty turned to Marcus. "Is that true?"

"Of course not," Marcus said. "I said nothing about having sex with her. I'm a married man, after all. With six children," he added piously.

Hypocrite. I felt my mouth twist in disgust. "He's right," I said as Monty turned back to face me. "He didn't actually mention the word *sex*. What he said was 'All you have to do is be nice to me.' And then he said he was sure I knew what he meant by that."

"Did anyone else hear him say that?" Monty asked.

"No. Mike came into my office right after he said it, and Marcus said I'd misunderstood him. But I know what I heard."

"But you haven't reported it to me, Doctor," Monty said. "Why am I just now hearing about it?"

"I've been to your office twice," I said. "You weren't there."

"Consider it reported," Monty said. "I'll let you know if I need more information."

"Thanks," I said and turned to go back to my office. I could feel their eyes following me, and just before I closed my door behind me, I heard Monty say just three words to Marcus Manning: "My office. Now."

Hah! I thought exultantly. *Who's in trouble now?*

But Marcus Manning wasn't done with me.

CHAPTER 9

Much water goeth by the mill
That the miller knoweth not of.

—John Heywood

My first inkling that Marcus Manning was still on my case came not as an attack on me but on Lucille Harper, my senior histotech.

Lucille, a large, loud bleached blonde who wore her hair on top of her head in a disorderly pile of curls and dressed like an explosion at the Crayola factory, had worked at Perrine Memorial since 1982, predating me and the majority of the physicians here. When Lucille had graduated from a vo-tech program somewhere in the Midwest and come to Twin Falls with her first husband, Perrine Memorial had had only ten physicians on staff.

What Lucille lacked in formal education she made up in experience and mechanical ability. She could fix anything. Her somewhat coarse and ungrammatical speech belied her native ingenuity and quick mind. But on paper, she didn't measure up to the other techs, who had bachelor's degrees and formal training in laboratories accredited by the American Society of Clinical Pathologists and had passed the ASCP registry examination. But since Lucille hadn't been educated in an ASCP-accredited program, she was ineligible to take the ASCP examination and did not have the right to put MT(ASCP) after her name as the other techs did. As a result, she had been hired at a significantly lower pay scale than the other techs, even though she did the same job.

However, back in the late seventies, the United States Department of Health, Education, and Welfare had decided to require all medical technologists without bachelor's degrees to pass a federal examination in order to continue working. Many older techs had quit rather than take the chance of failing the HEW examination. Not Lucille. She had taken the exam and passed it on the first try. Only 30 percent passed on the first try. I had fought hard to get Lucille on the same pay scale as the other techs, and her test score had been the ammunition I'd needed to get the job done.

Nevertheless, the hospital's current requirement was that all medical technologists hired after 1995 be ASCP certified or eligible, and although Lucille had been grandfathered in, on paper she still didn't measure up, which made her a target.

So when Lucille stormed into my office, pink slip in hand, I really wasn't terribly surprised. I'd been halfway expecting something like this.

It was the white-underbelly syndrome, I had figured out. The white underbelly represented any weakness that could be exploited by a predator. In this case, the predator was Marcus Manning, and the white underbelly was Lucille's lack of education, at least on paper.

Right behind Lucille came Natalie, my other histotech, who had trained at Massachusetts General and had the right to put both MT *and* HT(ASCP) after her name and whose workload would double without Lucille.

Natalie had come to us five years earlier. She'd been on the run from an abusive ex-fiancé at the time and had shown up just in time to fill in for Lucille when she'd been severely injured in a car accident and nearly died. With her gleaming long black hair, glowing complexion, and cobalt-blue eyes, she'd attracted the attention of every male in the vicinity and was now happily married to one of my techs.

Those cobalt eyes flashed now with indignation. "Why?" she demanded. "Lucille hasn't done anything wrong."

"That's what I said," Lucille added. "What the hell is this all about, Doctor?"

I knew perfectly well what it was all about, but this wasn't the time to talk about it. "I'll find out," I said. "In the meantime, both of you get back to work."

"But what about this?" demanded Lucille, waving the pink slip in my face.

I snatched it out of her hand. "I'll take care of this. You're not fired. Get back to work."

Oh goody, I thought. *Personnel management. Whoop-de-frickin'-doo.* As if I didn't have anything else to do. This was a job for Margo.

But Margo, when I asked her, knew nothing about it. "Fired? What for? I haven't heard any complaints about Lucille. Not only that, but there's a protocol for firing people, and this isn't it."

Perrine Memorial's employee handbook specified that an employee had to have three formal reprimands on his or her record, for documented complaints, to be placed on probation. Once on probation, another documented complaint would result in termination. The employee had the right to appeal, and there was a protocol for that also. Employees were not supposed to find pink slips in their paychecks without any warning, as Lucille had.

Under normal circumstances, the next step would be to talk to the person in charge of ancillary personnel. But these weren't normal circumstances. I knew that talking to our COO would be an exercise in futility.

So I sought out Monty, but he wasn't in his office. Charlie Nelson wasn't in his office either. As I stood undecided outside Charlie's door, Marcus Manning accosted me. "Anything I can help you with, Doctor?"

Of course not, asshole. You're the fucking problem. I waved Lucille's pink slip in his face. "Know anything about this?"

Marcus folded his arms. "Ah. Mrs. Harper. Not unexpected, is it, considering how many complaints we've received?"

Riiight. "And I'll bet you're not at liberty to tell me what they are and who made them."

"That's right."

"Where's Monty?"

"Off for the rest of the day. Charlie too."

I wished that I could slap that smug smile right off his face, but that would only get me in trouble and not help Lucille at all.

"Well, you just have a swell day," I said. "How about you utilize it to familiarize yourself with the employee handbook, particularly the part about the proper way to fire someone?"

I turned and strode purposefully away, just as if I actually had some idea where I was going, and then decided maybe it'd be a good idea to talk to Mitzi. Who knew, maybe the same thing had happened to her too today.

But no, it hadn't. Mitzi was appalled. I could tell because her mouth twisted slightly, almost imperceptibly, to the left. "How can they just fire Lucille without any warning? I mean, unless there *were* warnings?"

"No, and Margo hasn't heard anything either. Marcus just gave me that smug smile and said he wasn't at liberty to say."

Mitzi's mouth twisted a little more. "He would."

"Do you have anybody in your department with any kind of weakness that Marcus could exploit?"

"What kind of weakness?"

"Well, for instance, Lucille doesn't have as much education as my other techs, and she tends to mouth off at people. There have been complaints on her record but nothing recent. Stuff like that."

Mitzi shook her head. "No, nothing like that, but I've got a tech who's a recovering alcoholic. Goes to AA every day during lunch hour. But that's supposed to be confidential, so I can't tell you who it is."

That was a white underbelly if I ever saw one. "Well, keep an eye out," I told her. "He may be next."

Though Mitzi didn't say which tech, I knew who she was talking about. I'd had some experience with recovering drug addicts and alcoholics during my psychiatry rotation in medical school. Many of them had been Vietnam vets and had problems with anger, unprovoked violence, hallucinations, night terrors, and bad dreams—what we now knew as post-traumatic stress disorder—on top of substance-abuse issues. Most had also been heavy smokers, with reeking clothes and yellow fingertips, greasy hair, and pasty skin. No matter how well they'd cleaned themselves up, there had been a look about them, something in the eyes, a look of defeat and hopelessness, mixed with a little bit of fear, like the way an abused dog looked at you.

Only one person in Mitzi's department fit that description. He was an ex-marine who'd served in Desert Storm. He'd been clean and sober for at least ten years, and to look at him, nobody would ever guess that he'd had a substance-abuse problem.

Yet, in his eyes, he had that look.

Marcus, the predator, would see it and zero in on it. It was only a matter of time.

I'd made a slight miscalculation with regard to who might be next on Marcus's hit list. I was too busy thinking about what Marcus could do to Mitzi's tech to remember that he had not yet called Mitzi herself into his office to harangue her about some real or imagined slight, as he had with me.

He did it that very afternoon.

CHAPTER 10

I'll get you, my pretty, and your little dog too.

—Wicked Witch of the West, **The Wizard of Oz**

I'm not sure if Mitzi would have said anything to me about it; she's rather secretive about her personal affairs. But I happened to glance out of my office door to see Jackie Romero sprinting in that direction, cell phone in hand.

"Psst!" I said.

She turned, and I stepped out into the hall to meet her. "What's going on?"

"Mr. Manning is in the doctor's office insisting that she come to his office right now, and she's arguing with him, so I'm gonna plant my cell phone in his office and record them," she told me gleefully.

"Better hurry," I said and sprinted after her to administration, where she disappeared into Marcus's office. Seeing that Monty was back in his office and clearly not off for the day as Marcus had said, I took the opportunity to tackle him about Lucille. I knocked on his door.

"Come in," he said, and I did so.

"Do you know that Marcus fired Lucille this morning?" I began without preamble.

Monty sat back in his chair, a startled look on his face. "Whatever for?"

"He wouldn't tell me."

"Didn't he tell her?"

I shook my head. "There was a pink slip in her paycheck. That's the first she knew of it."

"I've heard nothing," he said. "Nobody complained to you? Or Margo?"

"Nope."

Monty took his glasses off and rubbed his hands over his face as if he were trying to wash it. "Where is Lucille now?"

"Working. I told her she wasn't fired."

"Good," Monty said and pushed a button on his phone. "Kay, could you bring me Lucille Harper's personnel file, please?"

"Coming right up," Kay replied.

Monty leaned forward and put his elbows on the desk. "You know, Doctor, when we divvied up the administrative duties among the three of us, I was relieved not to have to deal with ancillary services anymore. Marcus hasn't even been here a week yet, and already you're going over his head by coming to me. I feel quite strongly that if Marcus is to someday be CEO, he needs to be allowed to handle things as he thinks best, unless there's a very good reason not to. I'm nearing retirement, and this is the last thing I want to be dealing with at this time in my life."

I was about to tell him that there was a dandy reason not to when Kay, the administrative assistant, stuck her head around the door and said, "Excuse me, Mr. Montgomery, but Lucille's file isn't in the file cabinet where it belongs. Do you want me to check with Mr. Nelson or Mr. Manning?"

"No, Kay, that's all right," Monty said. "I think I know where it is." As Kay withdrew, he rose from his chair. "Doctor, how about we pay our COO a little visit?"

I remained seated. "He's got Mitzi Okamoto in his office, threatening her like he threatened me the other day. You do know that he sexually harassed her too, same as me?"

"All the more reason to disturb him, then. Let's go."

Marcus appeared somewhat flustered at our appearance but tried very hard to be gracious about it. "What can I do for you, Monty?" he asked, rising from behind his desk. "Doctor? Why are you here? This is a private conversation."

I merely smiled. *That's what you think, bub.*

"I'm looking for a personnel file," Monty said. "Lucille Harper?"

Marcus shook his head. "Sorry, I don't have it."

"Kay didn't find it in the file cabinet," Monty said.

"She must not have looked very hard," Marcus said, folding his arms over his chest and giving Monty the same smug look he had given me when he'd told me he was not at liberty to say what the complaints were. He was lying through his perfect white teeth. Again.

Monty pulled up a chair and sat down next to Mitzi, who looked pale. Following his example, I pulled a chair around to Mitzi's other side and sat in it.

Marcus sat back down and looked angrily at me and then at Monty. "Dr. Okamoto and I are done here," he said, "and I have work to do." He clearly expected us to just meekly get up and leave him to it, but nothing doing.

"As long as we're all still here," Monty said, "I think we need to have a conversation about the way we do things around here, just to get things straight. As COO, you are in charge of ancillary services, but as far as I can tell, you're not managing it very well. You've threatened Dr. Day and fired one of her employees without any reason. I expect you were doing the same to Dr. Okamoto just now."

Marcus assumed his most pompous air. "I did nothing of the kind."

I glanced at Mitzi, who had said nothing up till now. Her face showed no expression except that her almond eyes were slitted. "You lying bastard," she said softly. I'm not sure Marcus even heard her.

"Really?" I said to Marcus. "Let's find out." I bent down, retrieved Jackie's cell phone from underneath Mitzi's chair, and pressed the play button. The color drained from Marcus's face, and sweat broke out on his brow as his voice issued tinnily from the tiny microphone.

"The executive committee has decided that, under the circumstances, you can no longer be a member of this medical staff. We strive to adhere to a much-higher moral standard than that here."

Whoa. I pressed the rewind button and started over. *"It has come to our attention that you had a child by another man while still married to your husband."*

Mitzi: *"How? Whose attention?"*

Marcus: *"Mine, and the executive committee's. It's cause for some concern because—"*

Mitzi: *"This is nobody's business but mine. It has nothing to do with my ability to do my job."*

Marcus: *"That's where you're wrong, Doctor. A person of loose morals in her personal life can be expected to have loose morals professionally, and in our increasingly litigious society, we simply can't afford even the faintest hint of impropriety."*

Mitzi: *"So the executive committee expects me to just quietly resign? What if I don't?"*

Marcus: *"Then we will have no choice but to initiate disciplinary action."*

Mitzi: *"Discipline for what? There's nothing in the bylaws about losing one's privileges because of one's child's parentage!"*

Marcus: *"Ah, but there is a clause pertaining to moral turpitude, Doctor. Don't make us spread your little secret all over the hospital. That's what will happen if we have to take formal action, you know."*

Feeling slightly nauseated, I pressed stop. "Does that clause also pertain to blackmail?" I demanded. "That's a hell of a lot worse than having a child by someone other than your husband. You can go to *jail* for blackmail!"

Without giving Marcus a chance to reply, I pressed play again.

Marcus: *"Of course, none of this needs to happen, you know. Have you given any more consideration to my proposal?"*

Mitzi: *"How dare you suggest such a thing to me!"*

Marcus: *"Why not? You had sex with Mr. Burke. God only knows how many other men there have been. Why stop now?"*

"That's enough." Monty stood up. "This is reprehensible. I hope this is the last time I hear anything like this. I intend to research this matter thoroughly, and in the meantime, no action is to be taken regarding Drs. Day and Okamoto or Lucille Harper. Do I make myself clear?"

Marcus's face was back to its more familiar purple. A vein pulsed in his forehead. If looks could kill, all three of us would have died on the spot. "Crystal," he murmured.

"Good," Monty said crisply. "We're done here." He strode out, followed by Mitzi and me. I didn't dare look back. My intention was to accompany Mitzi back to her office for a nice, soothing gossip fest, since I had to return Jackie's cell phone anyway, but she excused herself and went into the ladies' room, where I heard her retching.

I didn't blame her. The whole thing was enough to make anybody sick, even me.

"Of course, Mitzi's little secret really isn't all that secret," I told Hal at home while we freshened up and got ready for the first Business After Hours in which the hospital would participate.

A few years ago, Mitzi had had an affair with a lawyer who'd involved the medical staff in a financial scandal and had affairs with a long succession of doctors' wives and other women, gotten them all pregnant, and then dumped them. Mitzi had been the last of his conquests, and her husband had divorced her while she was still pregnant. The result, her daughter, Stephanie, was now three years old.

"What I want to know," Hal said, "is why Monty didn't can his ass right then and there."

"I guess it has to be done by committee," I said.

"That figures," he growled. "That dickhead can fire you and Mitzi, but you guys can't fire him without a goddamn staff meeting."

"Oh, they'd need a staff meeting to fire us too. And what's the big deal anyway?" I asked furiously. "Doctors in general aren't known for their marital fidelity. They have affairs and cheat on their spouses every five minutes. They divorce the wives who put them through medical school and marry their nurses, secretaries, or any other young, attractive hospital employees who tickle their fancy. They don't, as a general rule, have their hospital privileges taken away or lose their medical licenses over it."

That is, male doctors didn't. Hal and I had had this discussion before.

"Well, hon, you know that the good old double standard is still as alive and well now as it was a hundred years ago. Female doctors are still as vulnerable as any other woman when they dare to claim equality in the infidelity department. Maybe more. With your mostly male medical staff, Mitzi could very well be voted out, if the asshole really wants to make an issue of it."

"You think Marcus could actually get away with this?" I demanded.

"What do you think?" Hal demanded back. "You and Mitzi both complained about sexual harassment, and what did Monty do? Nothing. Marcus is getting away with it even as we speak." He took me by the shoulders. "The rest of your colleagues overlooked what Mitzi did when it happened because the same thing had happened to so many other people. But Mitzi's the only *doctor* it happened to. Up till now, nobody's made a fuss. Who knows what they'll do now that somebody's making a big stink?"

"But ..." I began.

"Look. Jack brought this guy on board. His brother recommended him. He's supposed to be a big deal. He's worked in California. Everybody respects Jack; otherwise he wouldn't be chief of staff all the time. Jack may feel he needs to support this guy, and if everybody decides to support Jack, well ..."

Hal didn't have to finish the sentence; the rest was a given. This was so totally unfair, as Bambi would say. The only way this could happen to a male physician was for him to have an affair with a patient. That was a huge no-no for a physician of either sex. That was actually prohibited by the Idaho Medical Practice Act, and a physician *could* lose his or her license for it.

This was Mitzi's white underbelly. Her lawyerly lover had been one of our patients. Of course, as a radiologist, Mitzi didn't actually have patients of her own, but if the Idaho State Board of Medicine received a complaint about her, they'd have to deal with it, and even if she didn't lose her license, she'd get reprimanded for it.

What other white underbellies would Marcus find among our medical staff and hospital employees to exploit for his own nefarious purposes? And what was it going to take to get Monty and Charlie and the rest of the medical staff to see Marcus for what he really was? It seemed that neither my accusation of sexual harassment nor Mitzi's would be the slam dunk I'd hoped they'd be.

Hal mistook my silence for assent and changed the subject. "Sweetie, I love you for the way you always stand up for people when you think justice hasn't been done, but this isn't really your fight anymore."

"The hell it isn't," I retorted. "Then why does it always start with me? Why do I have to be the sentinel event? Am I wearing a target on my back? Is there a boot print on my butt with an arrow pointing to it? And who is it Marcus wants to make sure never practices anywhere in the United States again?"

Hal didn't have a comeback for that, and I continued to steam and stew while we walked in silence back to the hospital in the late-afternoon sun.

The trouble was I had acquired some sort of reputation for starting trouble, and I knew nobody would believe it wasn't my fault until enough other people, preferably enough other physicians, found themselves in the same position as I did. In the meantime, I had to deal with it alone while everybody else blew me off. No, not strictly alone; Mitzi was in the same boat this time. But I was still getting damned tired of it.

What was my white underbelly? How was Marcus going to make sure I never practiced again anywhere in the United States? The only way to do that was to get my license revoked. If that happened, every other state in which I was licensed would also revoke my license, so I wouldn't be able to go back to California to work, and no other state would issue me a license after checking with the Idaho State Board of Medicine.

What did Marcus think he had on me that would guarantee revocation of my license? I couldn't think of a thing. What was I missing? What did Marcus know about me that I didn't?

Sex with a patient? I was pretty sure I hadn't. Except for Hal, who was a patient, as was I, ever since we'd been here in Twin Falls.

Drug or alcohol abuse? Did my nightly scotch count? I didn't frequent bars. I'd never had a DUI. Nobody had ever smelled alcohol on my breath at work. I hadn't smoked pot since college. I didn't even smoke cigarettes anymore.

Failure to adhere to the community standard of care? Not that I knew of. Someone would have to complain. If so, the state board of medicine would contact me. They'd want me to send records.

But what if the complaint hadn't been to the state board? What if it had been to the hospital administration?

Monty would tell me.

Charlie would tell me.

Marcus would hold on to it. Savor it. Keep it to himself until he could use it to his advantage. Withhold it to prevent me from doing damage control. He "wasn't at liberty to say," my ass. Nothing was keeping him from telling me what the complaint or complaints were or who made them except his own twisted motives.

I supposed I could ask around some more ... but where would I start? This could take up enough time to adversely affect my ability to get my work done.

Hello. Of course it would. Maybe that was the whole point—to render me unable to do my job to the satisfaction of the medical staff. Reason enough to get me kicked off. Losing my hospital privileges could result in my having my license revoked or at least being disciplined, and that would follow me everywhere for the rest of my career.

At this point I had an epiphany. Or maybe it was an apostrophe. Anyway, I realized what my white underbelly was. Marcus hadn't threatened me until I'd defied him, made him a figure of fun in front of the front-office staff, humiliated him, and made his sexual innuendoes known to countless employees. And now I'd made it even worse by horning in on his first attempt to threaten Mitzi and putting Monty wise to what he was doing.

It was possible that the number of complaints he'd mentioned had all come from comments made after the staff meeting regarding my interruptions during the meeting. Of course, it hadn't been just me; Mitzi and Jeannie had been pretty vocal too.

My white underbelly was my own big fat mouth.

CHAPTER 11

Man's love is of man's life a thing apart;
'Tis woman's whole existence.

—Byron, **Don Juan**

As part of the new public-outreach program, the hospital was hosting this Twin Falls Chamber of Commerce Business After Hours.

The patient waiting room had been transformed into a welcoming space with buffet tables along the walls, with the catering staff standing behind them to serve the guests. Hot and cold hors d'oeuvres in tastefully decorated trays lined the tables, along with coffee urns, ice buckets filled with soda cans and water bottles, and (oh my God!) a no-host bar.

Tasteful low lamps had replaced the overhead fluorescent lighting that accentuated every line and crag and made us all look twenty years older. All the rows of ugly chairs were gone, except for those that circled the small number of round tables that would fit comfortably into the space—not nearly enough seating for everyone who came. That was supposed to keep people on their feet and circulating.

Accordingly, Hal and I got our drinks from the bar and circulated. The mayor was there, as were several members of the city council. The president of the chamber of commerce sat at one of the tables, chatting with Debra Carpentier and a man I presumed was her husband. I identified a couple of car dealers, the owners of several downtown businesses, and the chief of police.

Jodi and Elliott had come, as well as Fritz Baumgartner, the district attorney; his wife, Amy; and a few other lawyers. Monty and Charlie and their wives stood in a small group in a corner of the room, not circulating. I didn't see Marcus anywhere.

Jeannie Tracy sat at one of the tables talking to a woman I didn't recognize. Hal went over to talk to Elliott and Fritz, and Jodi and I went over and sat with Jeannie, whom Jodi knew. To my surprise, she knew the other woman too. Jodi knew a lot of people because of her beauty salon, which was patronized by nearly all the doctors' wives, as well as some of the doctors, including me.

"Toni, this is LaNae Manning; she's the wife of your new COO," she told me. "LaNae, this is Toni Day, one of the pathologists here. Oh, and look, here comes the other one!"

I turned to see Mike and his wife, Leezie, coming toward us. They took the remaining two seats. I performed introductions. Jodi knew who Mike and Leezie were but had never actually met them. Mike grabbed LaNae's hand and shook it vigorously. "Glad to meet you," he said. "How do you like it so far?"

Poor LaNae seemed overwhelmed by all the attention she was getting. She murmured something in response, but the noise level in the room drowned her out. She was a study in beige. Slender and graceful, with chin-length light brown hair, she wore a matching beige turtleneck sweater and skirt and a string of pearls. Next to Leezie Leonard, who was tall, blonde, and stylish to the point of glamour, LaNae looked almost dowdy. She tended to keep her eyes downcast, and her hair swung forward, covering the sides of her face, so I had difficulty getting a good look at her. The facial features I could see were pretty enough, but I knew I'd forget them the minute we left the party. Or maybe even sooner.

Marcus came up behind her and put his hands on her shoulders in a familiar and affectionate-looking gesture that wouldn't have caused concern if Elliott or Hal had done it to Jodi or me, but LaNae reacted like a nervous cat. She jumped guiltily and looked up at Marcus with unmistakable fear in her eyes, which were an unusual golden color, like a cat's. It happened so fast that I couldn't be sure I'd actually seen it.

Marcus said, "Time to go, dear," without any particular inflection, but LaNae stood up so precipitously that her chair fell over. She gasped, her eyes as big as saucers, while Marcus leaned over and casually righted it. She picked up her purse with shaking hands, dropped it, and knocked over her water. While Jeannie, Jodi, Leezie, and I quickly sopped the water up with napkins and told her it was okay, don't worry about it, no harm done, Marcus took her by the arm and hustled her away.

Jodi was the first to speak. "Well!"

"Poor thing," I said. "She acts like she's scared of her own shadow."

"Not *her* shadow," Jeannie said darkly. "His."

Jodi said, "Oh, no. You don't mean …"

"Oh, yes, I do mean," Jeannie said. "You couldn't miss the shiner."

Well, I'd missed it. "That must be why she wears her hair like that," I said, "and never looks anybody in the eye."

"That explains the makeup too," Leezie said. "She must have put it on with a trowel."

"She did have a lot of makeup on it," Jeannie said. "But from a certain angle, you could still see the bruise. And did you notice the bitten nails? Right down to the quick. And I'll bet there are bruises all around that arm Marcus hauled her out of here by."

"Maybe on her neck too," Leezie said. "I mean, *really*, who wears turtlenecks in July?"

"He's an abuser," I told Hal at home later.

"You want to be careful, sweetie," Hal said. "You could get into trouble, spreading rumors like that, especially without any proof."

"He's right," Elliott agreed. "He could sue you for slander if you go around saying things like that."

"I wasn't planning to go around saying it to anybody but you guys," I protested. "Why does she put up with it? I sure wouldn't."

"It's not the same for her," Jodi said. "She's been married to Marcus since she was nineteen. She's never had to work. She's totally dependent on him for everything, and besides that, they have six children between the ages of four and twelve."

I knew that in the Mormon world, men went on missions at the age of nineteen and were gone for a year and a half or two years. This meant that their college educations were interrupted and they came back as sophomores, two years more grown up and mature than their non-LDS peers. They usually married during college or right after graduation, and they were encouraged to have as many children as they could as soon as possible. I also knew that married couples were usually "sealed" in a temple, so that they would be together for eternity. I wasn't sure how divorce fit into that scenario.

I wondered if Marcus would continue to abuse LaNae for eternity too.

Then I began to wonder if Marcus could be targeting non-Mormons instead of women or ancillary services, but I discarded that idea almost as soon as I thought of it.

The Church of Latter-day Saints hadn't become one of the biggest religious organizations in the world by doing away with non-Mormons. They just kept making more Mormons by either birthing them or converting them. They had missionaries all over the world. They'd have them on the moon if there was anyone there to convert.

I felt pretty sure that the police would look unfavorably upon domestic abuse, Mormon or not. The problem would be getting it to their attention without committing slander. Or libel. Or getting myself kicked off the medical staff.

This might be the white underbelly I was looking for. But what the hell was I going to do with it?

CHAPTER 12

But to my mind, though I am native here
And to the manner born, it is a custom
More honored in the breach than in the observance.

—*William Shakespeare, **Hamlet***

Those who live in glass houses shouldn't throw stones. I decided to make sure I wasn't living in one before I went any further with this fight.

"Can anybody pull a credentials file and look at it?" I asked Monty.

"Sure," Monty said. "That material is public record. The board of medicine posts all that information on their website. Didn't you fill out one of their forms online?"

I did a mental head slap. Of course I had.

"How about peer-review records?" I asked.

"Those are protected," Monty said.

"Even in a malpractice suit?" I asked. "Or what if the board of medicine wants to see them?"

"They'd have to subpoena them. Doctor, what is the point of all these questions? What are you looking for?"

"I'm on a white-underbelly hunt," I said.

"Huh?"

I pulled my chair up close to his desk. "Monty, our esteemed COO threatened to make sure I never practice again anywhere in the country. What does he have on me that makes him think he can do that?"

Monty threw up his hands in frustration. "As far as I know, there's nothing in your file. You've never been subjected to peer review, and to my knowledge, there are no plans to do so. Is that what you wanted to know?"

Yes, but I wasn't through. "He threatened Mitzi because she had a baby by the wrong guy. Who else is he likely to be able to threaten?"

"You know I can't tell you what's in another doctor's peer-review records."

Well, there it was. I'd have to talk to the other doctors to find out if any of them had a white underbelly. Then all I had to do was convince them they should tell me about it. Conceivably, they might think it was *me* who was trying to blackmail them, not Marcus. As if I would do such a thing.

Well, I would, but only to Marcus, and then only if I could get away with it. Especially now that I knew what *his* white underbelly was. Not to mention his sexual harassment of Mitzi and me.

I would "hoist him by his own petard," as Willie Shakespeare would have said. I decided to create a "petard" by talking to my colleagues, who I was sure had no clue about what Marcus was up to.

George was in the middle of a procedure when I called, so I left a message, and he called me back about half an hour later. I hurried down to his office, went in, and closed the door after me. George, in green scrubs and surgical cap with a mask hanging around his neck, looked up from his paperwork in surprise. "Wow. Is it that serious?"

I pulled up a chair, sat down next to his desk, and told him all about Marcus's threats to me and Mitzi. George was disinclined to believe it until I told him it was all recorded on cell phones.

"Cell phones?" George said with skepticism. "You're just making that up."

Drag yourself into the twenty-first century, George. "Mike and I have it all saved on our computers. But that's not the point. I just want everybody to know what Marcus is doing. I think he's going to be an absolutely awful CEO, and I think the executive committee needs to reconsider. Maybe he wants to get all the non-Mormons fired and replace them with Mormons. Or get all the women fired and replace them with men. And I'm not sure he means to stop with the medical staff either. He tried to fire Lucille too."

George rubbed his hands over his face and combed his moustache with his fingers. "Jesus. I can't deal with this now."

"I know it's a bit much to absorb all at once, but we as a medical staff need to deal with it sometime. We can't let him do this. Come listen to what I've got on my computer."

But at that moment George got paged to the GI lab, and right after that I got paged for a frozen section.

"The first chance you get," I begged George. "Please. I need your help."

"Later," he said, and he was gone.

After my frozen section was done and I had grossed in the morning run of surgicals, I had a similar conversation with Dave Martin.

Dave was a family doc who did a lot of emergency room call, and he had patched up both Hal and me on multiple occasions. Dave and I went way back. He was a mild-mannered guy of average height, with brown hair and hazel eyes and a wry sense of humor, and he had come to Perrine not too long after I had.

Dave, conveniently, was a member of the executive committee this year. Not only that, but he was about to head to the cafeteria for lunch and agreed to stop on the way and listen to Marcus on my computer. He was aghast at what he heard.

"My God," he said. "What is he trying to do by getting rid of you *and* Mitzi? Does he have any idea how long it took to recruit the two of you? What's his problem?"

"That's our problem," I said. "We don't know what his problem is. Is he trying to get rid of female physicians? Or is there more to it?"

Dave took off his glasses and rubbed his eyes. "Has Monty said what he plans to do about this? Or doesn't he plan to do anything?"

"He told Marcus that he planned to investigate and that Marcus was not to do anything with regard to me, Mitzi, or Lucille until further notice," I said. "What I'm saying is, do we want somebody like this to be our CEO? I sure don't."

"I don't either," Dave said. "This is unbelievable. I'm not sure it's even legal. Okay, I'll bring it up at the executive committee meeting. Jack needs to know what's going on; after all, he's responsible for bringing the guy in here in the first place."

No wonder Jack had blown me off. He had a good reason for not wanting to hear it.

"Be careful," I advised Dave. "He might decide to fire you next. Keep your cell phone handy."

Debra Carpentier walked into histology while I was grossing the surgicals and asked me if I had time to talk.

"Sure," I said. "What about?"

"About these interviews I have planned," she said. "I thought I'd start with you."

Whatever I may have expected from her, it certainly wasn't that. "Start with me? Why?"

"Because you're a woman, for one thing. And you aren't afraid to speak your mind."

Well, I thought, *that's one way to look at it.* "When do you want me to do it?"

"I thought next week sometime. Wednesday work for you?"

"I guess so. What do you want me to talk about?"

"Oh, I'll interview you on camera right here in your lab, if that's okay. I wondered if you could kind of show me what you do here so I know what questions to ask."

"Good idea," I said and gave her the same spiel as I did visiting doctors. I was probably overwhelming her with information, but I kept talking anyway. Once I get going, it's hard to shut me up. She idly reached into the cupboard and pulled out a jar at random, reading the label as I continued talking. Suddenly she interrupted me.

"*Cyanide?* What in the world do you use *that* for?"

I took the jar from her. The label read "potassium ferrocyanide." "That's for the iron stain," I explained. "It's the Prussian blue reaction. If there's iron in the tissue, it turns blue."

"Isn't it poisonous?" She seemed agitated, and I tried to calm her down.

"Sure," I said. "I don't think any of the reagents in here would do you much good if you swallowed them or inhaled them."

"But ferrocyanide! I mean, would this turn into cyanide if someone took it by mouth?"

Jeez, Debra, get off it already. "Probably. I should think gastric acid would break it down and create hydrocyanic acid, which would kill you pretty fast. Why this sudden interest in cyanide?"

She turned away from me. She seemed shaken and suddenly anxious to get out of histology. "Oh, I don't know … Just curious, I guess," she mumbled. "I'll let you get back to your work now." With that, she left.

I stood looking after her, wondering what the hell had just happened.

CHAPTER 13

The law hath not been dead, though it hath slept.

—William Shakespeare, **Measure for Measure**

When I got home, Hal informed me that we'd been invited to a backyard barbecue. Elliott's partner John Stevenson and his wife, Trish, had just moved into a new house in one of the more upscale neighborhoods, a gated community called Canyon Crest. Many of the houses had a gorgeous view of the Snake River Canyon and the Perrine Bridge.

A picture of the sun going down behind the bridge and reflecting off the river could be seen on most of the chamber of commerce literature about Twin Falls. I'd often wondered whose backyard that picture had been taken from. The downside, of course, was that the afternoon sun blazed into the huge floor-to-ceiling windows of all these gorgeous houses, making it necessary to draw the drapes on that gorgeous view.

We'd been invited for six o'clock; the sun wouldn't be going down for another three hours. In the meantime, sun hats, dark glasses, and sunscreen were the order of the day. Once the sun went down, mosquito repellent would be needed as well. John's house was right on the canyon rim, and that famous picture could well have been taken from his house.

Besides John and Trish, Jodi and Elliott, and Hal and me, there were Elliott's other partner, Stan Snow, and his wife, Cherie, and Fritz and Amy Baumgartner. It was a nice, comfortable group, sitting around in lawn chairs, enjoying beers or cocktails, and eating crudités, barbecued ribs, corn on the cob, potato salad, coleslaw, and the like. The sun set behind the Perrine Bridge, and the sky reflected pinkly off the river even after the sun had gone down.

The only problem was that I felt as if I was about to have an allergy attack. My nose began to feel stuffed up, and my eyes itched. Small wonder—the vegetation beyond the limits of John and Trish's patio consisted of wild grass and weeds, even sagebrush.

That was when we heard it. Voices raised in anger, first a man's voice, then a woman's, followed by a slap, a scream, and then sobs. I couldn't actually make out any words. The man's voice boomed again. Then we heard another slap, another scream, and more sobs. The absolute hopelessness of those sobs tore at my heart. The man continued to hurl abuse at the woman. The woman shouted back. More slaps and screams and sobs ensued. The timing wasn't lost on me either. Did that man turn into a vampire or a werewolf when the sun went down?

I sneezed.

John got up. "That's it," he announced. "I've had enough. I'm calling the police." He went into the house.

I retrieved my purse from under my chair and rummaged around for tissues.

"Jeez," Hal said, "I wonder who lives there."

Trish overheard me. "They moved in just before we did," she said in a low voice. "I think their name's Manning. They've got a whole bunch of little kids. I don't know how she does it. He doesn't help at all, and he yells at her like that all the time."

"And hits her like that all the time?" I asked.

John came out of the house in time to hear my question. "Yeah, he does. I swear, if I'd known who lived next door, I'd have never bought this house. It's not just her; he yells at the kids and hits them too. What a flaming asshole!"

I sneezed again and blew my nose. *Why the hell didn't I take an allergy pill before coming over here?* I wondered.

"But she's really nice," Trish said. "Just this week she went up and down the street and gave all the neighbors jars of homemade peach-and-apricot jam."

"So are the police coming?" Hal asked.

"Yeah," John said, "but they didn't sound real jazzed about it."

Apparently they weren't jazzed at all. By the time Hal and I went home, they still hadn't come.

Hal and I were silent all the way home, except for my sneezing and blowing. I didn't know what Hal was thinking, but I felt traumatized, as if I had been beaten and yelled at, instead of LaNae. It was one thing to know that someone had a reputation for being an abuser; it was quite another to actually witness the abuse. I felt guilty and soiled at the same time for having been an inadvertent witness to LaNae's ordeal and her shame. I found myself identifying with her to the point where I even looked at my own husband with a jaundiced eye. I found myself shrinking away from Hal, huddling over on my side of the car, and I felt the utter despair that had to be LaNae's constant daily companion. Had it been like that when she first married Marcus? Had she lived like that since she was nineteen years old? Had Marcus abused her when they were engaged? Had she been forced to marry him anyway?

Since the police had been called, Marcus would now be on record as having had a domestic violence complaint against him. That is, if LaNae filed a complaint. If it had been me, I would have filed one in a heartbeat; it would have given me an escape from an impossible situation. Who the hell would *live* like that if she didn't have to?

Obviously she felt that she *did* have to.

I couldn't fathom such a thing, but then, I was a doctor and self-sufficient. Plus Hal and I didn't have children, except for Bambi, who was already twenty-one and married.

But this line of thinking was absurd. Hal was a gentle and loving man, a big teddy bear. I'd never known him to resort to violence with anyone, ever. Throwing up his hands and yelling "Oy gevalt!" to the ceiling was about as violent as he ever got.

By the time we'd gotten home and walked into the kitchen from the garage, I'd come around to feeling so profoundly grateful that I'd married such a man that tears came to my eyes, and I felt a sob coming up from my chest. I hurried over to the counter, grabbed another tissue, and blew my nose, but it didn't fool Hal. He put his arms around me and tilted my face up to his. "Honey, what's wrong?"

Mere words failed me, so I did the next best thing. I burst into tears, which stuffed me up even more than before. Hal held me close and stroked my hair while I cried myself out. "I know, sweetie," he said softly. "It made me feel sick too. How can anyone treat someone they love like that?"

I was about to say I hadn't a clue when the doorbell interrupted me. Hal went to the door and admitted Jodi and Elliott. Jodi looked as ragged as I felt, her eyes red and her mascara smeared. "You too, huh?" was all she said, and I hugged her. Hal went to the bar and, without asking if anybody wanted anything, poured four shots of brandy, neat. I let our dogs, Killer and Geraldine, inside and gave them Milk-Bones and took an allergy pill. We sat around the kitchen table, sipping.

"The cops came right after you left," Jodi said. "But they didn't do anything."

"That's not exactly true," Elliott said. "They talked to John, and they asked who else had heard what happened, and pretty much all of us had. But then they went next door, and when they came back, they told us that Mrs. Manning wouldn't make a formal complaint, so there was nothing they could do."

"Shit," Hal said.

"Was Pete there?" I asked.

"No, it wasn't Pete," Elliott said. "It was Bernie Kincaid and that other young fellow—Darren? Dylan? Something like that."

"Darryl?" I asked. "Looks like Merlin Olsen?"

"That's the one."

"So if there was no formal complaint, there won't be any record of this?" I asked.

"Well, there'll be a record of the call in the call ledger, and a report, but without a formal complaint, there's not one freakin' thing they can do about it."

"Hey," Jodi said, "you know what's weird? Where were the kids? How come they weren't crying and screaming too? Six kids under the age of twelve, Daddy beating up on Mommy, and not a peep! What's up with that?"

"Those kids are probably used to it," Elliott said grimly. "If they know what's good for them, they were probably huddled under the freakin' covers, hoping Daddy wouldn't come after them next."

I shuddered. "Now let me get this straight," I said. "As long as LaNae won't file a formal complaint against Marcus, there's nothing anybody can do to him, right? So the neighbors can call the police until they're blue in the face, and it won't do any good?"

"That's right," Elliott said, "and we wouldn't have heard anything if it hadn't been summer, with the windows and doors open and us outside on the patio."

"So what if he beats her up so badly that she ends up in the hospital? What then?"

"If she won't file a formal complaint with the police, she's unlikely to admit to the doctor that her husband beat her up. She'll claim she ran into a door or fell down the freakin' stairs."

"But what if the *doctor* thinks her husband caused her injuries? Can't he tell the police?" Jodi asked.

"He'd have to be awfully damn sure about it," Elliott said, "especially if the wife herself denied it. If a doctor filed a complaint of domestic abuse, he'd have to testify about it in court. Who are they going to believe, the doctor or the wife? The plaintiff could sue for defamation of character. What doctor in his right mind would do that when the plaintiff is the freakin' COO of the hospital he works in?"

Jesus H. Christ on a crutch. The possibilities boggled my mind. "I see what you mean," I said. "While all that grinds slowly on in court, Marcus could file a complaint with the board of medicine, the doctor could lose his privileges, and LaNae could sue him for malpractice. He'd lose everything."

"Okay, I can see your point," Jodi said. "But again, what about the kids? What happens if they show up in school with a black eye or a broken nose or cigarette burns on their hands—"

"No cigarette burns," I interrupted. "Mormons don't smoke."

"But I bet they barbecue," Hal said. "Matches, butane lighters, glowing charcoal briquettes …"

"They're kids," Elliott said. "Kids are always getting hurt. They fight with each other, fall out of trees or off playground equipment, stick their fingers in electric outlets, play with matches, and stuff like that. Who's gonna give them a second glance if they show up with a bruise or a broken arm?"

"Those kids could fall into the canyon," I said.

"See what I mean?" Elliott said. "How could anybody prove the injuries are due to abuse?"

"There is one way," I said. "Look for patterns. The same injuries over and over. X-rays that show lots of old fractures—more than you'd see in a normal child."

"So if we could get x-rays of all the kids, we'd have something to go on!" Jodi said excitedly.

"Not quite," I said. "I hate to rain on your parade, but how would we justify doing that? We can't just ask parents to bring in their kids and x-ray them without a reason. Even if we saw one of the kids with a fracture, we could only x-ray the fracture, nothing else. Apart from the liability issues, like a kid getting bone sarcoma years from now and suing us for the unnecessary x-ray, there is also the cost. Without a clinical indication, insurance won't pay, so Marcus would never allow it, and he'd be within his rights."

"Bullshit," Hal said. "You got a total-body x-ray on a baby once, I remember."

"It was an autopsy," I reminded him. "The baby was already dead. Besides, it takes years of abuse to show a pattern, and these folks have only been here a month or so."

"What about in California?" Hal asked. "Maybe there are hospital records where they came from."

"We'd have to subpoena them," Elliott said, "and no judge would issue one, not with so little information."

"How about if one of them dies from their injuries?" Jodi asked.

"Well, that would be a freakin' horse of another color," Elliott said. "That would be murder."

CHAPTER 14

Men are seldom blessed with good fortune
and good sense at the same time.

—*Livy*

Hal and I both slept late Saturday morning. Apparently we'd worn ourselves out the night before; either that, or we'd drunk each other under the table. Brandy and Allegra made a dandy sleeping concoction. I couldn't remember what time Jodi and Elliott had gone home.

The ringing of the phone in the upstairs hallway woke us at noon. Hal groaned and buried his head under his pillow. The message was clear.

I hauled my reluctant butt out of bed and went out into the hall to answer the call.

"Antoinette," said my mother, "I'm here at the airport, right on time, and you aren't. I do hope you and Hal haven't forgotten that I was coming?"

We had, but I would rather have died than tell my mother that.

"Darling Mum," I said, as brightly as I could manage with my eyes still essentially glued shut, "of course not. We just overslept, that's all. Stay put. I'll be right there."

"Well, *really*," Mum retorted, her British turned up full blast, "I can't imagine where you think I might go. And there are such things as *alarm* clocks, you know, dear."

Oh jeez. I was in so much trouble.

I hung up the phone with a heartfelt "Bloody sodding hell!" and went back into the bedroom. Hal moved his pillow a careful millimeter and opened one eye. "Fiona, right?"

"You remembered? Why didn't you remind me? We could have set an alarm!"

We'd known since Christmas that Mum was supposed to come for my birthday and stay a week. With all that had been going on in the last week, I'd completely forgotten. My birthday was tomorrow.

"I didn't remember until just now," Hal said. "You don't usually cuss in British unless it has to do with your mother."

"So what are we supposed to do now?"

Hal swung his long legs out of bed, stood up, and stretched. "Go get her—what else?"

"Looking like this?"

"You look fine. Throw on some clothes and go. I'll start breakfast and have everything ready when you get back."

I supposed that made sense. Hal was much better at cooking a sumptuous breakfast than I, and Mum had seen me looking much worse than this. Of course, since I looked exactly as if I'd just gotten out of bed, everybody I knew would also be at the airport, picking up other people I knew. It's one of the rules.

However, by the time I got there, nearly everyone had picked up their passengers and luggage and departed. Mum sat bolt upright on a bench outside the door, suitcase at her side, purse and train case in her lap, ankles demurely crossed, head high, every curly red hair in place. The crown jewels would not have looked out of place. Oh, she was pissed, all right.

But she had taught me a long time ago, among other things, that the best defense was a good offense. So I attacked.

I rushed up to her, sat down on the bench next to her, and threw my arms around her neck. "Oh, Mum, I'm so sorry," I said in a small, shaky voice that sounded as if I was about to burst into tears, "but I've spent the last week fighting for my job, and I was simply exhausted!" Then I buried my head on her shoulder, not the easiest thing to do with a purse and a train case in the way.

But Mum rose to the occasion, as she always did. She calmly put the purse and train case aside and took me in her arms. "Oh, kitten, why didn't you say so?"

Well, after all that, it was a simple matter of getting her and her things into the car. By the time we got home, I had brought her up to date on Marcus Manning and his heinous misdeeds, and she was suitably outraged at someone other than Hal or me.

My mother had been born in England and had met my father, an American soldier, in London. He'd been killed in a car accident shortly after their marriage. Mum had been seventeen at the time, and pregnant.

I'd been expecting breakfast, but not a party. Jodi and Elliott were there when we got home, and so were Bambi and Pete. Hal had made a sumptuous breakfast, all right, one that included champagne.

"Champagne?" I asked.

"Mimosas," he answered economically. "Want to give me a hand here?" He maneuvered delicately through the open french window with a platter of waffles in one hand and a platter of bacon in the other, sidestepping Killer and Geraldine, who had their sights set on the bacon—turkey bacon, in deference to Bambi, who hadn't yet become a cafeteria Jew like her father. I grabbed the platter as it tilted precariously, nearly dumping its load right into the dogs' greedy mouths.

"Move it, you two," I commanded. "This is people food. You don't get any."

We finally settled around the table, the dogs safely occupied with Milk-Bones while we partook of a repast so delicious that I wondered what was in store for me when my birthday actually arrived.

Mum always said that she'd known she'd end up living in America someday when I made my first appearance on its Independence Day, and she'd been right. We were both naturalized citizens, having emigrated from the UK when I was three to make our home with my father's parents in Long Beach, California. They had both passed on, but Mum still lived in their house.

I had no idea how we were supposed to get anything done after being stuffed to the gills with high-fat, high-carbohydrate food, plus champagne, but I guessed that was the whole point. We weren't supposed to.

"This weekend is for Toni," Hal said. "She's had a perfectly awful week. Did she tell you about it, Fiona?"

"My goodness, yes," Mum said. "How did your hospital end up with such a bloody sod for an administrator?"

"He's not administrator yet," Bambi said. "He's a COO."

Mum looked confused. I filled her in. "Chief operations officer," I said. "He's in charge of ancillary services, which includes pathology and the lab."

"And radiology too," Hal said. "He also tried to fire the radiologist."

"Both of us are ancillary services, and both of us are women," I said. "We're not sure which one of those is his motivation."

"I'd guess both, dear," Mum said. "Don't both of you have partners? Did he go after them?"

"Yes, but they're both men," I told her. "And no, he didn't."

"There you are, dear," Mum said. "Unless he also goes after your partners, his motivation is gender and not ancillary services. Perhaps he doesn't want to deal with women doctors, period. But you haven't answered my question: How did you end up with him in the first place?"

"He was recommended by the chief of staff's brother, who's worked with him," I said.

"But surely he's got references other than that," Mum said. "Didn't anyone check them?"

Hal and I looked at each other. "Huh," I said finally. "That's a really good question. Maybe they just took Jack's brother's word for it. Maybe Jack just railroaded him through the executive committee, and that was it. I'll have to ask Monty on Tuesday."

"Maybe this Jack has an agenda too," Mum said.

"Good Lord," I said. "What kind of an agenda could he have?" But as I said that, I remembered how evasive Jack had been when I'd told him what Marcus had said to Mitzi and me. At the time, I had thought he was hiding something.

"If Jack's agenda is getting rid of female docs," Hal pointed out, "you wouldn't be there, and neither would Mitzi. He's been there longer than both of you."

"And Jeannie Tracy," I added. "Okay, so that probably isn't it. Do you suppose Marcus has something on Jack, so that he has to go along with anything Marcus does?"

"You mean blackmail?" Pete said.

"That makes more freakin' sense than anything I've heard so far," Elliott said. "Either Marcus has something on Jack, or he has something on Jack's brother, and Jack has to go along to keep his brother out of trouble."

"Or maybe Jack's brother has something on Jack," suggested Jodi.

Elliott gave her a patronizing look. "Don't make it more complicated than it has to be, okay?"

Jodi stuck out her tongue at him. "You're just speculating," she said. "You don't know any more than the rest of us."

"Well," Hal said, "maybe next week Marcus will attack somebody else. Depending on who that is, it might give us more of a clue about what his agenda is."

"Whoever he attacks," I said, "will have to be someone in an ancillary service, because that's what Marcus's jurisdiction is right now. We'd have to wait six months before he could attack anybody else."

"But maybe he could do a smear campaign on somebody else so that one of the other administrators would fire them," Bambi said.

"Wow," Jodi said, "that opens up the *rest* of the medical staff for him to attack."

"Why stop there?" Hal asked. "What about the rest of the employees? He did try to fire Lucille, don't forget."

"Hell," I retorted, "he tried to fire *everybody* in the lab and diagnostic imaging, remember?"

"Whatever for, kitten?" asked Mum.

I laughed. "Because when he called me and Mitzi into his office and threatened us, our respective chief techs recorded the whole thing on their cell phones, and Mike put it on his computer and let everybody listen to it. It was quite a party. We even had pizza."

"Good heavens," Mum said. "What next?"

"That's what we're all wondering," Hal said. "It's kind of difficult when we don't know what it is he wants."

"Think about it, Hal, dear," Mum said. "Surely it's not rocket science. If you were in his position, what would you want?"

"To keep my ass out of trouble," Hal said with a smile.

"No, dear," Mum said with monumental patience, "you wouldn't. You'd want to run the whole show. Wouldn't you?"

"But, Mum," I objected, "he's gonna be CEO anyway in another year. That's the plan. Unless he screws it up by pissing us all off."

Mum gave me a green-eyed glare I had no trouble interpreting. It clearly said, *Antoinette, really, your language!*

"Antoinette, *really*," Mum said, "didn't you just tell me that your hospital is going to become part of a hospital system? Maybe he's not going to be satisfied just being a hospital CEO. Perhaps he wants to be *system* CEO. Have you thought of that?"

CHAPTER 15

Any fool can tell the truth, but it requires a man of some sense to know how to lie well.

—*Samuel Butler*

Of course. Why hadn't we thought of that? It made perfect sense.

Hal stood up and bowed to her. "Fiona," he said reverently, "you have just done a masterful job of clearing away the trees."

"Trees, dear?"

"So that we could see the forest," I explained.

"Ah," Mum said. "But who *is* the forest?"

Hal and I looked at each other, not sure what she meant. Bambi got it, however. "She means who are the trees Marcus is going to have to chop down to get to his goal?"

"Aha!" I said. "You mean who is he going to have to get rid of, right? Well, I'd say that would include anybody he doesn't think he could work with, or anybody that won't just go along with whatever he wants to do."

"Anybody who'd get in his way, you mean," Jodi said.

"That's Toni in a freakin' nutshell," Elliott said. "If she didn't argue, she'd die."

For the sake of our company and to avoid slowing the conversation down, I decided to overlook the possible insult. Besides, I felt pretty sure Elliott didn't mean it that way.

"It's Mitzi and Jeannie too," I said. "We all disrupted that staff meeting, and that was the first time Marcus met us."

"Don't forget your partner," Hal said.

"Oh yes, and now George and Dave—"

"And your chief techs," Hal interrupted.

"Not just them," I said. "It's everybody in the lab and diagnostic imaging. They were all out in the hall when Marcus threatened to fire them. They all made it pretty clear whose side they were on."

"So Marcus could continue to attack you and Mitzi by systematically firing your best employees, thereby weakening your departments, so that the freakin' medical staff would demand new leadership, and then he'd get rid of you and Mitzi and Mike," Elliott said.

"All in one swell foop," Hal added.

"My stars and garters," Mum said, "what a horrible thought."

"It's worse than that," I said. "He's going to keep Mitzi and Mike and me so busy defending our employees and getting Monty to bail them out that we won't have time to get our own work done."

"Monty could get so disgusted that he might just go ahead and retire now," Hal said. "Then what would you do?"

"Go to Charlie, I suppose," I said.

"Good luck with that," Hal said. "I get the idea that Charlie, however nice and comfortable he may be, is nothing more than window dressing. He never seems to make decisions; he just passes them on to Monty. You may just be dead in the water if Monty leaves and Charlie doesn't want to antagonize Marcus."

This was getting worse and worse. I got up from the table. "I think I've had just about as much joy and rapture as I can stand," I said.

"Where are you going, kitten?" asked Mum.

"Honey," Hal said, "while you're up, could you bring more coffee?"

I bared my teeth at him and went into the house. There was very little coffee left in the pot, which figured. I set up a new pot, stuck my head out the open kitchen window to tell everybody that they'd have to wait, and went upstairs to the computer, where I made a list.

When I was done, I e-mailed it to myself at work.

I needn't have worried about what Hal had planned for my birthday.

Being the Fourth of July, there was already a host of activities for us to partake in. It wasn't until I'd started school in Long Beach that I'd learned, rather cruelly, that they weren't there just for me. Other children can be so mean, especially to a kid who talks like a bloody Englishman.

But those days were long gone, and I'd long since learned that I could have fun anyway. First there was the parade, which started at nine in the morning and wound its way through downtown on Main Avenue and then up Shoshone and Blue Lakes until it ended at the Magic Valley Mall. Hal's and my house, at 205 Montana Street, was close enough to Shoshone that we could see pretty much everything from our front porch while we enjoyed our coffee and the doughnuts I'd gone and gotten earlier from Jim Bob, who, bless his heart, was open on holiday mornings.

Then there was the country-club picnic down at Bass Lake, followed later in the afternoon by a golf tournament. That night we'd have a fancy dinner, and that *would* be just for me.

Most of the doctors belonged to the country club, and I saw several of them cavorting in the lake with their kids. I did not see Marcus Manning, which pleased me. I had no doubt that if he saw a country-club membership as an aid to advancement, he'd waste no time seeking one, but right at the time, there was a waiting list.

Thank God for small favors, I thought.

I did see Charlie, however, lying in the sun on a raft anchored out in the middle of the lake, all by himself. Seeing that as an opportunity, I swam out to the raft and hauled myself up beside him.

I must have dripped on him or something, because he started and sat up suddenly as I sat down next to him. "Oh, Toni," he exclaimed in relief. "I must have fallen asleep or something."

"You are getting a little pink," I said. "Maybe you'd better turn over."

He did so.

"I thought Marcus might be here with his family," I said, as innocently as I could manage. "I thought you or Monty might have brought him as your guest. His kids would love it here, with the lake and the games and all."

He grunted. "Not hardly. Monty doesn't have a membership, and I can't stand the guy. What a phony. I hope he doesn't ask me to sponsor him, because I won't."

Well, that took care of the question of Charlie being a Marcus supporter. Could the rest of the story be far behind?

Our Charlie being the gossip that he was, I knew I would soon know everything he knew, unless somebody else decided to swim out here.

"I imagine Jack will be glad to sponsor him," I said, "seeing as it was his brother that recommended him to us. And I was just curious: Did you or Monty check his references or just take Jack's brother's word?"

"Are you kidding?" Charlie snorted. "You know Jack as well as I do. His brother was singing the guy's praises to the skies. Monty and I didn't have a chance to check anything."

"Did either of you actually talk to Jack's brother, or did this all come through Jack? What's his brother's name anyway?"

"It's Bob," Charlie said, "and no, neither one of us actually talked to him."

"So basically, you took Jack's word. Is that right?"

"What are you getting at, Toni?"

"You do know about what he did to me and Mitzi, don't you?"

"I heard about it," Charlie said. "I could hardly believe it. Like I said, I don't like the guy, but that seemed outrageous even for him."

"Well, believe it," I told him. "What I want to know is, did Jack have anything to say about it?"

"I haven't talked to Jack," Charlie said.

"Well, I have," I said, "and I got the distinct impression that he was trying to hide something. In fact, I was wondering if maybe Marcus was blackmailing him or his brother. Have you heard about anything like that?"

Charlie rolled over and sat up. "Good grief, Toni. Who have you been talking to?"

"You mean there *is* something?" I asked eagerly.

"Monty said something like that to me just the other day."

"Exactly what did Monty say?" I asked.

Charlie scratched his head. "It was right after Marcus threatened you, when you put on that deaf act in his office. Monty heard about that, and he said something to the effect that he didn't think the guy was going to work out but he didn't hold out much hope of getting rid of Marcus anytime soon, because Marcus seemed to have, and I quote, 'a stranglehold on the chief of staff.'"

Hot damn! I knew it!

"What about the other docs?" I asked. "What do they think of Marcus?"

"Mixed reviews," Charlie said. "I think most of them like the guy. He seems real easy to talk to, from what I hear, a really nice guy, and he seems to have some good ideas about how to run a hospital. And then I hear about how he treated you and Mitzi, and that makes me wonder what's really going on here. Did we screw up big time, not checking him out more thoroughly?"

"Mitzi and I would say so," I replied. "But maybe it's not too late to do that now. We certainly don't need a CEO who targets people before he knows anything about them."

"That's not entirely true," Charlie said. "He certainly knew something about Mitzi when he targeted her."

"True, but what he knew was common knowledge around here."

"Maybe he didn't realize that," Charlie said, "but you've gotta admit, he really did a number on her even so. Didn't you say that she got sick afterward?"

"She did. I heard her."

"If it was common knowledge, why would she react like that?"

Guys. What do they know? "He made her feel dirty," I said. "He threatened her on the basis of moral turpitude. He made it sound like he could really get her voted off the staff for it, even though nobody's had a problem with it until now. What Mitzi did was wrong, and she knows it. That makes her a target. And now I'm worried that he's going to dig until he finds something unsavory about everybody who gets in his way, so he can blackmail them or get rid of them."

Charlie turned his palms up in bewilderment. "What for?"

"This is just speculation," I said, "and don't tell anybody I said this, but maybe he wants to be system CEO of Cascade someday and is systematically eliminating all opposition to get there."

"Holy shit," Charlie said. "This is incredible, if it's true. But, Toni, all we have is his treatment of you and Mitzi to go on. Chauvinistic as it is, the rest of the staff is just gonna shrug that off as he-said–she-said stuff."

"Not exactly," I said. "It was all recorded on cell phones. Ask Mike. Ask Dave Martin. Ask Monty, for God's sake. They heard it too. Monty's been on Marcus's case about it."

"And can't do anything about it, because Marcus has a stranglehold on Jack," Charlie said. "Okay, Toni, you made your point. I'll start making phone calls tomorrow. No, Tuesday. Tomorrow's a holiday."

Ordinarily I like having days off from work—who doesn't?—but that Monday made me feel like my hands were tied. I was champing at the bit to find out more about Marcus Manning and couldn't do anything about it. My list of things to do was just sitting there in cyberspace, and I couldn't get anything done.

Or could I?

I had a computer at home, for God's sake. I could Google people on it. I didn't have to be at work. This was even better, because nobody would come into my office and catch me doing it. Like Marcus. I could just see him barging in and catching me Googling him. I wasn't sure he could do anything to me, but he'd certainly cause a scene.

I grabbed my coffee and went upstairs to the den, where I fired up the computer and got on the Internet. When Google came up, I typed in "Marcus Manning."

Several links came up. Most were related to an obituary of a Marcus Manning who had been killed in a drive-by shooting somewhere in Utah. After choosing and rejecting about ten links, I found him. Education: undergraduate, Brigham Young University, double major in economics and marketing. Funny, I'd always thought those were the same thing, but I guess that was just me. Postgraduate: UCLA, business administration. Positions: assistant administrator, Tustin Community Hospital, Tustin, California; assistant administrator, Fountain Valley Community Hospital, Fountain Valley, California; quality assurance officer, St. Joseph's Hospital, Orange, California; office manager, Seaside Medical Associates, Huntington Beach, California; assistant operations officer, Hoag Memorial Medical Center, Newport Beach, California.

He'd sure held a lot of positions, our Marcus. And none of them for longer than six months. Interesting. One tended to wonder why.

I hit print and went downstairs to get more coffee. Hal and Mum were sitting out on the back deck, deep in conversation, so I didn't bother them. I went back upstairs, intent upon my quest.

I Googled Tustin Community Hospital. The homepage came up. I wrote down the particulars—the address, phone number, and website. I went to the website and bookmarked it. I clicked on the link marked "Medical Staff." A list of names came up, all of them hyperlinks. I clicked on one at random. Up came an advertisement for the medical practice group that person belonged to, complete with address, phone number, and website. I ran down the list. Under anesthesiology, I found a former classmate.

I wrote down the particulars and moved on to Fountain Valley Community Hospital. There, under internal medicine, I found another former classmate.

Sheesh. This was almost too easy.

At St. Joseph's, I found someone in vascular surgery who'd been a fellow intern. Then, at Hoag Memorial, I hit pay dirt. In pathology and laboratory medicine, I found a fellow resident. A woman.

Aha! Now we were getting somewhere.

Next I Googled Jack's brother. Entering the name "Robert Allen" into Google brought up several gazillion entries. Adding "hospital administrator" to it narrowed things down a bit. Robert David Allen, one of the administrators of John Wayne Memorial Hospital in Newport Beach, California, was second on the list. I clicked on him and found his curriculum vitae online. He'd been in the same position for fifteen years. A hyperlink to the hospital website led me to the hyperlink for the medical staff, where lo and behold I found another former fellow intern, who'd also been a classmate, in anesthesiology. I clicked on him, got his group practice website, and wrote down address, phone number, and e-mail address. Then I had a brainstorm.

Bambi was from Newport Beach. Her mother, Hal's ex-wife; her stepfather; and her two brothers lived in Newport Beach still. Her stepfather was a car dealer there, selling Mercedes and BMWs, among other foreign, sporty vehicles that might appeal to wealthy doctors, which Newport Beach had in abundance.

I couldn't really expect Hal to contact his ex-wife, but Bambi could call her parents and ask some questions in the course of her weekly conversations with them.

In the meantime, I'd already come up with a tidbit of information that told me the Newport Beach connection might be the best one yet. Marcus hadn't put John Wayne Memorial on his curriculum vitae. Why not? If he hadn't been there in some capacity, how would he know Jack's brother? Bob Allen had been in the same place for fifteen years. Marcus had been all over the map, but Bob hadn't. Marcus had to have worked at John Wayne Memorial at some time, and something awful must have happened for him not to include it in his résumé.

What could it have been? Had he been fired? What for?

Whatever it was, Jack's brother had praised him to the skies. Why would he do that if Marcus had left there in ignominious circumstances? Was Marcus blackmailing him? What about?

According to Charlie, Monty had said that Marcus had a "stranglehold" on Jack. Could those two things be related?

Jack had been at Perrine Memorial for over ten years. Where had he come from originally? Could he have known Marcus in a previous life? That was difficult to imagine. Jack was in his early fifties, and Marcus was still in his thirties, early forties at the most. They weren't contemporaries by any means. But was it possible that Marcus had been working in some capacity at the same hospital where Jack had been a resident or intern or even a medical student doing a clinical rotation? No, that didn't make sense. Jack was nearly twenty years older than Marcus.

I went to the Idaho State Board of Medicine website and clicked on the Idacare forms we had all filled out back in the nineties. These were public record and accessible to patients. Jack had attended medical school at UCLA and done a straight internal medicine internship, internal medicine residency, and pulmonary medicine fellowship there.

Well, well. Marcus had gotten his MBA from UCLA. They had been there at the same time.

But they'd been in different departments. How would they have known each other? It couldn't have been through work. It would have had to have been social. Perhaps they'd met at a party. Maybe they'd dated the same girl. Maybe they'd had friends in common. Maybe their parents knew each other. No, that couldn't be it. Marcus's parents lived in Twin Falls.

And Marcus was LDS. How likely would it be that he'd have been socializing with the likes of Jack, who, I'd been told, could put away a good deal of alcohol and had become the life of the party on several occasions? I personally had seen him pretty well lit up at a Christmas party a couple of years ago, so chances were good that Jack wasn't LDS. In fact, come to think of it, I knew he wasn't. The Allens went to the Episcopal church. I'd seen them there on the occasions that I took Mum to Midnight Mass on Christmas Eve.

So how could Marcus get close enough to Jack to know something to blackmail him with?

That question would have to wait until tomorrow.

CHAPTER 16

And I thought he had been so cunning and so valiant in fence,
I'ld have seen him damned ere I'ld have challenged him.

—*William Shakespeare,* **Twelfth Night**

My list was right there waiting for me when I got to work Tuesday morning, and so was a pile of mail. An envelope from the Idaho State Board of Medicine sat on top of the pile. I eyed it as if it were a snake coiled up and ready to strike while Marcus's words reverberated in my brain. *"Doctor, you had better be careful ... I can make it very difficult here for you. I can make sure you never practice medicine anywhere in the United States, if need be. You will be very sorry you ever decided to tangle with me."*

Well, there it was. He'd done it—made sure I would never again practice anywhere in the country.

My first impulse was to throw the thing into the wastebasket, but I knew that wouldn't solve anything. I may as well open the damn thing and get it over with.

But then a frozen section arrived. I closed my list and shut down my computer before I left my office. If Marcus came snooping, he'd have to reboot, and he didn't know my password.

Sure enough, he came. Right in the middle of the frozen section.

"Doctor, we need to talk."

I sighed. "Right now? I'm in the middle of a frozen section."

Marcus didn't take the hint. "Yes, Doctor, right now."

"Marcus," I said, "your timing stinks. You're interfering with patient care if you delay me in giving the surgeon a diagnosis."

He ignored that. "I've been talking with Charlie Nelson."

Uh-oh. "How nice for you. Did you enjoy it?"

"He told me all about his conversation with you at the country club."

Shit. "That must have been fascinating."

"Oh, it was, it was," he assured me. "How dare you tell him that I'm blackmailing Dr. Allen!"

"I didn't," I said. "Would you mind moving over a bit, please? You're standing right in front of the cryostat."

Marcus didn't move. "Then how did he find out?"

"Beats me. Move, please."

He moved enough for me to put the specimen into the cryostat to freeze but then moved right back into my personal space. "Then how did you find out?"

"Find out what?" I was damned if I was going to make this easier for him, even if it meant that Russ Jensen would have to scrub out and come down here to find out what was happening to his frozen section. In fact, maybe that would be a good thing.

"That I'm blackmailing Dr. Allen."

That sounded like an admission, although I was sure Marcus hadn't intended it to be.

"Oh, are you really?" I asked him with mock eagerness, as if it were a totally new topic. With luck, maybe I could confuse him into admitting it. "With what?"

"Doctor, I'm asking the questions here."

"Toni, what the hell's going on down here?" asked a new voice. Russ Jensen, in green scrubs, paper cap on his head, mask hanging around his neck, came into histology. "I've been waiting … Marcus? What are you doing, interfering with our pathologist?"

"That's exactly what he's doing," I said. "I asked him to leave, but short of physical violence, I don't know how to get him out of my hair."

"Now look, Doctor, I don't appreciate your telling lies about me," Marcus said. "I demand an apology."

You won't get one, asshole, I thought. I opened my mouth to speak, but Russ forestalled me. "Now you look, Manning, I don't appreciate you coming in here and interfering with Toni when I'm in the operating room with a patient under anesthesia waiting for an answer to tell me what I need to do next. So I'd appreciate it if you'd get your butt out of here and let her do her job."

Russ was a gentle soul, not given to physical violence or even raising his voice in anger, but the short-sleeved scrub top accentuated his burly shoulders and arms, covered with curly dark hair, and gave him the aspect of a thoroughly pissed-off black bear. Marcus obviously thought better of antagonizing him further and departed hastily.

"Now," Russ said to me, "just how far did you get?"

"I managed to get it into the cryostat, though I practically had to push him out of the way to do that," I said. "It should be frozen by now. All I have to do is cut it and stain it, and you'll have your answer."

Since Russ was already scrubbed out, he stuck around while I did that and followed me into my office when I took the slide in there to look at it under the microscope. The case was a bowel obstruction in a patient with a colon mass. Russ had found a nodule on the liver and wanted to know if it was a metastasis.

It was. But Russ didn't leave right away. "Does he do that often?" he asked. "Harass you like that?"

"This is the second time he's done it," I said. "The first was right after the staff meeting. Why?"

"He's been doing it to Mitzi too," Russ said. "I've caught him in her office a couple of times, talking to her like he was talking to you. What's up with that?"

"He's trying to get rid of us," I said, and I told him about Marcus's conversations with Mitzi and me.

"My God. Does Monty know?"

"Yes, he does."

"Well, isn't he going to do something about it?" Russ demanded.

"Shouldn't there be some kind of peer review about that? Shouldn't the executive committee get involved?"

"You'd think so, wouldn't you?"

"You mean they're not?"

"Neither one of us has a witness. As far as Monty's concerned, it's a he-said–she-said situation."

"What was that about blackmailing Jack?"

"Charlie told me that he heard Monty say something about Marcus having a 'stranglehold on the chief of staff,'" I said, making air quotes. "Maybe that's why nobody's going to do anything about him. Charlie must have told Marcus about having told me that, and Marcus got the idea that I accused him of blackmailing Jack, but I didn't."

Russ shook his head disgustedly. "Shit. If that's true, we'll never get rid of him."

After he left, I allowed myself a smile. Chalk up another nonsupporter for Marcus Manning.

But my elation was short-lived. The letter was still there, still unopened. I gritted my teeth and opened it.

The board of medicine was requesting records on a certain James Cameron Wilson, who had had a pigmented skin lesion removed two years earlier. The lesion had recurred and had been diagnosed as a melanoma, and the sentinel lymph node had been positive. His wife, Kathy Lynne Wilson, was suing me, Russ, and the hospital for failure to diagnose a melanoma on the original biopsy.

I felt as if I couldn't get enough air into my lungs. I broke out into a sweat. With shaking hands, I booted up my computer and looked up James Cameron Wilson. When I did, I remembered the case.

I had diagnosed the lesion as an atypical nevus, or mole, and sent it out for expert consultation. The expert had concurred with my diagnosis.

Kathy Lynne Wilson was a hospital employee. She worked in medical records. I knew her. At the time of her husband's original biopsy, she'd asked me if I was sure it wasn't a melanoma, because her husband's brother had died of melanoma. I'd told her that I didn't think it was but that I'd sent it to an expert just to be sure. That was the last time we'd spoken about it. I'd assumed that when Russ had gotten his copy of the consultant's report, he'd told her about it.

Our pathology reports were all in the computer, as were reports from the University of Utah, because their lab was interfaced with ours. But our melanoma expert was at the University of California, San Francisco.

That meant that the hard copy in the file cabinet in the basement was the only copy we had. I had filed the expert's report with our own report, as we did with all expert consultation reports.

Suddenly I couldn't get my hands on that report fast enough.

I raced downstairs to the basement. Our file cabinets stood practically under the stairs in the darkest corner of the basement and were usually swathed in cobwebs and covered with dust, but strangely enough, the drawer that contained reports from two years ago wasn't.

My heart sank.

Somebody had gotten there before me.

Of course, there was always the chance that someone had been looking for another patient in that drawer, but somehow I didn't think so.

I pulled the drawer open anyway and looked through the reports, which were filed by surgical accession number. I found the hard copy of my report, but the consultant's report wasn't there.

Frantically, I looked through reports on either side of the one I was looking for. But no dice. I looked for the same number in the year before and the year after. While I was doing this, I heard footsteps on the stairs. Marcus Manning materialized before me, haloed by the light behind him. Suddenly I knew exactly what had happened to that report.

"Find what you're looking for, Doctor?"

"No," I replied. "But you knew that, didn't you?"

"I'm sure I don't know what you're talking about," he said airily and turned to leave. I stood and listened while he climbed back up the stairs, thinking furiously. There had to be a way to get a copy of that report.

Back in my office, I placed a call to San Francisco. Eventually, after countless transfers, I was connected to the pathology department. The secretary who answered the phone told me that the consultant had retired last year and asked for the accession number of the report I wanted. I told her that I didn't have it, and couldn't she just look up the patient by name?

Grudgingly, she assented and asked if I wanted it mailed or faxed. "Both," I told her and gave her our address and the lab's fax number. Now all I had to do was wait.

But I didn't have to wait long. Russ was back in my office almost as soon as I hung up the phone with an envelope in his hand. He opened his mouth to speak, and I held up a hand to stop him. "Is that from the board of medicine?"

"Yes. It seems we're both being sued. Thank God you sent that out, or we would be in real trouble. We need to send them records. Can you give me a copy of the consultant's report? There doesn't seem to be one in the chart."

I explained to him why I couldn't do that. "Oddly enough, Marcus showed up while I was looking for it and asked me if I was finding what I was looking for. How do you suppose he knew where I'd be at that precise moment? And why do you think there's no report in the chart?"

"What are you saying, Toni?"

"Marcus threatened that he could make sure I never practiced anywhere in the United States ever again. What would be a way to make that happen?"

"It would have to be something to have your license revoked for," Russ said. "But isn't that kind of chancy? Doctors get sued all the time, and they don't lose their licenses for it."

"It depends. If the doctor is found to be at fault and the mistake resulted in a patient's death, he might."

"Do lawsuits get reported to the board of medicine?"

"In Idaho, all medical malpractice lawsuits are submitted to the board of medicine for prelitigation screening. That's how they know. That's why they're asking us for records."

"And if they don't get them?"

"We could both be found guilty ... No, wait—*I* would be found guilty, because the misdiagnosis was my fault, not yours."

"But there was no misdiagnosis," Russ protested. "The consultant agreed with you."

"Only I can't prove it."

"What I don't understand is why Kathy Lynne is suing. I talked to her at the time and told her that you'd sent the case out to an expert and that he agreed with you. She knows you did nothing wrong."

"Unless someone suggested it to her."

Russ turned up a palm. "Why?"

I shrugged. "As a way to get money to pay her medical bills. Her husband's cancer treatment has got to be expensive, and sometimes insurance doesn't cover it."

"Who would do such a thing? The hospital's being sued too, you know."

"That wouldn't be the first time someone has sued to get money for medical bills," I said. "But that's chancy too. What if they lose? They still have to pay the lawyer."

"It's a gamble," Russ agreed. "I'm going to go talk to Kathy Lynne. Maybe she'll tell me who put her up to it."

The executive committee was supposed to meet at noon. Mike and I wanted to be there, but Dave advised us to stay away. No doubt he didn't want the free-for-all that might result if Marcus and I were in the same room.

"But he's just going to lie to you," I protested. "He lied about all those complaints, didn't he?"

"Don't worry," he said. "I've heard the recordings, don't forget, and so has Monty. He won't get away with anything, believe me."

Dave sounded confident, but I wasn't so sure. Jack had a forceful personality and was well respected among the physicians. That was why he was chief of staff so often. He liked to lead, and he was good at it.

But he'd been responsible for bringing Marcus on board, and he had a stake in keeping Marcus here. Dave would not have an easy time convincing Jack and the other members of the executive committee that they'd made a mistake.

If he even tried. Uneasily I recalled Mitzi's dire pronouncement: "Unless they're all in on it."

Even if they weren't, Marcus, the slime, would manage to lie his way out of anything they accused him of. They underestimated him. The man was pure evil, in my opinion.

I was beginning to doubt the existence of a conspiracy. By now, even if there were one, I felt pretty sure that Dave, Russ, and George weren't in it. Charlie wasn't either. Or Monty.

So, while I slogged my way through tray after tray of surgical slides, my mind stubbornly went round and round on what I could do next if Dave's attempt at damage control backfired onto me.

Marcus would no doubt come storming into my office after the meeting and rip my ass a new one for spreading rumors and trying to get him fired. The fact that he'd done the same thing to me and Mitzi wouldn't matter to him. In his mind, getting me fired would be righteous; my getting him fired would be underhanded and sneaky. It would be a toss-up whose reputation would suffer most, although I was doing my best to tarnish his. I was savoring the anticipation of juicy gossip fests, especially with Patti, my former fellow resident.

I had e-mailed Charlie all the links to Marcus's previous places of employment but had kept the links to my former classmates and colleagues for myself.

Marcus's white underbelly wouldn't do me any good in this situation—not unless he went to jail for it, which was so unlikely as to be considered a miracle, somewhat along the lines of seeing the image of the Virgin Mary on a tortilla chip. His abusiveness at home had nothing to do with his ability to do his job at work, in the same way that the identity of the father of Mitzi's daughter, Stephanie, had nothing to do with her ability to do her job. Hal and Elliott were right: bringing that up at work would just get me in more trouble than I was already in.

Right on the heels of that thought came anger. I felt outrage that I always ended up being the scapegoat whenever a difficult person invaded our normally amicable medical staff. Such people seemed to make a beeline for me right off the bat. Why? Did I have a scarlet *A* inscribed on my forehead? Or perhaps an *I* for *i*ncompetent, *i*nept, or *i*ncapable? Or maybe just a big red *F* for *f*ucked.

Hal called and asked if I wanted to go to lunch. I told him I couldn't because (a) I had too much work to do, (b) I was expecting Marcus to chew my ass right after the meeting, and (c) if I ate anything, I would puke it right back up. On the other hand, projectile vomiting might be just the ticket to get Marcus off my back. Particularly if it were malodorously hemoccult positive from the bleeding ulcer I was no doubt incubating.

But it would mess up my office. Possibly my clothes also. Mike came in between frozen sections and asked how I was doing. "Want me to be here when Marcus comes after you?" he asked. "Because it's not just you, you know."

I told him I'd holler if I needed help, and he went back to his office.

The meeting had started at twelve, and they usually ended by one thirty or two, but two o'clock came and went with no sign of Marcus. By two thirty I was so hungry that I just had to eat something regardless of the effect Marcus might have on my digestion. Unfortunately, the cafeteria was closed until five. So I went across the street to Starbucks, hoping they'd have a cookie or something that would take the edge off.

I'd been there barely five minutes when I heard the door open and felt a blast of hot air. I hadn't even taken a bite of my cookie yet, and perhaps that was just as well.

I turned to see Marcus striding purposefully toward me with a look on his face that could have curdled my latte. A vein throbbed in his temple. "Dr. Day, you need to come back to the hospital. We have to talk."

"Right this very minute? I haven't even had lunch yet. Can't it wait?"

He stepped into my personal space, looming over me, his Pacific-blue eyes as dark as a storm at sea. "No, it cannot."

"And why not, pray tell?"

A smirk curled his lips. "Because the executive committee has voted to terminate you, that's why. You're to vacate your office within the hour."

CHAPTER 17

*You may as well say, that's a valiant flea that dare
eat his breakfast on the lip of a lion.*

—*William Shakespeare,* **King Henry V**

Involuntarily, I gasped. My heart jumped into my throat and started pounding. I broke out in a sweat, despite the air-conditioning.

Then common sense intervened. Medical staff was never terminated in that way. It required the entire medical staff to meet and vote on it. "I don't believe you."

The clerk who'd waited on me had stopped what she was doing and was listening avidly.

Marcus glanced at her. "I'd prefer that this be a private conversation, Doctor."

"I don't care."

Marcus grabbed me by the arm and unceremoniously hauled me out the door and into the parking lot, spilling my latte in the process. "Well, I do. You're coming with me."

"The hell I am. You say what you came to say right here, in front of God and everybody."

Marcus continued to pull me by the arm. "You thought you were going to get me in trouble with the executive committee by spreading rumors?" he hissed. "Well, it didn't work. I was perfectly justified in doing what I did. I was following instructions."

Huh? "You had *instructions*? From whom?"

Marcus still had hold of my arm, and he shook it so hard that I dropped my latte, splashing his trousers. An elderly woman walking by looked at us curiously. "Let go of me," I said loudly, trying to pull away. The elderly woman reached into her purse and took out her cell phone. Marcus noticed.

"From Dr. Allen and Mr. Montgomery, that's who. Please keep your voice down. You need to come to my office so that we can discuss your termination package."

"Not on your nelly. Are you telling me it was Jack and Monty who told you to get rid of Mitzi and me and Lucille too?"

"Yes, it was."

"Will they back you up on that if I ask them?"

"Of course they will."

"Did they tell you to sexually harass us as well?" If that were actually the case, it would certainly explain why Monty had done nothing about it.

Marcus opened his mouth, but nothing came out.

"If I ask to read the minutes of the meeting, will I find it there?"

"That's enough!" Marcus grabbed me by both upper arms and shook me, hard. "Now you listen to me!" he hissed through gritted teeth. "I'm just doing my job. Now you shut your mouth and keep it shut, or termination won't be the only thing I can do to you. And you know I can do it too."

Jesus, Mary, and Joseph, but that man had a strong grip. He was hurting me, but I knew the bruises he'd leave on my arms would make a dandy photograph to introduce into evidence when we ended up in court. I looked him straight in the eye and endeavored to show no pain. He gripped me even harder.

"Unhand me, sir! Unlike your wife, I will press charges."

He let go of me as if he'd been burned. "And just what do you mean by that, Doctor?"

"My husband and I were at your next-door neighbor's house

Saturday night, with a bunch of lawyers and their wives. It was one of them who called the police."

He stepped back into my personal space. I tried not to recoil, but it wasn't easy. The man looked ready to kill someone, and that someone was me. He grabbed my arms again. "Now you listen to me. That is none of your business, and I resent you dragging my personal life into this discussion. How would you like it if I did that to you?"

I stared defiantly into his eyes. "Knock yourself out. I don't beat up on *my* family."

The Pacific-blue eyes narrowed. The perfect teeth were clenched. His face was millimeters from mine and slightly blurred. Damn, was I already getting presbyopic? "My private life is just that: private. You interfere, and by God, you'll wish you hadn't." He let go and shoved me, so that I was forced to step back to keep from falling.

I shrugged and tried to cross my arms. It hurt. My hands felt numb from the pain radiating down into them. He must have done more damage than I thought. "Dear me," I said, "that sounded like a threat." The elderly woman was across the street now but still in earshot, unless she was deaf. "You threatened me!" I accused. "You hurt me!"

The elderly woman, now talking on her phone, turned around and looked at us. Obviously she wasn't deaf.

Marcus glared at her and turned back to me. "Do we understand each other, Doctor?"

I palpated my arms gingerly, wincing. "You understand this: what you just did to me is *not* part of your private life, nor is it part of any termination package. Like I said, I'm not your wife, and that *was* assault and battery, and I can and *will* press charges."

Marcus paled. Monty came out of the same door that I'd used and crossed the street toward us. Marcus saw him and grew paler still.

"Did I hear something about pressing charges?" Monty asked as he reached us.

"You did," I said, gently stroking the sore bits. "Marcus grabbed me by the arms and shook me so hard I thought my eyeballs were going to fall out and go rolling down the street, followed by my head."

Monty sighed and took Marcus by the arm. "My office. Now." They left.

I took my time getting back to my office. I went back into Starbucks and got myself another latte first. The clerk looked at me curiously. "What was going on out there? I could hear it from here."

"Just a little argument with one of the administrators," I said casually. "It's all right now."

No sooner had I gotten back to my office than Dave Martin showed up. "Toni, I'm so sorry," he said. "I meant to come back from the meeting and tell you what happened, but I had an emergency. Monty told me what happened just now. What did he do to you? Did he hurt you?"

My first instinct was to act brave and not make a fuss, on the principle that if I did, it would look like just another reason why women didn't belong in medicine, but on second thought, what for? The more sympathy the better. "Well, yes, he did, as a matter of fact. He grabbed me by the arms and shook me, and it still hurts."

"You need to go talk to the police about this," Dave said. "I can't believe that asshole actually assaulted you."

"I'd call it *aggravated* assault," Mike chuckled. "I heard she *aggravated* the pure livin' bejesus out of him. The lady's got a tongue on her, I tell you what."

"So am I to assume that my immediate termination was just a figment of Marcus's fevered imagination?"

Dave's eyes narrowed. "Is *that* what he told you?"

"Yeah. I didn't believe him. We argued about it."

Dave snorted. "Argued? Is that what you call it? That's not what Monty called it. You need to go talk to him."

"I think Monty has his hands full right now," I said. "We can talk about it tomorrow."

"Well, if you're going to press charges," Dave said, "you need to go to the police and get a lawyer, and the sooner the better."

"Don't worry," I told him. "My next-door neighbor's a lawyer, and my son-in-law's a cop."

And when Hal hears about this, I thought, *Marcus is gonna need a bodyguard.*

CHAPTER 18

I'm mad as hell, and I'm not going to take it anymore!

—Howard Beale, **Network**

"Antoinette!" Aghast, Mum stared at my arms. "What on earth happened to you, kitten?"

Marcus had left a nice ring of dark purple fingerprints around each of my upper arms, somewhat like a tattoo of a flower garland. One could almost see the whorls and ridges, or whatever they called them, they were so sharply demarcated. They were damn sore too.

"Kitten," Mum said, "you need ice on those, and the sooner the better." She bustled about the kitchen, opening the freezer and scooping ice cubes into ziplock bags. "I'm making you some ice packs," she said. "The very idea, assaulting you at work! What the bleedin' hell is the world coming to, I ask you?"

Mum didn't swear like that unless she was very, very angry. I wouldn't have given a plugged nickel for Marcus's chances if she got her hands on him about now.

"It wasn't exactly at work," I told her, but it didn't make any difference. "Humph!" was all she had to say on that subject.

Hal was predictably outraged. He was all ready to go charging off to Marcus's house to punch the son of a bitch's lights out, but Elliott restrained him.

"How the hell can Toni press charges if you go off half-cocked and get yourself in the same freakin' predicament, you freakin' idiot? Use your freakin' head!"

"You know if you do that, he's just going to make his wife and kids wear it," I told him.

"He's probably doing that anyway," Jodi said darkly. "Sounds like Toni was pretty hard on him today."

"The hell you say," I remarked. "Who was hard on who? Look at my arms!"

"Whom, dear," my mother predictably interjected.

Hal subsided, growling. "All right, all right already! Let go of me, or I'll look just like Toni!"

Elliott let go. "You know Toni's gonna have to go to the police station to file charges, and the sooner the better, before those bruises fade."

Hal groaned. "This isn't what I wanted to be doing tonight, sitting on some damn bench in the police station for hours. It's gonna take forever, and we'll be up all night."

"Maybe not," I said. "Why don't you call your son-in-law, the cop?"

"I'll do it," Elliott said.

Pete arrived about five minutes later. He whistled when he saw my bruises. "Holy shit. He did quite a job on you, didn't he? Do they hurt?"

"Of course they do," I said. "Mum's making ice packs for them."

"You can do that later," Pete said. "Right now we need to get some pictures. Relax; it won't take that long, half an hour maybe. I'll take you to the station myself. No, not you," he said to Hal. "You'd just get in the way. I need Elliott, though. Want to ride with me or take your own car?"

Elliott chose to take his own car. Pete was right: it didn't take long to file a charge of assault and battery against Marcus Manning. But I'm sure that if Pete hadn't been there and if I hadn't already had a lawyer, it could have taken much longer. The only thing I needed to do was have my injuries examined by a doctor. That would be easy. I was sure Dave would be happy to do it.

Elliott brought me home and followed me inside. "We need to talk," he said. "Marcus will be arraigned tomorrow, and I need you there."

"I know. What time?"

"Nine o'clock."

"Okay. That'll give me time to go to work first and let Mike know. How long will I need to be there?"

"It'll go pretty quick. All we do is discuss the charges, inform the defendant of his rights under the court system, see if he needs an attorney appointed, and set a date for his preliminary hearing. Since he hasn't been arrested—"

"What do you mean he hasn't been arrested?" I demanded.

"Okay," Elliott said with a sigh, "here's the deal. Assault and battery is a misdemeanor, unless it's done with intent to cause grievous bodily harm. All Marcus did to you is cause bruises. So for right now, it's a misdemeanor. Therefore, Marcus is free for the time being, as long as he appears for his preliminary hearing. Got it?"

I nodded. I didn't like it, but what could I do? "Do I need to tell Monty to be there?"

Elliott shook his head. "No witnesses. Just a magistrate judge and the district attorney. If Marcus has a lawyer, he'll be there too. One other thing—if you, the victim, want a no-contact order, that gets done at the arraignment."

"Is that like a restraining order?"

"Sort of. Do you want one?"

"That would be great," I said. "But can they do that? I mean, Marcus and I work in the same place. He wouldn't be able to go to work."

"Think of it this way," Elliott advised. "Whose problem is that? Not yours, right?"

"So that means Marcus can't bother me at work anymore."

"If you get the order. Marcus's lawyer will argue against it, and the judge could deny it on hardship grounds."

Damn. There's always a catch. Why does everything have to be so difficult?

Trying to sleep with ice packs taped around my arms was really difficult. I prefer to sleep on my side, and I couldn't. Even without the ice packs, it hurt to lie on either arm. So I didn't sleep very well, and in the morning, my arms hurt even more, in spite of the ice. The clear, well-defined fingerprints had turned into a wide band of amorphous purple blobs blending into each other all the way around both arms and extending down toward my elbows. It hurt to move my arms at all. Hal had to help me get dressed. The fact that it was summer was a mixed blessing, since anything with sleeves would probably have hurt, but wearing anything sleeveless exposed my bruises to the world. Like a badge. Maybe that wouldn't be such a bad thing. Everybody who saw me would ask about it, and word would get around. It probably already had. Marcus's reputation would be in the toilet, and his name would be mud.

Or possibly Bruiser.

Mum urged me to call in sick and stay home. "Your arms look simply awful," she said. "You can't possibly want to go to work looking like that, dear."

"I have to, Mum," I said. "I have to have a medical exam and a statement from a doctor who isn't me."

"Well then," Mum said, shifting gears, "come home right after, then."

I assured her that I felt quite capable of doing a day's work, and I quite meant it at the time I said it.

"Jesus," Dave said when he saw my purple arms. "That son of a bitch sure did a number on you. That bruising must go all the way to the bone. And speaking of bones, how do your arms feel? Can you raise them above your head? Bend your elbows? No? Maybe we'd better get some x-rays, just in case. Boy, I'd like to see the executive committee try to sweep *this* under the carpet."

No fractures showed up on the x-rays, though. My next stop was to talk to Monty, but he wasn't in. Neither was Marcus, which didn't surprise me. I'd hoped that he was languishing in one of those ancient cells under the police station, redolent of urine and vomit, with a drunk retching in the next cell. I'd had occasion to spend some time in one of those cells, and it hadn't been pleasant. But no, Marcus was free as a freakin' bird, as Elliott would have said.

Charlie Nelson came out of his office to welcome me. "Boy, oh boy," he greeted me, rubbing his hands together. "Did the shit ever hit the fan around here this morning! Monty's been trying to find a lawyer for Marcus, and boy is he mad! Monty got a hold of the hospital's counsel to defend Marcus in court, and he said he couldn't, because he's *your* lawyer."

With a start I remembered that Elliott was the counsel for the hospital. I hadn't even considered that and what an anomalous position it would put him in. He'd said nothing about it last night. He'd probably gotten one of his partners to take Marcus's side, conflict of interest being what it is, which is whatever a lawyer says it is.

"The gossip mill's going great guns around here. There's been a steady stream of folks in and out of my office ever since I got here. Jesus, is that what he did to you? Have you seen a doctor? Dave? What'd he say? They aren't broken, are they? No, I guess not, or you'd be in casts. Do they feel as bad as they look?"

"Worse," I told him. "Hal had to dress me."

"Are you gonna be able to work?"

"I thought I'd try, but Mike said he could handle it and I should go home."

"Well, I think you should too," Charlie said. "You don't want to be here when Monty gets back here with Marcus after the arraignment."

"I have to be at the arraignment too," I said. "But seriously? He's bringing Marcus here? I should think he'd be on administrative leave after what he did, at the very least. I think he should be fired. Are you guys really going to let him run loose around here? He's a menace."

"Only to you, Doctor. Nobody else has had the guts to stand up to him like you have, let alone make him look stupid."

I laughed. "Stupid? Is that all I did? I was hoping to make him look like a criminal."

CHAPTER 19

The law is a sort of hocus-pocus science,
that smiles in yer face while it picks yer pocket;
and the glorious uncertainty of it is of mair use
to the professors than the justice of it.

—*Charles Macklin*

I didn't have time to ask Charlie how he was getting on with his phone calls. I had an arraignment to go to. Luckily, the courthouse was only two blocks from the hospital, and I actually got there five minutes early.

Elliott directed me to a seat in the front row. The defendant, Marcus, sat at the table in front of the judge, with his lawyer on one side and Fritz Baumgartner, the district attorney, on the other. Marcus's lawyer was a long drink of water whose legs stretched beyond the width of the table and whose bald head would have rivaled Fritz's for the glare from the overhead lights if it weren't for the yarmulke he wore.

LaNae sat in the front row on the other side, dressed in one of those long-sleeved Laura Ashley–type dresses that make everybody who wears them look virginal and pregnant at the same time. Only I was quite sure that she had made it herself. Word around the workplace was that LaNae was some kind of superwife whose talents didn't stop at having battalions of children. She made all her own clothes and those of her daughters. She grew vegetables and fruit and canned them. If she didn't grow them, she acquired them in bulk through other church members. Her "Mormon closet" must have been bulging at the seams.

Debra Carpentier sat on one side of her, and a severe-looking, gray-haired man whom I didn't recognize sat on the other. Someone from her church? The bishop, maybe? Only I thought Monty was the bishop. Maybe it was her father. Or Marcus's.

Elliott hadn't been kidding when he'd said it would go quickly. The judge wasted no time opening the proceedings and advising the defendant of his rights. Marcus already had an attorney, so that didn't need to be addressed. Since he wasn't in custody, bail wasn't discussed. The judge denied the no-contact order without even discussing it with the attorneys. The date of Marcus's preliminary hearing was set for July 20. The whole thing was over in ten minutes, and I could see no reason why I'd needed to be there in the first place.

I took Charlie's and Mike's advice and went home. I was no longer feeling so fine. My arms were so swollen that they were beginning to remind me of blood sausages, and that was probably exactly what was going on under the skin. They were hurting more too, actually throbbing. I needed to lie down with my ice packs and maybe take a nap, since I hadn't slept well the night before.

I opened the front door and the french doors leading to the backyard to let the summer breezes blow through, locking the screen doors. Hal was teaching summer school at the college, so aside from the dogs, Mum and I had the house to ourselves. Mum insisted on preparing me a lunch before I went upstairs to bed, and I didn't argue with her.

Sometime later, I awoke to the doorbell ringing and the dogs barking. I heard Mum answer the front door, accompanied by the dogs. I heard a man's voice, and a brief conversation ensued. I couldn't make out words, but I did hear Mum's voice raised in anger and Killer growling. At that, I became fully awake and alarmed. I heard Mum close and lock the front door. At least I hoped it was Mum and not some serial killer preying on sixtyish Englishwomen.

I jumped out of bed and ran to the head of the stairs. "Mum!" I called. "Are you okay?"

"Yes, kitten," she answered. I heaved a sigh of relief and ran down the hall to the den and opened the window that looked out on the front yard and Montana Street. Marcus was heading down the walk to his car, a bright-red Porsche that sat at the curb. A *Porsche*? Had to be his; it was the only car parked there. A midlife crisis car if I ever saw one. Wasn't that a bit premature? I wondered. Marcus didn't look that old, late thirties at the most. A nice Mormon family man with six kids shouldn't be driving a car like that. Where the hell did he get the money? No doubt LaNae's car was a minivan. Or a school bus.

"Fuck!" I heard him exclaim as he opened the door to his Porsche. *Tut-tut. A nice Mormon boy shouldn't talk like that.* Then he got in, slammed the door, and peeled away in a small shower of gravel.

"Dear me!" my mother exclaimed, joining me at the window. "What a thoroughly unpleasant young man!" Killer and Geraldine had accompanied her up the stairs. Killer leaned against me, and I scratched his head absently.

"What did he say?" I asked her. She moved away from the window and sat in Hal's recliner. Yes, we had recliners up there too. Comfort rules. I flopped into mine, and Geraldine jumped up into my lap.

"He asked for you," she said. "I asked him who he was, and he told me. I said, 'Then you're the one responsible for nearly breaking my daughter's arms,' and he said that it was all a misunderstanding and he was hoping to get you to drop the charges. Well! I told him he had a hell of a nerve coming here and that under no circumstances was he to come harassing my daughter in her own home. 'If you want to talk to her,' I said, 'you can talk to her at her office, like any civilized person.' The very idea!"

"Good for you!" I said. "I'll bet he didn't like that."

"No, he didn't," Mum said. "He was extremely rude. I slammed the door in his face."

Curious, I asked her what he had said.

"I simply cannot repeat it," she insisted haughtily.

"Come on, Mum," I wheedled. "Didn't I hear you say 'bleedin' hell' not too long ago?"

"Antoinette!"

It was no use. Mum was keeping mum on the subject.

I left the window open. A nice breeze was blowing in from the west, and it felt good. I called Pete at the station. He was out, so I left a message.

Since I was home for the rest of the afternoon, I figured it would be a good time to make some phone calls, uninterrupted by frozen sections, incoming phone calls, or Marcus. Before I'd left work, I'd modified my list and e-mailed it to myself at home. I'd then deleted it from my e-mail at work, emptied the deleted-items folder, and shut down my computer. I knew that one couldn't ever really delete things off a computer and that somebody could always find them if they knew how to go about it, but I was damned if I'd make it easy for them. I fired up my computer, brought up my e-mail, and stared at my list. The first two items, warning Mitzi, Mike, Margo, and Jackie and talking to George and Dave, could wait. I might have a lot more to say after talking to former colleagues.

So I started at the beginning with Tustin Community. My former classmate was on vacation. And who might I be? A former classmate, just catching up? Would I like his cell number? *Well, duh.* I added it to the list. Then I had an inspiration.

"Actually, I'm trying to locate somebody he might know. Does the name Marcus Manning ring a bell?"

The receptionist thought for a minute. "It sounds familiar," she said. "What did he do?"

"Hospital administration," I said.

"Oh, I think I do remember that name," she said. "Wasn't he that guy who got in trouble for sexual harassment?"

Bingo. "Dear me," I said with mock concern, "that doesn't sound very good, does it? Who was he supposed to have harassed?"

"I don't really know," she said doubtfully, "a secretary or something. I heard she quit. He's not here anymore either."

"Do you remember her name, by any chance?"

"I don't think so," she said. "Why do you want to know all this?"

I couldn't think of a suitable lie on such short notice, so I told the truth. "Because he's here at my hospital now, and he's harassing me."

Apparently that had been the right thing to say. The receptionist became all hush-hush and confidential. *"Really?"* she breathed. "You're a doctor, and he's harassing *you?"*

"Actually he's harassing two of us," I said.

"Are you going to sue him?"

"I don't know," I said. "I don't want to lose my job. I'm trying to get *him* fired."

"Hey, I hear you, girlfriend. Good luck with that. My name's LaShondra, by the way. Call me anytime and let me know how it goes, okay?"

I added LaShondra to the list and moved on to Fountain Valley. My classmate, a gastroenterologist, was in the middle of a procedure. The receptionist was new and did not remember Marcus Manning. I left a message.

My fellow intern at St. Joseph's, now a surgeon, was in surgery. The receptionist didn't have time to talk to me; her phone was ringing off the hook on multiple lines. I left a message.

My fellow resident at Hoag Memorial, Patti, was really surprised and excited to hear from me after all this time. We had been quite friendly with each other during our residency together, and it was as if no time had passed at all. After catching up on each other's accomplishments, I mentioned Marcus Manning.

Dead silence.

"Patti?" I said.

"Toni, can I call you back tonight?" she asked. Her voice had become hushed and somewhat muffled, as if she'd cupped her hand around the receiver so nobody could hear her. "We've all been told not to say anything about him, so I can't talk here."

Wow. That bad? "Sure," I said. "We're not going anywhere tonight."

Oh boy, this was gonna be good! I was almost tempted not to call Tom, my former fellow intern/classmate at John Wayne Memorial, but I was on a roll here, so I did. Since Tom was an anesthesiologist, I figured he'd be in surgery, but to my surprise, he was between cases and had a few minutes. At least he did until I mentioned Marcus Manning.

"That son of a bitch?" he erupted in anger. "Don't mention that name to me! The asshole broke up my marriage, okay? That what you wanted to know?"

"Tom," I said, "calm down. This is Toni. We're friends, remember? The only reason I want to know about you-know-who is because he's here at my hospital now, and he's harassing me."

"Sorry, Toni," Tom said, sounding contrite. "It's still pretty raw. We fired his ass, and he won't get a reference from us, but we're not supposed to talk about it to any prospective employers."

I laughed shortly. "Oh, I think we've gone beyond prospective," I told him. "I'm trying to get him fired from Perrine."

"Well," he said, "I can't talk about it from here. How about I call you tonight from home, where there's nobody to overhear? No wife, no kids ..." He sounded as if he was about to cry.

"Tom, I'm so sorry," I said.

"It's okay, Toni; I know you are. Talk to you tonight."

We said our goodbyes and disconnected.

I didn't have a chance to call Charlie. Hal came home at four, surprised to see me already there. "Are you all right?"

I told him what had happened with Marcus.

"You mean he's not in jail?" he demanded. "He's out on bail?"

"He was never in jail in the first place, remember? Elliott said assault and battery is a misdemeanor unless it's done with intent to cause grievous bodily harm."

"Jesus," he said, putting his hands on my arms, then removing them hastily as I winced. "Still sore?"

"Oh yeah," I said. By this time my arms were a mottled dark purple with burgundy streaks. Some of the color had begun to drain into my lower arms as well. Bad as I looked, I suspected that LaNae looked worse. At least in places that didn't show.

Hal smacked his fist into his palm, no doubt wishing it had been Marcus's face. "I'm gonna call Pete. This is harassment."

"I already did," I told him.

"Then I'm gonna call Elliott."

Pete, Bambi, Jodi, and Elliott showed up around five thirty, with food. They figured that I wouldn't want to cook, although Hal could have done so if necessary; he's no slouch in the kitchen, and neither is Mum. But as they bustled around, putting things in the microwave and in the oven and setting the table, I felt glad of the company, not to mention the opportunity to discuss the situation with people who actually knew what they were talking about. Speculation got us nowhere.

Hal was still grousing about Marcus not being in jail. Elliott tried to explain.

"Marcus isn't in jail," he said, "because assault and battery is a misdemeanor, unless a weapon was used. That would make it aggravated assault. His preliminary hearing has been set for July 20, and then he'll go to trial. He could end up with jail time, but probably all he'll have to do is pay a fine."

Bambi, busy chopping up salad ingredients, glanced over at him. "That's just wrong," she said. "Sick and wrong. Somebody like that shouldn't be allowed to run around free."

"If you ask me," Mum said, "the bloody sod wants flogging."

"How much jail time are we talking about?" I asked.

"Not much," Elliott said. "The most he can get is six months. However, if we can convince a jury that this was aggravated assault, he could get as much as five years."

"Okay, I'm confused," Hal said. "You just said that aggravated assault requires a weapon. Marcus didn't use a weapon."

"That's usually the case," Elliott said. "But according to the Idaho Code, aggravated assault is also defined as 'by any means or force likely to produce grievous bodily harm.' If that can be shown, Marcus could get as much as five years."

"You mean," I said, "if my arms look like 'grievous bodily harm' to the jury, Marcus would definitely go to jail."

"Well," Elliott said, "he could get away with a fine for that too. The only way to guarantee that he gets a jail sentence is to get him convicted of aggravated *battery*. The Idaho Code says that one of the conditions is that the battery resulted in 'grievous bodily harm, permanent disability, or permanent disfigurement.'"

I shrugged. "So all you have to do is convince the jury that this is 'grievous bodily harm.'"

"It's possible," said Elliott, "but unlikely. What I'd have to do is show it at the pretrial hearing, where the judge decides whether the case gets tried at the magistrate or district level. If the judge decides it's a misdemeanor, it gets tried in magistrate court, and if Marcus gets a jail sentence, it'll be in the county jail. But if the judge decides it's a felony, it gets tried in district court, and any jail sentence will be served in the state penitentiary, and he could get as much as fifteen years."

"Sounds good to me," Hal said.

"Not so fast," Elliott said. "Toni's injuries look like hell right now, but they're not likely to result in permanent disability or disfigurement. By the time the freakin' hearing rolls around, they'll be gone. So more than likely, as a first-time offender, Marcus'll get off with a fine."

"Terrific," Hal said with disgust. "So he's free to come after Toni a second time and try again; *then* maybe he'll go to jail."

"Or he could go after Mitzi or Jeannie Tracy or any other woman he wants to get rid of," I said.

"I could try to get a restraining order," Elliott suggested.

Hal and I both snorted. We knew very well how ineffective restraining orders could be, because I had been stalked before. The stalker had gone to prison, but not for aggravated assault and battery. He was serving a life sentence for the kidnapping and attempted murder of my husband.

"Oh, that'll work," Hal scoffed. "They work in the same place, for Christ's sake. They'd have to *fire* Marcus for that to do any good."

"Or fire Toni," Jodi said.

"No way," Bambi objected. "That would be *so* totally not fair."

"Why *haven't* they fired Marcus?" Mum wanted to know.

"Probably because it didn't happen on hospital grounds," I said. "It happened across the street at Starbucks. Not only that, but if Marcus is to be believed, Monty and Jack Allen *instructed* him to do what he did."

CHAPTER 20

So, naturalists observe, a flea
Has smaller fleas that on him prey;
And these have smaller still to bite 'em;
And so proceed ad infinitum.

—*Jonathan Swift*

I went back to work the next day, despite Mum, Hal, and Mike urging me to take it easy for another day. My e-mail list, which I'd sent from home, was waiting for me on my computer.

I didn't think it was fair to Mike to make him do my work as well as his for another day. I did ask him to take care of the frozen sections, though, because my arms had swelled up to about twice their normal size, and cranking the cryostat microtome hurt them. The skin had gotten so tense that I thought it might actually split at some point. Actually, practically everything hurt them, even propping them up on the desk to work the microscope stage.

But I thought it best to get the surgicals from the previous day signed out before bearding Monty and Jack in their respective dens with regard to their "instructions" to Marcus. Not to mention finding out how Charlie had fared with Marcus's references. I could hardly wait to share what I had already found out from my own personal sources.

Mike offered to talk to Monty about whether or not he and Jack had given Marcus instructions to get rid of me. I accepted the offer, as I figured he could infiltrate the good ole boys network better than I could.

Mike returned after about an hour. He plopped himself down in my visitor's chair and said, "Okay, here's the deal. Monty and Jack both denied having given Marcus any kind of instructions with regard to you or anybody else. Marcus isn't here, by the way. Monty told him to take today off and not to come back until Monday. He told me we'd made a big mistake and that our new COO is a loose cannon. But until the medical staff wants Marcus gone, Monty can't do anything, because they sign his paycheck."

"My, my," I said. "You two must have had a real heart-to-heart. He didn't happen to mention that Marcus might be blackmailing Jack, did he?"

"Huh?"

"Oh, that's right. I didn't have a chance to tell you. I heard that from Charlie. So go on. How'd it go?"

"Oh, we male bonded like you wouldn't believe, I tell you what. We talked about hunting and fishing a lot—you know, all that guy stuff. I also asked for a copy of the minutes of the meeting."

"He gave you a copy?" I asked in disbelief.

Mike handed me a sheaf of papers. "Yeah, I told him your lawyer might need it and he'd just subpoena it if he couldn't get it any other way, and how would it look if Marcus got hold of it in the meantime and altered it—you know, like altered medical records are practically an admission of malpractice ..."

I shoved the papers into my purse. "Oh, good point. Did you happen to talk to Kay?"

"Kay who?"

"Kay Osterhout, the medical-staff secretary."

"And why would I talk to her?"

"To find out if there was anything said at the meeting that they asked her *not* to put in the minutes."

"Jeez Louise," Mike complained. "Why the hell would I even *think* of that?"

Oh well, I thought. *He's only a guy. Real deviousness takes a female brain.* Once again, it just went to show that if you wanted a job done right, you had to do it yourself.

I needed to talk to Jeannie. I needed to talk to Kay. I could see my day getting longer and longer, just when all I wanted to do was go home and put my arms to bed.

I picked up the phone and called Jeannie's office number. She didn't answer. I called her nurse, Donna. Donna didn't answer either. Instead I got a girl-child with a high-pitched voice who told me that Dr. Tracy was in with a patient. Then, instead of asking if she could take a message or pull the chart of a mutual patient, she simply hung up. Wow, sucky telephone manners. Where were these kids getting their training, at recess? And where was Donna anyway?

Oh, well, it was summer, I rationalized, and doctors and employees alike had kids in high school or college who needed summer jobs. Perhaps Donna was on vacation. But I didn't think that filling in for an office nurse was a job for a summer intern; it actually required some training. I couldn't be sure that this fourth grader would even think to tell Jeannie that I'd called.

Groaning, I hauled myself and my swollen arms up out of my chair and prepared to hie myself down the hall to Jeannie's office, but I didn't have to. As I swung my office door wide, Jeannie herself materialized in the doorway. "I have to talk to you," she hissed. "Close the door."

I sat back down, and so did she. "Holy crap, look at your arms!" she exclaimed. "Is that what Marcus did to you? Maybe I got off easy. All he did to me was fire my nurse."

"No shit," I said. "On what grounds? How did he do it? A pink slip in her paycheck?"

"How'd you know?"

"That's how he fired Lucille. Did he tell you why?"

"No, he just smiled that smug smile and said he wasn't at liberty to say."

"Well, I know *that's* bullshit," I told her. "Go talk to Monty. He'll fix it."

"He will?"

"Lucille's still here," I pointed out. "So who's the kindergartener he's replaced her with?"

"Her name's Sabrina," Jeannie said in a falsetto voice with just a hint of a lisp. "Sabrina Kimball. Long blonde hair and dreat, big boo eyes. She's apparently Mrs. Manning's niece," she went on, in a more normal tone. "She makes a nice desk ornament, I suppose, but she's not good for much else as far as I can see."

"Is she as young as she sounds?" I asked.

"No, she's actually a CNA," Jeannie said, "a certified nursing assistant, which means she at least has a high school diploma. Although in my opinion, she doesn't have two brain cells to rub together. She's a *feeb*."

"A what?"

"*Feeb*. Feebleminded. I have to explain the simplest things to her over and over, and she still gets them wrong. Her telephone manners … well, let's just say she hasn't any. It takes me twice as long to see a patient as it used to because I ask her for something I need and then end up having to get it myself. And if she's ever used a computer before, I'll eat my lab coat. *Feeb*," she reiterated, just in case I hadn't gotten it the first time.

"What you're telling me is that she's interfering with patient care."

"What?"

"Well, isn't she? How many patients do you usually see in a day when Donna's here? And how many are you seeing now?"

Jeannie looked as if she'd just had an epiphany. "Then that's what I'll tell Monty."

"Not just that," I said. "It's affecting patient satisfaction too. Patients who have to wait a long time and then get rescheduled are not going to be happy. They might decide to go to Jerome or Gooding or Boise. That's not going to help the bottom line. Plus, if she's as dumb as you say, she could make mistakes—mistakes that would reflect poorly on *you*. Why, she could cause you to actually get sued."

"Jesus, Toni. I never thought of all that."

"Well, no. You're too new. I've been here fifteen years, and I hear that same crap over and over at staff meetings. Patient satisfaction is a big deal. They're a lot more informed than they used to be, and pickier too. They go on the Internet and Google stuff. Wait a minute." Now it was my turn to have an epiphany. "Hello. She's not a feeb. She's a Trojan horse."

Jeannie looked confused. She waved her hands as if to chase away a swarm of gnats. "What the hell are you talking about?"

"Maybe this is Marcus's way of getting you booted off the medical staff—by firing your nurse and then replacing her with someone who'll make you look bad. The boys'll look at the figures and say you're not keeping up with the others and you're hurting the bottom line, and they'll say that if patients are unhappy and going elsewhere, maybe you don't need to be here."

Jeannie looked as if she'd been poleaxed. But I wasn't through. "I'll bet Miss Sabrina Kimball is a lot smarter than she acts. Somebody *told* her to act like a feeb. Any guesses who?"

"I'm not saying you're not right, Toni, but what the hell can I do about it?"

"This is Marcus's project, not Monty's. Monty has no interest in hurting the hospital's bottom line just to get a particular doctor off the staff. He's spent too much time trying to recruit them. Go talk to him and get your nurse back."

Jeannie rejected my offer to accompany her to talk to Monty. "You've got enough to do, Toni, and I can see you're not feeling too good." When I told her I had to talk to Kay and why, she offered to do that too.

It was only after she'd left that I realized I could have gotten the same information from Dave. Oh well. It was always best to have two sources corroborate each other as far as evidence was concerned—or at least that was what the Commander, Pete's boss, always said.

Mike came in, and when he saw the pile of slide trays I still had to go through, he offered to take some of them off my hands. "What were you and Jeannie talking about in such secrecy? Or am I not supposed to know?"

"Marcus fired her nurse and replaced her with a CNA who just happens to be his wife's niece."

"I don't get it. Why fire Donna? She's worked here for a hundred years."

I told him my theory. His reaction was unexpected. "This is your theory du jour, huh?"

"What do you mean, my theory du jour?"

I must have sounded offended, because he flapped his hands at me as if I'd launched a squadron of fingernails at his eyes. "Well, hell, Toni, first you decide that since Marcus is COO and in charge of ancillary services, he's out to get rid of you and Mitzi. Then you think he's out to get Margo and Jackie and the female heads of all the departments, even though he has no authority, mind you. And now you think he wants to get rid of all three of our female physicians. It's making my head spin, I tell you what."

Poor baby. I bet Leezie would have gotten it in a heartbeat.

But Hal wouldn't, and neither would Elliott or Pete. Maybe I should apologize.

Naaah. Instead I smiled sweetly. "Well, hell, Mikey, I belong to so many minorities around here, sometimes it's hard to figure out which one I'm being attacked for."

"Huh?"

"I'm the first one he came after, remember? Why? I'm not the only female physician here. So why start with me instead of Mitzi or Jeannie?"

"Well, Jeannie isn't ancillary services," he began.

"So why not start with Mitzi?"

Mike rubbed his face with both hands, as if trying to wash it or perhaps to remove the fog of mystery surrounding the motives of our COO. Apparently if it was a guy thing, it wasn't one that my partner was familiar with. "I don't have the foggiest notion. Why? What do you think it is?"

I just shook my head. I didn't have the foggiest notion either.

Jeannie tapped on the door and came in. "Am I disturbing anything?"

We assured her that she wasn't, and she parked one butt cheek on the corner of my desk after gently pushing my dwindling stack of slide trays aside. "Donna will be back on Monday," she said, smiling.

"Yay, you!" I said. "What did Monty say?"

"That I was lucky to have someone like you in my corner."

Whatever I'd been expecting to hear Jeannie say, it sure as hell wasn't that. It rendered me temporarily speechless.

Mike had no such problem. "That's it!" he said triumphantly.

"That's what?"

"That's why Marcus started with you," Mike said. "Don't you see? If he could get rid of you, there'd be nobody to stick up for the others. Then he could get rid of them without any problem. Like knocking over dominoes."

Or shooting fish in a barrel. "Are you saying that Mitzi and Jeannie couldn't stick up for themselves? Should Jeannie be feeling insulted right about now?"

Jeannie, far from looking insulted, seemed to be enjoying the exchange. Her blue eyes darted from Mike to me and back again as if she were watching a tennis match. "Not like you, Toni. Oh, I heard about that scene at Starbucks the other day when you threatened to press charges for assault and battery, and then you actually did!"

"Well, of course I *actually* did," I said with asperity. "Did anybody *actually* think I wouldn't?"

"A lot of women wouldn't have had the courage," Jeannie said. "They'd fear for their jobs."

"I know," I said, "but we're doctors, members in good standing of a hospital medical staff. And despite rumors to the contrary, *we* hire administrators, not the other way around. Marcus can't fire us, not without the blessing of the rest of the medical staff. He's not supposed to be able to fire employees either, not without going through the protocol in the employee handbook."

"But he damn near got away with it," Mike said.

"It's an effective technique," I said. "Get rid of valued employees in order to adversely affect workflow, and then get rid of the doc because his or her performance is adversely affecting the bottom line. I wish we could warn the docs, but I'm afraid they wouldn't believe us."

"Not only that," Mike said, "but they'll think we're nuts. And besides, taking the time away from our work to do all that would adversely affect our performance."

"Thereby making him want to get rid of both of us, not just me," I said. "By the way, Jeannie, what did he say to Donna anyway?"

"I don't know," Jeannie said. "I came to work today, and she wasn't here, and Sabrina was. And speaking of which, I'd better get back to work if I'm gonna get through that backlog of patients anytime today."

"You know what that tells us," I said to Mike after she'd left. "The reason he fired Lucille was to slow us down. He might come after Natalie next for the same reason, although what his trumped-up reason might be is anybody's guess."

"Oh, I think I know," Mike said. "She's married to Dale. He'll claim that persons married to each other shouldn't work in the same department."

Dale Scott, Natalie's husband, was one of my techs. We'd been through the whole married / same-department issue with Monty when they'd gotten engaged, five years ago. But Marcus could very well dig it all up again and cause a big to-do that would slow a lot of things down, just because he could.

"You know what else it means," Mike pointed out. "If he could fire Donna, he's not sticking to ancillary services. *Everybody's* at risk."

"In that case," I said, "who on the medical staff might he attack next? There aren't any more female physicians to go after, so now what?"

"Hell," Mike said, "that's a crapshoot, I tell you what. Other than Jack, it might be anybody."

That was pretty much my take on the situation too, so we decided that we'd better get back to work before Marcus fired us for adversely affecting his bottom line.

Thank God it was Friday, and then I could stay off my arms for a couple of days, so to speak.

Mike was reading out, which meant that I was on call and normally would be grossing the surgicals and doing the frozen sections, but my arms were hurting too much. Mike offered to trade jobs with me on the condition that I remained on call, which I thought was eminently fair. Again I silently thanked God that I had a partner to help me. I could not imagine what it would have been like to have had to do it alone in my present condition.

While I waited for my slides, I called Elliott at his office and told him I wanted to have a meeting at his house to discuss what to do about Marcus Manning. I was thinking sometime the next week, but Elliott apparently felt a sense of urgency about the situation. "How about tonight?" he asked. "Around seven? I'll tell Jodi."

Terrific. Now I had to get hold of everybody and hope they were all free. I started with Charlie.

"I think I'm free tonight," he said. "I'll call my wife and check, but I'm pretty sure I can be there. And speaking of which, she told me she heard something about Marcus getting into some kind of trouble in California."

"What kind of trouble?" I asked, intrigued.

"She didn't say. She didn't know any details."

"Who told her?" I persisted.

"I don't know," Charlie said. "I think she heard it at the hairdresser or something."

"Who's her hairdresser?"

"Jeez, Toni, what difference does that make?"

"Who is it?" I persisted.

Charlie gave in. "First Resort, on Sixth and Addison."

Bingo, I thought, *that's Jodi's place.* She might have overheard something, and she'd be at the meeting too.

I let Charlie get back to work and tried Dave and George next. They were both free too, as were Mitzi and Jeannie and Russ.

My first few trays of slides had arrived, and I sat down and read them out. Jack Allen stopped by my office to inquire about a bronchial biopsy, and while I had him there, I threw caution to the winds and asked him what kind of trouble Marcus had gotten into in California.

"Jesus, Toni, leave the poor guy alone, can't you?"

Poor guy, my ass. "I'd be happy to, if he'd leave me alone," I said. "But he hasn't, and it might be pertinent."

"Pertinent to what?" Jack asked.

"Pertinent to whether he's the kind of guy we want as a CEO."

"That's the executive committee's business, not yours," Jack informed me.

That got my Irish up. "Not my business? He threatened my job. He physically attacked me. Look at my arms! How the hell is that not my business?"

"Now look, Toni, you stay out of this and let the executive committee handle it," Jack warned me. "Don't go interfering where you don't belong. Or else you might be the one who's out on the street, not Marcus."

CHAPTER 21

People who have no weaknesses are terrible;
there is no way of taking advantage of them.

—Anatole France

Without giving me a chance to respond, he left. *Wow,* I thought, *that sounded like a threat.* Under the circumstances, I decided maybe it wouldn't be such a good idea to run down the hall after him and ask what Marcus was blackmailing him with. At the very least he might bean me with a bronchoscope. At the most, well, he might get me fired.

Natalie came in with more slide trays at that point, and I decided I'd better get back to work. All this investigating might interfere with getting my work done, and that would never do.

When I got home at five, I found Hal and Mum busily carrying trays of food next door. Immediately I felt guilty. I hadn't really thought this through. I wasn't expecting Jodi and Elliott to feed everyone dinner, but that was what it looked like.

"I didn't intend to put you guys to so much work," I said.

"It's not so bad, kitten," Mum said. "Many hands make light work, don't you know."

"Jodi's got everything set up outside on the patio," Hal said, "and Elliott's barbecuing hamburgers. This is just salads and stuff."

Salads and stuff? I eyed the beautifully garnished bowls: potato salad with lettuce leaves around the edges and slices of hard-boiled egg on top, macaroni salad with parsley sprigs, and coleslaw with red cabbage leaves around it. Not to mention the tomato and dill pickle slices artistically arranged on lettuce leaves to be put on the hamburgers. "You guys did a lot of work here. I don't know how to thank you."

"No worries," Hal said. "Fiona did most of it. I just went shopping. Want to grab the other tray?"

The third tray contained rolls and condiments and a plate of brownies, each garnished with a Hershey's kiss. "Mum," I said, "you made all this stuff?"

"It's all from Walmart, dear," she murmured. "No work at all, really."

No work at all? In what universe?

That was so typical of my mother. I would have left those salads in the original containers and stuck a spoon in them. I would have left the condiments in their original containers instead of putting them in little dishes. Even as a child, I'd never been allowed to just plop the milk carton on the table. I'd had to pour it into a pretty pitcher, even if we weren't having company. As a child, I'd thought it was stupid. Now that I was an adult, I realized that if it looked as if one had taken the trouble to make the food look pretty, people would feel special, and there was nothing wrong with that.

I began to wonder, though, if we weren't overdoing it a bit. This wasn't supposed to be a party. I hadn't said anything about bringing wives or significant others, and I wondered if having Hal and Mum there would be considered inappropriate. Yet I couldn't tell them they couldn't be there after all the work they'd done. Besides, Jodi would be there. And we did have to eat sometime.

I needn't have worried. Everybody showed up, and nobody brought a spouse. Nobody thought the presence of Hal and Mum and Jodi inappropriate, or if they did, they didn't mention it.

I'd asked Elliott to run the meeting, and he had brought one of those big flip charts on an easel. But no sooner had he called the meeting to order than Charlie spoke up.

"Marcus fired me today," he said.

Gasps ensued.

"You're kidding," I said.

"No way," said Jeannie. "Did you get a pink slip too?"

"Wait a minute," I interrupted. "I thought Marcus wasn't supposed to be back until Monday."

"Well, he was there," Charlie said. "He just came in and told me that he and Monty had been discussing the various roles administration was involved in, and supposedly Monty told Marcus that he didn't think we needed two assistant administrators and that Marcus could handle both CFO and COO just fine. So I was no longer needed."

"But that doesn't make any sense!" I protested. "The executive committee just barely approved the changes in administration, and now Marcus goes and undoes everything they did?"

"I'll bet Monty said no such thing," Mitzi said darkly.

"From what I've heard," I said, "Monty'd be more likely to tell Marcus *he* was no longer needed and Charlie could handle CFO and COO, since that was what he was doing before Marcus came along. Did you check it out with Monty?"

"I couldn't," Charlie said. "He'd already left. And it's Friday, so I can't talk to him till Monday, unless I call him at home, and I hate to disturb his weekend."

"Why not?" Hal asked. "Marcus disturbed yours, didn't he?"

Elliott opened up the flip chart and started writing. Soon he had a list of all Marcus's transgressions. Almost.

"Y'all are forgettin' that, somewhere in there, Marcus physically assaulted Toni," Mike said, "and her injuries are interfering with her job."

"You didn't tell me that, Toni," Elliott said. "Interfering how?"

"She can't crank the cryostat to do frozens," Mike said, "and now she can't gross surgicals either. So she reads slides every day while I gross and do frozens."

"You didn't tell me that either, honey," Hal said. "I thought you were getting better. Now it sounds like you're getting worse."

"You'd better let Russ take a look after we get done here, Toni," Dave said. "What do you think, Russ?"

"She could have compartment syndrome," Russ said. "That's nothing to fool with, you know. She could lose her arms."

Compartment syndrome could occur with crush injuries, when the muscle bled and swelled but the fascia that contained it didn't stretch. So the swollen muscle compressed blood vessels and nerves, damaging the nerves and causing necrosis, or death of the muscle. Fasciotomy, or surgical slitting of the fascia, was needed to release the muscle and decrease the pressure on these vital structures.

My arms had continued to swell and throb even after having packed them in ice and elevated them for these last few days. I could barely stand to touch them. Russ could be right.

If I ended up needing surgery, a jury would certainly call this "grievous bodily harm." Maybe Marcus would go to jail and make all this plotting and planning unnecessary.

"So what's with this guy?" George growled. "What's his agenda?"

"Fiona has some ideas on that subject," Hal said.

"Yes, Hal, dear," Mum said. "I think he wants to not only be CEO of your hospital; he wants to be CEO of the whole system and will eliminate anybody who might want to stop him."

"That makes a hell of a lot more sense than all those harebrained theories of yours, Toni," Mike said, "I tell you what."

"Thanks a lot, bub," I retorted.

"No offense," he said.

"None taken," I said. "I happen to agree with you."

"If you're right," Jeannie said, "all we have to do now is figure out who he thinks would want to stop him."

"All of us, obviously," Dave said. "Do you think he's going to try to fire all of us, Toni?"

"No, I don't," I said. "I think he's going to fire your best employees so that you won't be able to do your jobs as well, and the rest of the medical staff will want to fire you because you're negatively affecting the bottom line."

"Jesus!" said George.

"Not only that," I said, "but I think there's a good chance that any employee who gets a pink slip in his or her paycheck may just not show up for work the next day, rather than telling you about it or going to Monty. So you're going to have to be on the watch for that happening and will have to contact the employee yourself to see if that's what happened."

Russ came over to me and sat down, pulling up his chair to face me. "Toni, let me take a look at your arms," he said, reaching out to touch both of them lightly with his fingertips.

"Ouch!" I objected.

"I barely touched you, and it hurt that much? Wow. This is worse than I thought. How far can you bend them?"

I tried to bend them. I couldn't even achieve a ninety-degree angle.

Russ took my right hand. "Toni, I'm going to just move your forearm and hand around and see what happens," he said. "Just relax and let me do the moving, okay?"

I nodded. He flexed and extended my forearm, wrist, and fingers. I gritted my teeth. "Does that hurt?" he asked. "Which motion hurt the most?"

"All of them," I said.

He went through the same routine with the left arm, and it hurt even more than the right had.

"Toni," he said finally, "your hands are cold as ice, and they look blue in this light. You've got fairly good radial and ulnar pulses, but ..." He ran a fingernail down the palm of my hand. "Can you feel that?"

"No," I said. I was beginning to get frightened. "It feels numb."

It felt numb in the other hand too.

"You've got compartment syndrome in both arms," he said, "both anterior and posterior compartments, and it looks pretty advanced. You need fasciotomies, and the sooner the better. I'll meet you in the emergency room in ten minutes." I tried to object, but he cut me off. "No. No arguing. If you want to keep your arms, Toni, you'll be there."

CHAPTER 22

The savage in man is never quite eradicated.

—*Henry David Thoreau*

Russ left. I looked at Hal. He stood up. "Let's go," he said.

"But ..."

"No buts. You heard what he said."

"Go, kitten," Mum said. "Jodi and I can take care of all this. Don't worry, darling; everything will be quite all right."

"I can handle things at work," Mike said.

So I went.

Russ was waiting when Hal and I got to the emergency room. After I checked in, a nurse whisked us into a cubicle, helped me out of my clothes and into a gown, and took my vital signs, using a thigh cuff to take my blood pressure. Russ came into the cubicle while she was doing that, accompanied by Rod Alexander, an orthopedic surgeon whom I knew but not well, as he was one of our more recent recruits.

Rod was tall and thin with light hair and ice-blue eyes. He reminded me of an icicle. But his eyes widened, and he sucked air audibly when Russ pulled up the sleeves of my gown so that he could see my arms in all their glory. "You didn't get her in here any too soon," he remarked.

He gently took my wrist, feeling for pulses. "Pulses are still pretty good, though," he said.

"Yeah," Russ said, "but her hands are numb."

"Then we need to get going," Rod said. "We don't want permanent nerve damage, do we?"

"I should say not," I said.

"Now," Russ said, "we have to measure your compartment pressures." A complicated procedure ensued, in which multiple areas of both my arms were anesthetized, small incisions made, and probes inserted and removed.

"All your compartment pressures are over forty millimeters of mercury," he told me. "That's an indication for an emergency fasciotomy in anybody's book."

"Okay," I said. "Now what?"

Russ pulled a felt-tipped marker from his pocket. He sat on the bed and pulled my left arm across his lap. "Here's what we have to do, Toni," he said. "We have to make an incision that goes the length of the affected area and accesses both compartments." He drew a line in an S curve that went from my armpit to the back of my arm and then across the bicep above my antecubital fossa and down into my forearm. "Like so."

I pulled my arm back in horror. "You're joking, right?"

He pulled it back. "No, this is no joke."

"You have to do that to both arms?"

"Of course both arms. What did you think?"

I looked at Hal. He looked as horrified as I felt. "Then what?"

"Then we dissect the skin back and expose the fascia. Then we dissect the fascia up off the muscle and slit it lengthwise. That relieves the pressure."

"Then what?" I asked, fearing the worst.

"Then, after twenty-four to forty-eight hours, we close it up again."

"You mean she's got to have her arms laid open like that for two days?" Hal demanded. "Won't it get infected?"

"It shouldn't," Russ said. "It'll be covered with sterile dressings, and she'll be on intravenous antibiotics."

Rod, who had been leaning against the wall and not saying anything, finally spoke up. "You know, there's a better way," he said. "I learned this procedure at the last meeting I went to. There's a laparoscopic method." He moved to the other side of the bed and took my right arm. "You make a small, longitudinal incision at each end of the affected area, like so." He drew a short line just below my armpit and another just above my elbow. "That's for the laparoscope. Then you make a transverse incision that crosses the septum between the two compartments, like this." He drew a line across the inner surface of my arm from back to front. "See?"

Russ came around the bed and peered at Rod's handiwork. "Then what? How do you get at the fascia?"

"What you do is a blunt dissection under the skin to access the fascia," Rod explained. "You free up all the skin down to and including the transverse incision and then start from the other small incision and do the same thing. When you have the skin freed up, you can slit the fascia of both compartments all the way from here to here and then sew up the skin incisions. Using the laparoscope, you can see what you're doing and not cut any vessels or nerves. You have a much shorter recovery time and less chance of infection. Of course, you have to leave drains in for at least twenty-four hours or until the bleeding stops."

Russ looked skeptical. "And how's that gonna relieve the pressure?"

"Fascia doesn't stretch," Rod said, "but skin does."

"That sounds a lot better to me," Hal said.

"Me too," I said.

"You do realize that I haven't actually done this procedure here," Rod said. "You'd essentially be a guinea pig."

"I don't care," I said. "I'm tired of this. Let's go for it."

And so we did, after I signed a consent form. A nurse started a large-bore IV in the back of my hand, and one of my techs drew blood from the back of the other hand, and I was given pre-op medications.

Hal kissed me goodbye. "I'm going home now, sweetie," he said. "Fiona and I will be back by the time you come out of surgery."

We exchanged "I love yous," and he left. I was asleep even before anyone came to take me up to the operating room.

I woke up in the recovery room, or postanesthesia care unit, PACU, as they called it nowadays. My arms were swathed in gauze fluffs, and I was sure I looked like one of those Madame Alexander dolls with the big, puffy sleeves. My arms still hurt, but my hands didn't feel numb anymore. My throat was sore, I guessed from the endotracheal tube. I felt freezing cold, even though they had me wrapped in one of those Bair Huggers, which was like a very heavy-duty electric blanket, to help prevent those awful postanesthesia rigors. It seemed to be working, for once.

Hal and Mum materialized at my bedside. Hal bent over and kissed me, bumping the nasal cannulas through which I was getting oxygen. As I raised a hand to adjust them, I noticed that I had a pulse oximeter on one finger.

"Sorry, sweetie," Hal said, and Mum, wisely refraining from touching me anywhere, said, "How do you feel, kitten?"

"My arms are still sore," I said, "but other than that I guess I feel okay."

Russ materialized on the other side of the bed. "She's going to be fine," he told them. "We evacuated hematomas from all four compartments. That relieved the pressure right there. We slit the fascia anyway and left drains in, just in case, but those can probably come out tomorrow or the next day."

Experimentally, I tried to flex both arms, and it didn't seem nearly as difficult as it had before surgery. I also noticed something else. "Where's my IV?"

"You've got a subclavian," Russ said. "We put in a central line because we're gonna need to push fluids the next couple of days. You had myoglobin in your blood from the muscle damage, and we don't want it to shut down your kidneys. You've got a Foley catheter too."

"Right," said Rod, coming up alongside of him. "With compartment syndrome, the two big dangers, aside from muscle necrosis and permanent nerve damage, are the elevated potassium, which can stop your heart, and the myoglobinemia, which can stop your kidneys. Sometimes we have to use hemodialysis, but I don't think you're going to need it. Your urine output looks really good so far, and your renal-function tests are normal."

Hal had a shocked expression on his face. "I knew she could lose her arms," he said, "but I had no idea it was *this* life threatening."

"Nor did I," my mother said. "I would have been *frantic* ..." She drew a deep, shaky breath and appeared unable to continue.

"Well, don't do it now!" I exclaimed in alarm. "That's not happening. Mum! Stop hyperventilating!"

Mum burst into tears. Hal put an arm around her and turned her away from the bedside. "Come on, Fiona. It's gonna be okay. Let's go. We'll be right outside," he said to me, and they left.

Where was my mother's stiff upper lip? Even when I'd been recovering from the effects of succinylcholine, even when I'd had broken ribs and a punctured lung and had been bleeding to death from an anticoagulant overdose, I'd never seen Mum cry. Why now? The other episodes had been just as life threatening as this, if not more.

With a slight sense of shock, I realized that my mother was now sixty-three years of age. Maybe she was having health problems of her own that she hadn't told me about. Maybe there was more stressing her than my situation.

Or maybe she just hadn't cried in front of me until now.

Mum and I were going to have to have a talk when I got home.

I more or less slept through the next two days. I became much more alert on the third day, which they informed me was Tuesday. Apparently my pain meds had been decreased, allowing me to wake up and actually be coherent when people talked to me. While I'd been sleeping, my room had been transformed into a branch outlet of the local florist. Bouquets, some quite elaborate, some with Mylar balloons, stood on every available surface. I wondered who they were all from, but that could wait. I didn't have the energy to get out of bed and check.

The fluffs were gone. The drains were out. My arms were now wrapped in Ace bandages and felt much less painful. I could flex them past a ninety-degree angle now, with only mild discomfort.

"You can go home tomorrow," Russ told me, "on oral antibiotics and pain meds. The drains are out. There was hardly any drainage yesterday. Your renal-function tests are still normal, and there's no myoglobinemia now. Your potassium is normal too. But your CK is still above a thousand, so we're going to keep you one more night and push fluids until that comes down more. We're also going to make you drink lots of water, to make sure you can hydrate yourself at home."

CK, or creatine kinase, was an enzyme released from damaged skeletal and cardiac muscle.

"Good," I said. Experimentally, I raised my arms above my head and flexed them, wiggling my fingers. Not too bad.

That was the last resting I got to do that day. Between the physical therapist, the nurses who got my lazy ass out of bed to make sure I could walk to the bathroom and back, all the visitors, and the meals, I was exhausted. *Oh well,* I thought, *I can sleep tonight.*

But it was not to be. The coup de grâce was yet to come. They removed the Foley catheter, sentencing me to a night of constant trips to the bathroom to get rid of all the fluid they were making me drink. I thought morning would never come.

But of course it did.

CHAPTER 23

The lady doth protest too much, methinks.

—*William Shakespeare,* **Hamlet**

My first day home I read and slept, read and slept. Hal went to work, but Mum woke me periodically to make me drink water and do my exercises. She fixed me an egg-salad sandwich for lunch, with chives in it, just as she had when I was in school.

"Do we have any potato chips?" I asked.

"Yes, but you don't want to overdo it right at first," she warned me. "Your stomach isn't used to it."

I knew she was right, but damn, I was still hungry.

Hal came home about four thirty, and Mike dropped by after work, about five. Hal offered him a beer, which he accepted. I would have liked a scotch, but my stomach wasn't used to that either. I contented myself with a few sips from Hal's beer.

Mike was full of news, about several more key employees who had received pink slips, gone to Monty, and gotten reinstated. Including Charlie. "And here's something else I nearly forgot," Mike said. "Guess what else Marcus is doing."

"I couldn't possibly," I said. "There are so many possibilities to choose from that it boggles the mind."

Mike rubbed his hands together in anticipation. "He's having an affair with Debra Carpentier."

"No!"

"I kid you not."

"But isn't she married?"

"Yes, but she's divorcing her husband."

"How do you know all this?" I asked.

"Charlie told me."

Our Charlie was quite the gossip, a handy thing to have around at times like this. If you needed any juicy information about anybody in the hospital, just ask Charlie.

"Apparently they're neighbors out there on Canyon Rim Road," Mike continued, "and their kids are friends. Besides working together, they get thrown together a lot at school things."

"Too bad," I said. "I like Debra. I would have hoped she had better taste than that."

"Not to mention that it's gonna screw up her divorce," Mike said. "Her husband can claim adultery and take her to the cleaners."

"Maybe Marcus threatened her job unless she put out," I suggested. "just like he did to Mitzi and me."

"That's certainly more his style," Mike agreed. "Well, that's the news from Lake Wobegon, so to speak. I'd better go and let you guys get to your dinner."

"Call me if you hear anything else," I called after him as he went out the door.

"Sure will."

Pete and Bambi came over after dinner. Bambi had prepared a tuna casserole and was disappointed that we'd already eaten.

"No worries," Hal told her. "We can heat it up and eat it tomorrow."

"Tonight," I said, "we ate the lasagna that Jodi brought over yesterday."

I hadn't eaten much of it, under Mum's watchful eye, but I'd had plenty of water, by golly.

"How do you feel, Toni?" Bambi asked.

"Not too bad," I said. "My arms are sore, but not anything like before. Mostly I'm just weak." *And hungry, damn it!*

"Not to change the subject or anything," Pete said, "but have you heard anything more about your junior administrator, the abuser?"

Bruiser the Abuser. It would slip easily off the tongue, rather like Vlad the Impaler. "Apparently," I said, "he fired another office nurse and the head nurse in the GI lab, and he's having an affair with the new gal they hired for community outreach."

"Talk about reaching out and touching someone," Bambi said.

"Inappropriately," I said. "Incidentally, it seems that before he came here, he was at John Wayne Memorial in Newport Beach."

Bambi's hand flew to her mouth. "Oh my God, was he *that* guy?" she asked. "There was a guy who was fired from there not too long ago, and there was a big hoo-hah. It was in the newspapers. My folks told me about it. Something about sexual harassment. My folks know the details better than I do."

"I'd love to know the details," I said. "Maybe you could ask them about it next time you talk to them."

"I will," Bambi said. "I want to know too, since he's here harassing you now."

"I'd say it's gone way beyond harassment in my case," I said. "I think he's done with me, since I can probably put him in jail. This is surely grievous bodily harm if it required surgery to fix." I held out my bandaged arms. "Apparently this could have killed me."

The phone rang. Hal answered it and handed it to me. "It's a man," he said. "I don't recognize the voice."

I took the handset. "Hello?"

It was Tom, my fellow intern who was at John Wayne Memorial. "Hi, Toni," he said. "I'm sorry it took me so long to get back to you. I got busy. You know how it goes."

I allowed as how I did.

"Well, I can talk now," he said, "since I'm calling from home on my landline. Nobody's gonna pick it up on a police scanner or anything. Here's what happened. My wife, Marcie—did you ever meet her? I married her in our third year."

I tried to recall, but the name Marcie rang no bells. "I don't think so," I said.

"Well, anyway, she got a job as an administrative assistant here, so she was working in constant contact with Marcus Manning, and they ended up having an affair. She left me for him. She said he was going to get a divorce too."

"That old story," I commented.

"Right. Well, we got divorced, and she started pressuring him to do the same. Of course there was no way *he* was going to get divorced, being a Mormon and all. I guess they don't do the polygamy thing anymore, do they?"

"No, not anymore."

"Well, she kept after him, and I guess he'd had enough, because one night he beat her up and dumped her on our doorstep."

"Jesus, that's cold."

"You should have seen her, Toni. Her stockings were torn, her dress half ripped off, and he'd blacked both eyes, broken her nose, and cut her lip. She'd even lost a couple of teeth ... He really did a job on her."

I could imagine it all too well, having been beaten up in a similar fashion by an old boyfriend myself, back in college. "Did you call the police?"

"She asked me not to. I did take her to the emergency room, and they called the cops, but she wouldn't press charges."

I could understand that. I hadn't either. "She probably thought it was all her fault," I said. "So then what happened?"

"She asked me to take her back," he said. "But I ... I couldn't. I just ..." His voice broke. I heard him blow his nose. When he spoke next, he sounded more under control. "She wasn't the Marcie I married. She looked and acted like a cheap call girl. She was wearing this really tight, short red dress, and she had all this makeup on. I was ... revolted."

"Oh, Tom. That must have been awful," I said. "Was that why he was fired?"

"Oh, no." He sounded relieved not to be talking about Marcie anymore. "Not that I didn't try. No, what he did next was try to make a move on one of our administrators."

"A woman?"

"Yes. A quite attractive one too. But she's a real lady," he said. "I mean she's got class. She's feminine but doesn't flaunt it. She's a good administrator too. I mean, there's a reason she got that position over all the others who applied. She knows what she's doing. She's really likable, but she can be tough when she needs to."

Jeez, Tom, are you sure you're not in love with her yourself? "So what happened?"

"He kept coming on to her—you know, telling her how nice she looked, that he liked the way she smelled, asking her out, patting her arm, putting his arm around her, making sexual innuendoes. Stuff like that."

"She's not married?"

"No, she's divorced. No children."

"So did she file a complaint of sexual harassment?"

Tom laughed. "No, she just fired his ass. Then he sued *her* for sexual harassment."

"Oh, so that was it."

"That was what?"

"My stepdaughter told me there was a big hoo-ha in the Newport Beach papers about a sexual harassment suit and a guy being fired."

"Oh, does she live in Newport Beach?"

"Her parents do. Shawna and Marty Bloom."

"Marty Bloom, really? I know him. I bought a car from him. He's a good guy. So you have a stepdaughter, huh? Your husband's daughter?"

"Yeah. Shawna Bloom is her mother. She's Hal's ex-wife."

"Small world."

"Sure is. Hey, how did the lawsuit turn out?"

"Your pal lost."

"Good. Couldn't happen to a nicer guy."

"Jeez, what did he do to *you?*"

I told him all about my compartment syndrome.

"Holy shit, Toni, that's serious business. You could have lost your arms. You could have died."

"I know."

"You could sue him for that."

"I am. Tom, I really appreciate you calling me back. Can I give our administrator your number in case he wants to talk to you? You know, to help us get Marcus fired from here?"

"Sure. Anything I can do to help."

"Thanks."

"No problem, Toni; it was good to talk to you. Don't be a stranger, okay?"

We said our goodbyes and hung up. I turned to Hal.

"Did you get the gist of that?"

"Sort of. Marcus got fired for sexual harassment?"

I nodded. "They've got a female administrator. Marcus harassed her, and she fired him, and then he sued *her* for sexual harassment."

"No shit," Hal commented. "Who won?"

"She did," I said.

"Good. Who was that anyway?"

"Tom Parker. We were interns together. He's at John Wayne Memorial Hospital in Newport Beach."

"I'm surprised your hospital would hire Marcus with that sort of thing in his background," Mum said.

"They didn't know about it," I told her. "He didn't put John Wayne Memorial on his résumé, and Jack Allen's brother recommended him to Jack, and Jack just kind of pushed it through without anybody checking his references."

"Then how did you find out?" asked Bambi.

"I Googled him," I said. "It's amazing what you can find on the Internet. I found former classmates who'd worked with him and former fellow interns and even a former fellow resident, who has yet to call me back, by the way."

"But if he didn't put John Wayne Memorial on his résumé, how did you find it?"

"I Googled Jack's brother. That's where he is."

"Pretty thorough," Pete said. "Are you sure you don't want to come and work for the police department?"

"You can't afford me," I said.

"You were lucky Tom agreed to talk to you," Hal said. "Usually they tell everybody not to say anything except 'Yes, the guy worked here.'"

"Usually that's the case," I said, "and Tom wouldn't talk to me from his office. But Marcus broke up his marriage, so he's got a grudge against him."

Pete and Bambi left shortly thereafter, and Hal and I went to bed. He and Mum both urged me to just stay there on the couch, but I wanted my own bed. I figured if that didn't work, I could always come back downstairs.

Of course they were afraid I'd get light-headed and fall or something, seeing as it was my first day home from the hospital. It didn't seem possible. This morning seemed light-years ago.

With the help of my pain pills and my general state of exhaustion, I slept like a rock.

Hal didn't.

"I was afraid I'd roll over on you and hurt you," he complained. "I was afraid to move."

Hal went off to work, and Mum fixed me tea and crumpets for breakfast. That left me with the rest of the day to do ... what?

Mum had her own ideas on the subject. "You need to just rest, kitten," she said.

Easy for her to say. I was already bored out of my skull. "I rested yesterday," I objected.

"Not really, dear," she replied. "You just came home from the hospital yesterday and had all those visitors and phone calls, and you were exhausted. Today you need to just rest, without all the excitement. Besides, we need to talk."

"About what?"

"My week is up. I'm scheduled to fly home on Sunday, but I hate to go home and leave you like this."

"Leave me like what? I'll be okay. I'm going back to work on Monday."

"I don't think you should, kitten. I can easily extend my stay for another week or two if necessary. But that creates another problem."

"I know. You have to go back to work too."

"No, dear, I don't. I have the whole month off."

"You were planning to stay that long? Mum ..."

"No, I wasn't. Antoinette, I should have told you about this before."

I was beginning to lose patience. "About what?"

Mum heaved a giant sigh. "I took the time off for a wedding and a honeymoon."

CHAPTER 24

Whoever loved that loved not at first sight?

—Christopher Marlowe

"A wedding? Whose?" Then it sank in. "Mum!"

"I know, dear. His name is Nigel Gray, and I've known him nearly three years."

Aha! At this point I had yet another epiphany. I remembered teasing Mum about a man in her life way back in 2008, but she wouldn't admit she had one. Over the next two years, I'd heard nothing more about it—until now.

"Darling Mum!" I tried to throw aside my ice packs and get off the couch, but Mum stopped me. She sat delicately on the edge of the couch, and I attempted to hug her. Very carefully. "What's the problem? Get him up here! You can get married here."

"Oh, no, I couldn't do that. We were going to keep it small and quiet—just a quick ceremony by a justice of the peace."

"And you were planning to tell us about this when?"

"Antoinette, I would have told you, all in good time."

"All in good *time*? Like the next time Hal and I came to visit and there just happened to be a man in the house?"

"Don't be silly, dear."

"And as far as keeping it small and quiet, we can do that here.

Just Hal and me, and Bambi and Pete, and Jodi and Elliott and their kids ...”

“You call that small, dear? And quiet, with all those kids?”

“Please, Mum. For your only daughter? Please with marmalade on it?”

For an answer, Mum rose and went to the phone.

Hal got the news when he got home at noon.

“You’re kidding. A wedding? Here? Fiona? Well, shit.” He hugged her and proceeded to pepper her with questions. “Who is this guy? Where’d you meet him? What does he do? How long have you guys known each other?”

“Really, Hal darling,” Mum said. “One question at a time, if you don’t mind.”

Hal sighed. “Okay. Who is this guy?”

“That’s better,” Mum said. “His name is Nigel Gray. He’s retired from Scotland Yard, and I met him around Christmastime two years ago.”

“Scotland Yard?” I gasped. “How neat!”

“Two years ago?” Hal yelped. “How come you never said anything?”

“Hal,” I said, “let her talk already.”

“Thank you, kitten. I was out shopping with my friend Doris from the office, and we went to Harbor Village—you know, down where the *Queen Mary* is—to look in all those cute little shops, and then we thought it might be nice to treat ourselves to lunch on the *Queen Mary*. Nigel was there with a tour group. He’d recently lost his wife, and instead of staying home alone at Christmastime, he decided to go on this tour.”

“So your eyes met across a crowded room, and it was love at first sight?” Hal said.

“Something like that, dear,” Mum said. “He came over to me and asked me if I was Susan Hayward.”

As a young woman, Mum had borne a close resemblance to Susan Hayward, a gorgeous redheaded actress from the forties. She’d even worn her curly red hair the same way. Of course, it was mostly gray now, but the resemblance remained even so.

"Well, then, of course, he noticed I was British, and we got to talking, and he asked me for my phone number. And the next thing I knew, he'd left the tour and decided to stay. I helped him find a flat, and we started seeing each other regularly."

"So when you get married, he's going to move in with you?" I asked.

"He already has, dear."

"Mother!"

"Well, really, kitten, why should you young people have all the fun?"

"Jesus," said Hal, "I've got to call Bambi."

"I already did," I told him. "Jodi too. They'll all be over later. We have to make plans. I also called Father Fred from the Episcopal church. It's going to be next Saturday morning at eleven, right here in the backyard."

"Nigel will be here tomorrow," Mum said. "He's coming in on the noon flight."

I resolved not to oversleep this time. Mum would make sure of it.

And so it was that in the middle of all the celebrating and arguing over who was going to be responsible for what, my fellow resident Patti finally called me back.

"Toni, I'm so sorry it took me so long to get back to you, but my sister's daughter got married last weekend, and you know——"

"How it goes," I finished. "Yes, I certainly do. My mother's getting married here next weekend."

She gasped. "Your mother? Oh my God! Why, she's been a widow for … how long?"

"Well, let's see … How old am I? Forty-six years."

"Wow. How wonderful for her. What do you think of *him*?"

"I haven't met him yet," I told her. "He'll be here tomorrow."

"You must be so excited!"

"Oh, I am, believe me. So what can you tell me?"

"Well, you remember Sydney, who used to share an apartment with me?"

I did remember Sydney. She'd been a nurse in the ICU where we'd been residents.

"Well, I don't know if you realized it, Toni, but we're a couple."

Oh. I hadn't, but I'd been such an innocent in those days.

"Okay," I said cautiously. "And you guys are still together after all this time?"

"We are," she said, "but it hasn't been easy, and Marcus Manning certainly didn't help."

"What did he do?"

"He nearly broke us up is what he did."

"How?"

She hesitated, obviously uncomfortable with the subject. "He started coming on to me. I told him to stop. But he didn't. He told me he knew all about me and Syd and claimed that he was so good in the sack that he could even satisfy a lesbo. He said if I didn't put out, he'd put my … preferences on Facebook."

"Eww!"

"I know gays are pretty much accepted nowadays, but I sure didn't want him plastering me and Syd all over cyberspace, so I … er … put out."

"Jeez. How awful. So did it shut him up?"

"No. Instead he put on Facebook that I put out."

"Oh my God. Did Syd see it?"

"Not then, but I thought she had, because she started acting really strange. She got really quiet and didn't want to talk or go anywhere with me. I thought she knew and was giving me the silent treatment."

"Oh, Patti. So what happened?"

"After that went on for about a week, I confronted her, and we had a big fight. I threatened to leave. She threatened to leave. Then she finally confessed to me that Marcus had done the same thing to her that he'd done to me. He'd posted about her on Facebook too. She thought I'd be mad at her."

"Jeez, what a slime dog."

"You got that right. Anyway, once we got all that out in the open, we kissed and made up. But the whole thing made us both feel really … dirty. Exposed. Out there."

"Did you get any hate mail?"

"Some. There's always some homophobe or other out there. But it didn't last long. We never responded to it."

"And I don't suppose you ever complained?"

"There really wasn't anyone we felt comfortable complaining *to*, if you know what I mean."

I could see that.

"But somebody must have," she said. "He's gone now."

"And now he's here."

"And what did he do to you?" she asked.

I told her. I also told her what had happened at John Wayne Memorial. I think it made her feel better.

She was shocked and concerned about my ordeal, but I told her not to be. My pain would go away. Hers and Syd's would always be there.

"Give Syd a hug for me," I said, and we hung up, after I got permission to give Charlie her phone number.

For Patti's and Syd's peace of mind, I hoped he wouldn't have to use it.

The weekend passed in a blur of wedding plans and frequent naps. Hal and Mum picked Nigel up at the airport Saturday morning, as my arms were in no condition to drive just yet.

Picture a gray-haired, much less pompous version of Dr. Bombay from the old sitcom *Bewitched*, and you'd have Nigel. Jodi and Bambi and I adored him on sight, and he sure did seem to adore Mum. His whole face lit up when he looked at her, and vice versa. Any misgivings I may have had about my mother remarrying vanished. And Bambi ... well, when she found out Nigel was retired from *Scotland Yard*, she practically swooned.

I went to work Monday morning. Hal wanted to drive me there so I wouldn't tire myself out, but I insisted on walking. My arms were still in Ace bandages to keep the swelling down, but I no longer needed the ice packs. So far there was no evidence of post-op infection. Stitches would come out tomorrow.

The first thing I did when I got to work, after everybody had greeted me and commiserated with me over what that bastard had done to me that had required such extensive surgery, was go talk to Charlie.

Actually, the first thing I did was get a cup of coffee and sink into my chair to close my eyes and rest for a bit. Walking to work had indeed tired me out. Then I went to see Charlie.

"Damn, Doc, are you a sight for sore eyes! Are you glad to be back?"

I sat down in one of his visitor's chairs. "That depends," I said. "What's happening?"

Charlie launched into a litany of more employees that had been fired and subsequently reinstated, including both Margo and Natalie. I had to stop him in order to ask if he'd had a chance to talk to Marcus's references.

"Not really," he replied. "Nobody would talk about the guy. All they'd say is that yes, he worked there from such and such a date to such and such a date, and that was it."

I got up, closed the door, and came back. "Well, have I got a deal for you." I hauled out the slip of paper upon which I had written phone numbers and put it on his desk. "This," I said, pointing to Tom's number, "is a guy who was an intern with me who's now at John Wayne Memorial Hospital in Newport Beach, where Marcus worked last, and this number is the administrator who fired him. This one is a gal who was a resident with me who is now at Hoag Memorial, but please don't use it unless you have to."

"Wait," Charlie said, puzzled. "John Wayne Memorial? That's not on his résumé."

"That's because he was fired from there. Don't you want to know why?"

"How'd you find out about it?"

"I Googled Jack's brother. That's where he is."

"So why was he fired?"

I told him about the hospital administrator and the sexual harassment lawsuit. Then I pointed to Patti's number. "This gal, my fellow resident, is in a lesbian relationship with a nurse. They've been together since we were residents. Marcus approached each of them separately and told them that if they didn't have sex with him, he was going to expose their sexual orientation on Facebook."

"Jesus Christ!"

"They each gave in, but they almost broke up over it. And then he put it on Facebook anyway, that he got these two lesbos to put out for him."

Charlie put his face in his hands. "I feel sick," he mumbled. "Why would Jack's brother recommend such a sleazebag to us?"

"Marcus must have something on him," I said, half joking, and then it hit me. "Of course! That's it!"

"That's what?"

"He's blackmailing Jack's *brother*."

"Then why did Monty say he had a stranglehold on the chief of staff?"

"Because Jack's trying to protect his brother. It's not Jack who's being blackmailed."

"So now what?"

"I think you should call Jack's brother," I said. "Tell him about the two lesbians and about how Marcus posted about them on Facebook even after they did what he wanted. That tells me that even if Jack and his brother do everything Marcus wants them to, Marcus will still do whatever he threatened to do to Jack's brother anyway. So Jack's brother has got nothing to lose by talking to you."

Charlie cringed. "If you're so sure about this, why don't *you* call him?"

"It's not my place," I told him. "Jack told me pretty forcefully to stay out of the executive committee's business or I'd regret it. Unlike Marcus, he *can* fire me. You can tell Monty all this, and maybe he'll do it, but there's no way in hell I can, and you know that as well as I do."

At home, Nigel prepared drinks while I gave him an encapsulated version of the Marcus Manning story.

"Dear me," Nigel said. "Quite a shemozzle, what? Does this Marcus person have it in for you for some reason?"

"Yes," I said. "I think he wants to fire me and replace me with somebody who will support him in his quest to become CEO of our whole hospital system. Plus, I'm female."

Nigel stopped what he was doing and stared at me incredulously.

"Surely not that old thing? In this day and age? Aren't there laws against that sort of thing here in the colonies?"

"Certainly, but this is Idaho. We're still living in the Wild West here. Plus, he's a Mormon."

"And what's that to do with the price of tea in China?"

"It's a very male-oriented society," I told him. "Women are supposed to stay home and have as many children as possible and then run the relief society."

Nigel handed me Hal's drink and mine. "Rather a potential drain on the welfare system, all those children, eh what?"

I passed Hal his drink. "Not the Mormons. They take care of their own."

"Ah, well then." Nigel gave Mum her drink and sat down next to her on the couch. I sank into my recliner and took a healthy swig of my scotch.

"Does that mean," Nigel persisted, "that sex discrimination is rampant here because of the Mormons?"

"Not necessarily," I said. "There are plenty of good ole boys who get drunk and treat their wives like servants and carry that attitude into the workplace who aren't Mormon."

"Toni's no stranger to sex discrimination," Hal said. "She's got some great stories to tell about medical school. Remember that time you got in a knock-down, drag-out fight with a resident because he wanted the bed you were sleeping in?"

Nigel looked horrified. "What on earth?"

I laughed. "It's not quite that bad. There was a call room on the ward that had four beds in it. I was on call, and when I was done with all my emergency admits and it was quiet, I lay down on one of the beds and went to sleep. I had just dropped off when one of the residents—"

"Male residents," Hal put in.

"Of course male. Anyway, he shook me awake and told me to find someplace else to sleep because that room was for men only. So I told him I had just as much right to that bed as he did, and then he grabbed me and tried to drag me out of it, but I grabbed on to the frame and wouldn't let go. So he dragged me and the bed right out into the hall.

By that time a crowd had gathered, and the attending told me to get my butt out of that bed and they'd find me someplace else to sleep. I told him I would, but until they did, I was just going to hang on to that bed and sleep in it."

By now, both Mum and Hal were grinning in anticipation, but Nigel was laughing so hard he was practically falling off the couch.

"As I recall, they found you something pretty nice," Hal said.

"They put up a cot in one of the doctors' offices in the clinic building and gave me a key," I said. "It was nice and private and quiet, and I had a phone. Then after that, they arranged to do that in several of the doctors' offices at night and on weekends. There were fifteen other women in my class, and up till then, no provisions had ever been made for accommodating female doctors or medical students when they were on call. I think we were supposed to make do with the nurses' lounge, on a lumpy old couch with broken springs."

"And speaking of that," Hal said, "wasn't there something about the nurses' lounge when you were an intern too?"

"Oh, yes, there was," I said, and I described the kerfuffle that had ensued when I'd insisted on watching TV in the doctors' lounge instead of the nurses' lounge. "I told them that I was a doctor and therefore had just as much right to the doctors' lounge as any of the other doctors. It wasn't as if I were using the men's locker room, after all."

"And I'd wager that wasn't the end of it, was it?" Nigel said.

"Of course not. The next thing that happened was that the director of the internship and residency program told me the same thing. I gave him the same argument and told him I was really disappointed that he wasn't backing me up, because I thought that was part of his job. I asked him if he'd actually ever *seen* the nurses' lounge, because it sucked, and told him that requiring me to use it instead of the doctors' lounge was sex discrimination. Plus, I wasn't a nurse, *hello*, and therefore, unless they were willing to create a separate lounge for *female* doctors, with all the amenities of the present doctors' lounge—the windows, the couches and easy chairs, the color TV, the tasteful lighting, the kitchenette, the refrigerator, etcetera—I was going to exercise my right to use the doctors' lounge."

"That's my girl," Mum said.

Nigel had hitched himself forward on the couch and appeared fascinated by my story. "What happened then?"

"He just stood there with his mouth open, so I concluded my argument by saying that I wasn't the only female intern or resident they were going to have to deal with. There were going to be lots more, so they'd better get their asses in gear and figure out a solution before the next intern class arrived on July first."

"So what did they do?" Nigel asked.

I shrugged. "They put in a door to the locker room, and that was the last thing I heard about it."

"Hell's teeth," Nigel said. "Haven't you Yanks had a law against sex discrimination for quite some time?"

"Since 1964, to be exact. Title VII."

"It didn't do Anita Hill much good," Hal said, "back in 1991."

"That wasn't sex discrimination, Hal, dear," said Mum. "That was sexual harassment. Quite a different thing, don't you know."

"I don't think it's done anybody much good," I said. "They meant well, but every woman who tries to claim sex discrimination or sexual harassment gets dragged through the mud, has her reputation ruined, and loses her job anyway, and frequently her marriage breaks up to boot. Once it gets into the news, nobody wants to hire her. Who'd voluntarily go through all that if she didn't have to?"

"But, my dear girl, aren't you required by law to have policies and procedures to deal with that sort of thing in the workplace?" Nigel asked.

"Of course we are, but as far as I can tell, it's just for show," I said. "Nobody's going to get anywhere claiming sexual harassment at this hospital, what with Marcus Manning around to fire them before they can cause any trouble and nobody to back them up."

"What about you, kitten?" asked Mum. "I know you'd back people up. Wouldn't you?"

"I do back people up," I said in frustration. "All it does is get me in trouble. I should just mind my own business."

Hal let out a sarcastic whoop of laughter. "Hah. That'll be the day.

You and Jodi couldn't mind your own business if your lives depended on it."

"How about yours?" I shot back. "If I'd minded my own business five years ago, you'd still be moldering away in Stan Snow's crawl space."

"Yes, Hal, dear," my mother said, "no thanks to that awful Robbie."

Nigel merely said, "Hmm." I had no doubt that he'd heard all about Hal's dramatic rescue and his subsequent bout with hantavirus pneumonia, as well as other adventures, including the awful Robbie, from Mum over the three years they'd known each other.

"The fact remains," said Hal, "that sexual harassment policies aren't worth the paper they're written on, at least around here. Anybody who sues for sexual harassment just gets fired. It doesn't matter what the verdict is."

I agreed. "It seems as though those antiquated attitudes are just going to have to die along with their owners."

Hal snorted. "Don't hold your breath. I'm seeing those same attitudes in my students. Apparently the old rednecks are teaching them to their grandkids."

"Well, I think charging Marcus with grievous bodily harm and sending him to jail will solve my sexual harassment problem a lot better than some policy about it," I said.

"Oh, that reminds me," Hal said suddenly. He pulled a folded document out of his shirt pocket and handed it to me.

It was a subpoena, requiring me to be present at the courthouse at nine the next morning for Marcus's second arraignment. This would be the one in which the charges against Marcus would be amended from misdemeanor assault and battery to assault and battery with intent to cause grievous bodily harm—a felony for which Marcus would no doubt be taken into custody and out of my life, unless he made bail.

This arraignment was quite different from the last one since we were now dealing with amended charges: a felony instead of a misdemeanor. One could have cut the tension with a knife. This time Marcus would be taken into custody, to spend an unknown period of time languishing in one of those fetid cells in the basement of the police station, which even Martha Stewart couldn't convert into anything approximating decent living conditions.

After a rather heated argument, Marcus's bail was set at $50,000, and LaNae wept as he was handcuffed and taken away by the bailiff. The gray-haired man I'd seen at the last hearing put his arms around her and tried to comfort her, but she appeared inconsolable. *Maybe she just needs to go home and can something,* I thought uncharitably. I felt majorly bummed because I hadn't needed to be there any more than I'd needed to be at the last one.

I walked back to the hospital slowly, enjoying the warmth of the sunshine on my sore arms and the knowledge that Marcus wouldn't be around to harass me when I got there. At least not until somebody bailed him out.

The day wasn't over yet, but I was exhausted. Mike urged me to go home and rest, and I did so as soon as I had been to see Russ to get my stitches taken out. Russ told me I could lose the Ace bandages too. It sure felt good to get fresh air and sunshine on my arms, which had developed significant tan lines in the last few days.

Mum and Nigel were out, and so was Hal, so I had the house to myself. I went upstairs, tore off my clothes, and lay down for a nap in my underwear. I must have really needed it, because the next thing I knew Hal was shaking me awake. "Sweetie, it's after six," he said. "Aren't we going to the picnic?"

I sat up groggily. "Picnic?" I said stupidly. "Oh, God."

"Don't you want to go?" he asked. "Are you not feeling up to it?"

Getting up and going to a picnic was the last thing I wanted to do right then. I wanted nothing more than to lie back down and sleep some more. But even in my semicomatose state, I knew that if I did that I wouldn't sleep tonight, so I forced myself awake.

"I want to," I told him. "Just give me a minute."

"At least that asshole Marcus Manning won't be there," Hal said. "He's in jail, right?"

I pulled on a sleeveless top and a pair of shorts and slipped my feet into Birkenstocks. "He was this morning," I said.

"Good, because otherwise I might forget myself and deck him."

"You'd better not," I said. "You might end up in the next cell if you do."

He shuddered. "Want me to spray you?"

I held out my arms while Hal sprayed me liberally with mosquito repellent, which made my incisions sting in the holes where the stitches had been. I usually got eaten alive at evening outdoor affairs in the summer. Mum was even worse; plus, with her red hair and fair complexion, she also needed industrial-strength sunscreen.

Mum and Nigel were there when we got downstairs.

"There you are," I said. "What were you doing all day, out having fun somewhere?"

"Not exactly, dear," said Mum. "We've been rather busy planning a wedding."

"And a honeymoon," Nigel added. "Replanning, actually, what with changing plane tickets, hotel reservations, and all that sort of thing, don't you know."

"Oh dear," I said.

"Not to worry, not to worry," Nigel reassured me. "Really, don't you know, I think Fiona's happier doing it this way, instead of doing it on the sneak, so to speak."

"Well, that's good," I said. "Would you two like to accompany us to the hospital picnic, or do you have other plans for the evening?" I knew how Mum felt about picnics, so Nigel's answer didn't really surprise me.

"I think we'll spend the evening in a nice, cool restaurant," he said. "You kids just run along and have a good time, and we'll see you later, alligator."

That sounded so comical in Nigel's British accent that I had to laugh. Nigel looked worried. "What? Isn't that right?"

"Of course it is. It just sounded funny in a British accent, that's all."

"So we're gonna go," Hal said. "See ya later, alligator!"

"After a while, crocodile," said Nigel, with a coy little wave.

It looked like the entire population of Twin Falls was already at the park, but it was only the four hundred or so hospital employees and their families. A volleyball game was in full swing over in the southeast corner, and the dunking tank had been set up on the north side of all the picnic tables and barbecue pits. Countless small children yelled and screamed and wove in and out of everyone's legs as they waited in line for food. Long tables groaned under the weight of huge platters of fried chicken, which had been provided by the medical staff, and the countless side dishes and desserts provided by the employees themselves. Hal and I hadn't brought any food, just our trusty picnic basket with the necessary utensils.

We picked a nice spot under a tree, out of the sun, and were spreading out our tablecloth when Charlie hailed us from the table where he was sitting, asking us if we wanted to join them, so we did. Monty was there too, as well as Jack, Dave Martin, and Jeff Sorensen.

"I find myself constantly rushing around putting out fires," Monty was saying. "Not a day goes by that I don't have to deal with a host of new problems. Frankly, I can't do this anymore. If something doesn't change, I plan to retire now."

"Oh, no," I said, alarmed. "That's not going to help, Monty. With you gone, there won't be anybody to control Marcus."

"Thanks a bunch, Toni," said Charlie. "Don't you think I can handle Marcus?"

Oops. Maybe I was judging Charlie too harshly. I'd never actually seen him in disciplinary mode, so I really didn't know. "Sorry, Charlie" was all I said.

"Has something else happened?" Hal asked.

"Oh yes, something new every day," Monty said sourly. "Just for starters, today our new community-outreach officer, Debra Carpentier, gave me her two weeks' notice. Two of our newly recruited doctors, Dr. Isaacs and Dr. Resnick, have told me they plan to go elsewhere at the end of their contracts instead of joining the partnership if Marcus becomes CEO. Valuable employees have been fired for no reason. Others have quit. Luckily, we've been able to reinstate most, if not all, of them, but we've had to spend a lot of precious time on matters we shouldn't have had to spend time on at all, to the detriment of other matters more pressing with regard to the new hospital."

"Not only that," Charlie said, "but the man is a pathological liar.

Employees have begun taking someone else with them as a witness when they go to his office, because if they don't, he'll tell them anything they want to hear and then deny it later."

Jeff spoke up. "Well, this seems awfully sudden," he said. "He hasn't even been here a month yet. Has anyone tried to talk to him about all this? Give him a chance to mend his ways?"

Jack, who was sitting next to Russ, answered Jeff. "We have. We all have. Monty and Charlie have tried to get him to lay off all these firings and treat employees with respect, regardless of gender. But this business with Toni is just over the top."

"Surely that was just an accident," Jeff said. "Surely he didn't intend to hurt her that badly."

"Oh yes, he did," I said. "You weren't there. You didn't see the look in his eyes. If he could have gotten away with killing me, he would have."

"Oh, come now, Toni, isn't that just a bit melodramatic?" Jeff asked.

Russ shook his head. "I don't know how much you all know about compartment syndrome, but I operated on Toni, and I'm here to tell you that she not only could have lost both of her arms but could have died. She had myoglobinemia, and her potassium was over six when she was admitted. It's a bloody miracle she didn't have a fatal arrhythmia or go into renal failure. So don't talk to me about melodramatic."

Jeff wasn't through. "The man has six children. Shouldn't we take that into account?"

"That's not our problem," I said.

Jeff glared at me. "Oh, yeah, right, Toni, we know where you're coming from. You don't have kids."

"Not for lack of trying," I said hotly, "and no, that's not where I'm coming from. We're not allowed to take that sort of thing into account when we hire someone, and we shouldn't take it into account when we fire them either."

Charlie spoke up. "Kids or no kids, there's no point in trying to keep this guy on and trying to rehabilitate him. I did go to the trouble of checking on places where he's worked before, and it's quite clear to me that the man is a sexual predator and most likely has a borderline personality disorder. Now, I'm not a psychiatrist, but abusive men like Marcus are like pedophiles. No matter how much you work with them, they always do it again. Furthermore, he was fired from the last place he worked, which he didn't even put on his résumé, for sexual harassment. He sexually harassed one of the *administrators*, for God's sake."

"Let's get something to eat," Hal suggested. "How about I get the food while you get the drinks?"

"Okay."

My appetite disappeared completely when I spied none other than Marcus Manning himself holding forth over by the beer kegs. He laughed and joked with everyone as he passed out beer in large Dixie cups to all comers. LaNae, quiet and demure by his side, passed out cups of lemonade, and Debra Carpentier stood next to her, passing out cups of fruit punch. LaNae held a cup out to Marcus, but he shook his head and didn't take it, so she set it down next to him on the table.

Oh my God. I really hadn't expected him to make bail that fast, although I didn't know why not. Maybe I hadn't expected his family and members of his ward to be able to put $50,000 together that fast, but then I remembered that they only had to put up 10 percent. In any case, there he was, big as life, laughing and gesturing as he exchanged pleasantries with everyone. I nearly turned around to go back to the tree, with the intention of telling Hal to get the drinks himself, when Marcus saw me. Too late.

"Well, if it isn't our little queen bee herself, the all-powerful and all-knowing Dr. Toni Day! Tell me, did you enjoy your day today?"

I knew exactly what he was getting at, but in the interest of not starting a knock-down, drag-out fight in the middle of all these people, I didn't take the bait. "Very much so, thanks for asking. Did you enjoy yours?"

His face, already alarmingly red from the heat and sun, turned even redder. I visualized a six-foot thermometer with the mercury rising precariously close to the top. Apparently he knew what I was getting at also.

"I think you know the answer to that as well as I do," he snarled. "You think you're pretty smart, don't you?"

I declined to engage. "Could I have two beers, please?"

He poured them and set them down on the table so hard they sloshed. I picked them up. "Thank you," I said politely and turned to go. But Marcus wasn't done with me yet.

"Not so fast, Doctor. You didn't answer my question. You thought you'd gotten rid of me, didn't you?"

I turned back, but I still didn't answer his question. "You don't really want to fight with me right here and now, do you?"

"Oh, don't I? Let me tell you something," he raged. His speech sounded slurred, and I wondered if he'd been sampling the beer. Unlikely, with his wife standing right next to him, I decided. Perhaps he was just having an aneurysm. One could always hope.

LaNae tugged at his sleeve. "Drink your lemonade, dear," she said. "You're getting dehydrated."

He ignored her. "You're not gonna get rid of me so easily as all that," he told me, breathing hard.

LaNae pulled at his sleeve again. He shook her off. "Damn it, quit nagging!" he said roughly.

"Marcus, you're overheated," she said softly. "You need to drink something so you won't get heatstroke."

He ignored her. His attention was on me. "Did you hear me?" he said. "I said you're not going to get rid of me that easily. I'll get rid of you first, if it's the last thing I do!"

With that, he picked up the lemonade and drained it. He crumpled the cup and threw it at the nearest trash receptacle. It missed. He didn't go after it.

Taking strength from the discussion I'd just heard, I said, "I wouldn't be too sure of that if I were you."

Marcus didn't reply. Instead, he grabbed at his abdomen, bent over, vomited, and then collapsed.

CHAPTER 25

Nothing in his life became him like the leaving it;
He died as one that had been studied in his death
To throw away the dearest thing he owed
As t'were a careless trifle.

*—William Shakespeare, **Macbeth***

LaNae screamed. "Somebody help him!" she cried.

People turned toward her, but most of them didn't respond to her cry for help. Several physicians came forward. Marcus writhed and thrashed on the ground, retching and foaming at the mouth. Then his eyes rolled back in his head, and his thrashing turned into a grand mal seizure.

Dave Martin, Russ Jensen, and George Marshall pulled him away from the beer kegs and the table upon which the carboys of lemonade and punch sat. They tried to restrain him from injuring himself by stabilizing his head and holding on to his arms and legs.

I ran over to see if I could help, but they seemed to have the situation under control, except for one thing. "Stay away from that vomitus," I warned Dave, who was closest. "The police are gonna want to take samples."

Dave sat back on his heels and looked up at me with a startled expression. "The police? What for? I thought he was just having a scizure. You think he was poisoned?"

"Well, he drank some lemonade and then collapsed," I said. "That seems suspicious to me. Doesn't it seem suspicious to you?"

"I suppose so. Hey, as long as you're not doing anything, how about calling for an ambulance?"

"Okay." I hauled out my cell, called 911, and asked for the police along with the ambulance.

Hal materialized behind me, putting his hands on my shoulders. "What's the story?"

"LaNae gave him a cup of lemonade, and he drank it and collapsed."

"Poisoned, do you think?"

"Possibly. Hey, watch where you're stepping!"

Hal looked down, made a face of severe distaste, and stepped away from the vomit.

Suddenly Marcus stopped seizing and went limp. LaNae gasped. Her children gathered around her. "What's the matter with Dad?" the oldest boy asked.

LaNae ignored him. "Are you going to just sit there and let him die?" she demanded. "Can't you do CPR or something?"

The youngest girl started to cry. I positioned myself between them and the vomit.

"He's still breathing," Russ said, "and he's got a pulse."

I thought that before the ambulance arrived it might be a good idea to cordon off the vomit, so that nobody else would step in it, and I looked around for something to use. An empty pot to cover it up with? No, they all had food in them. A paper plate wouldn't be sturdy or heavy enough; somebody could smash it or kick it, or the wind could blow it away. Then I had an idea. I grabbed a handful of plastic knives and started sticking them into the ground around the pool of vomit. I did this as much at arm's length as I could because I really hated being in such close proximity to vomit, but I couldn't help getting a whiff of it, and it didn't smell like any vomit I'd ever smelled before. "Hal. Come here and smell this."

"Are you out of your mind? Why—"

"Just smell it. What do you smell?"

"Huh. That's weird." ·

"What?"

"It smells like—"

"No pulse!" Russ yelled. "He's not breathing!" He started chest compressions while George tipped Marcus's head back, pulled his chin up, swabbed out his mouth with a napkin, and began mouth-to-mouth resuscitation.

"—almond extract," Hal finished.

"Bitter almonds!" we both said at the same time.

"George!" I screamed. "Get away from him!"

George ignored me. I went over to him and pushed him. He fell over on his side and looked up at me, looking ready to tear me a new one. I didn't give him a chance. "Cyanide!" I said.

George tried to tear me one anyway. "Are you fucking nuts? What the hell do you think you're doing, Toni? I didn't smell anything."

"Not everybody can smell it," I said. "Hal and I smelled it in the vomit."

"Christ," said George, struggling to his feet. "I'm getting too old for this nonsense."

The ambulance arrived. Two paramedics jumped out. One of them replaced George at Marcus's head with an Ambu bag and an oxygen cylinder. George, now on his feet, took a few unsteady steps, swayed, and then *he* collapsed.

"We're going to need a second ambulance," I told the other paramedic. "He's inhaled cyanide fumes from doing mouth-to-mouth." He gave me a slightly panicked look and hauled out his phone.

Russ knelt next to George's head and checked his pulse and respiration. Then he looked up. "He's breathing," he said to nobody in particular, "and he's got a pulse."

By now the paramedics had intubated Marcus and started an IV. One of them had attached the Ambu bag to the endotracheal tube and started bagging him while Dave Martin continued chest compressions. The paramedic doing the bagging looked up at me. "Did you say cyanide?" he asked me. I nodded. "Hey, Corey!" he called out to the other paramedic who was inside the ambulance. "Bring me one of those cyanide kits, will ya? And some activated charcoal?"

"Bring two!" I called.

Corey brought one. "There's enough in here to treat two people," he said.

"Then give half to him," I instructed, indicating Russ, who was still monitoring George.

Corey opened up the kit, took out what he needed, and then ran back to the ambulance and fetched an oxygen tank, a mask, and a second IV setup. Quickly he snaked a nasogastric tube through one of Marcus's nostrils and injected activated charcoal solution into it. "This may help," he explained to me. "But that stuff gets absorbed so quickly it may already be too late." He then went over to help Russ with George.

I picked up the open kit. "AKORN PHARMACEUTICALS," it said on the wrapper. "CYANIDE ANTIDOTE PACKAGE. Contents: amyl nitrite, twelve 0.3 mL ampoules; sodium nitrite, two 300 mg/10 mL ampoules; sodium thiosulfate, two 12.5 g/50 mL vials."

The paramedic bagging Marcus, who introduced himself as Josh, asked me to hand him one of the vials of sodium thiosulfate. He stopped bagging long enough to suck the contents into a syringe and injected it into Marcus's IV. Nothing happened.

"Do you want the sodium nitrite now?" I asked Josh.

"I hate that stuff," he said, but he took the vial nonetheless. "It causes methemoglobinemia. The methemoglobin binds the cyanide, but you can't reverse the methemoglobinemia with methylene blue, because it just releases the cyanide again. Seems like a waste of effort to me. The thiosulfate binds cyanide too and makes thiocyanate, which you can just pee out." He injected the sodium nitrite into Marcus's IV. "But the guidelines say you need to use both, so we do."

I was impressed. I mean, I was a pathologist, and that was more than I knew about cyanide poisoning. I looked over at George. Russ had put the oxygen mask on George's face. Corey, who had already started an IV in George's arm, snapped the top off an ampoule and injected the contents into the IV. Russ had snapped the top off another ampoule and removed the mask long enough to wave it under George's nose. When there was no response, he replaced the mask. "No, no," Corey said. "You have to hold it there for thirty seconds. Then wait thirty seconds, and then do it again. Three times."

George moved. He turned his head away from the ampoule Russ was holding to his nose, which I assumed was the amyl nitrite, and began to cough. Corey stood up. "You gonna be okay now?" he asked Russ. "Because we gotta get this other guy to the hospital."

"I'm okay," Russ said. "So's he. You guys go ahead."

The police arrived just as Corey and Josh loaded Marcus into the ambulance, with Dave Martin still doing chest compressions and LaNae and the children following them to the ambulance door, where the kids clamored to get in and "ride with Daddy."

LaNae gently dissuaded them. "We'll go in the car," she told them.

Bernie Kincaid and Pete Vincent jumped out of the squad car and came running over to us. "What happened?" Bernie asked.

"Marcus drank some lemonade and collapsed," I told him.

"So what's wrong with *him*?" asked Pete, pointing at George, who was trying unsuccessfully to sit up.

"He was giving Marcus mouth-to-mouth, and then *he* passed out," I said. "Probably from the cyanide on Marcus's breath."

"How do you know it was cyanide, Toni?" Bernie asked.

"Hal and I smelled bitter almonds in the vomit," I said.

"Vomit?" said Pete. "What vomit?"

I showed them.

"Clever," said Bernie, trying unsuccessfully not to laugh at my white plastic barricade. "Like a tiny little picket fence."

"Well, it was the best I could do," I said. "People kept trying to step in it."

He laughed even harder when I showed them Marcus's crumpled paper cup, which I had skewered to the ground in front of the trash can with a plastic fork.

"Where did the lemonade come from?" Pete asked.

"From that carboy over there," I said. "The orange one. But lots of people drank that lemonade before Marcus, and nobody else got sick."

"Did he pour it himself, or did somebody give it to him?"

"His wife gave it to him," I said. "She was passing out lemonade. He was passing out the beers."

"Did she pour it out of that carboy?" Bernie asked, busily writing in a notebook.

"I suppose so. I didn't see her do it. Marcus was trying to pick a fight with me, so I wasn't paying any attention to her."

"I saw her put a cup of lemonade over by the beer keg and urge Marcus to drink it," Hal said, "but he didn't drink it right away. She had to nag him a couple of times."

"So how long would you say it sat there before he drank it?" Bernie asked.

"A few minutes," Hal said. "Maybe five. Less than ten."

"And I don't suppose you saw anybody put anything in it while it sat there," Bernie said, a trifle sarcastically.

Hal shook his head.

"That figures," Bernie grumbled. "Nobody ever sees anything helpful."

Pete nudged him with an elbow. "Cheer up. Maybe we'll see something helpful in the vomit."

Bernie made a face. "Not me. The crime guys can do that." It wasn't common knowledge that Bernie was squeamish when it came to disgusting bodily fluids, but I knew for a fact that he'd never yet made it through an entire autopsy. I'd done him in with a gangrenous bowel the first time I'd ever met him, and I'm not sure he's ever forgiven me for that.

Bernie Kincaid, a detective lieutenant like Pete, was a transplant from California. He'd been going through a divorce at the time. He'd been responsible for me being arrested for murder five years ago. For some reason, he'd taken an instant dislike to me. Then he'd tried to have an affair with me. I'd been tempted; with his black hair and black eyes and compact body, he was very attractive, and Hal and I had been having problems at the time. But all that upheaval was behind us now.

The crime van with its portable lab arrived right on the heels of the second ambulance. George, by now fully awake and grumpy, protested half-heartedly that he didn't need to go to the hospital, but Russ overruled him, and George apparently didn't have the strength to even sit up, let alone get on his feet and walk away. So away he went in the ambulance, Russ accompanying him.

The crime-scene techs got busy, one taking pictures, the other cordoning off the area with yellow crime-scene tape. I looked around and saw that nearly everyone had left. Most of the covered dishes on the food table were gone. The fried chicken remained, and someone had at least covered it with a red-and-white-checkered tablecloth.

"Hal," I said, "isn't that our tablecloth?"

"Yep. We're obviously not using it, and maybe it'll keep the flies and yellow jackets off the food. Hey, want your beer now? They're still sitting on the table by the beer keg."

"No," I said, "I don't think I'd better. You'd better not either."

Hal looked astonished. "What do you mean, I'd better not?" Then his eyes grew round as he realized what I was thinking. "Oh."

"In fact, I think you guys ought to take those beers for evidence," I said, pointing them out to Bernie. "I don't think anyone should drink those beers. Know what I mean?"

Bernie looked at me. "You mean …?"

"Maybe I did have a motive to kill Marcus," I said, "but he also had a motive to kill me."

Bernie said, "Oh." Then his eyes widened. "You had a motive to kill Marcus?"

"He threatened my job. He harassed me. He fired my histotechs and my chief tech. He attacked me. See these scars? I had to have surgery. I'm suing him for assault and battery with intent to cause grievous bodily harm. Yes, I had a motive."

"I don't think this is the time to be telling him that, hon," Hal said.

"No, it's okay," I said. "He's going to find out anyway from the first person he talks to."

"Oh, we'll be interviewing everybody here—don't worry," Bernie said. "What's left of them," he added, looking around. "Nobody's gonna leave until we do."

"Oy vey," Hal said to me. "Might be a long night. You'd better call your mother and let her know what's going on."

I hauled out my cell phone and called Mum's cell. After several seconds, she answered, sounding breathless. I heard laughing in the background and glasses clinking.

"So sorry, my darling," she told me. "One can hardly hear a phone ring in all this noise. You'd never guess who we ran into. Your friends Jodi and Elliott. They've joined us. We're just having a high old time, aren't we, Nigel?"

I heard Nigel's voice but couldn't make out what he said.

"Mum," I said, "we might be rather late getting home tonight, and I didn't want you to worry."

"Well, thank you for letting me know, kitten, but why?"

I told her. She sounded appalled.

"Antoinette, *really*, how could you think I wouldn't be worried with you mixed up in another *murder*?"

I heard Nigel's voice again but more clearly this time. "Murder? You don't say. Here, let me have that phone, Fiona, please? My dear girl," he continued, directly to me now, "now don't you say a word to those police johnnies until we get there."

I giggled. "That might be difficult," I told him, "since one of them is my son-in-law."

"Son-in-law? Fiona, dash it all, why didn't you tell me ..." Nigel's voice faded into the background, and the next voice I heard was Elliott's.

"Toni, Nigel's right. Why the hell didn't you call me? We'll be there as soon as we pay the freakin' tab."

"Pick up Bambi on the way," I suggested. "She won't want to miss this."

I pocketed my phone. "They're coming," I told Hal.

"Fiona and Nigel? They're coming here?"

"Yes," I said. "And Jodi and Elliott. They were having dinner together."

"Well, I suppose it makes sense to have a lawyer, but—"

"And Bambi," I finished.

"Oh, for God's sake!"

"Think about it. It'll be like a field trip for her. Extra credit."

Hal threw up his hands. "Only you, Toni," he said. "Only you would make a party out of a crime scene."

"Not a party," I objected. "A teaching opportunity."

"I doubt if Pete will see it that way," he said.

It took at least fifteen minutes for Elliott to get there. He parked behind the crime van, and everybody piled out and came running over to us. Mum pulled me into her arms and hugged me tight while Nigel harrumphed over her shoulder. Elliott asked, "What the freakin' hell is going on here, Shapiro?" Pete came over and asked Bambi what she thought she was doing there.

"Toni thought I could learn something," she said.

"Hmph," he said. "Well, as long as you're here, you might as well help." He slung an arm around her, and they went off together to the crime van.

Nigel cleared his throat and scratched his chin. "Possibly I could be of some assistance, eh what?" he said and ambled off in the same direction.

I shrugged, said, "Possibly I could too," and followed them.

The interior of the crime van was pretty small to begin with, definitely a one-butt kitchen. Pete, Bambi, Nigel, and I filled it nearly to bursting point. Bambi was poking around in the vomit sample with a pair of long, pointed forceps.

"Be careful!" Pete said. "There's cyanide in there. Keep it away from your face. I don't know what you think you're gonna find."

"I saw something," Bambi protested. "Something blue. There's no blue food, right? So what would be blue in vomit?"

"M&Ms?" Nigel suggested. "Cake sprinkles?"

"Not that color blue," Bambi said. "Aha! Here it is." With her forceps, she withdrew a bit of blue film. "That's not food!"

Pete reached up on a shelf and took down a small evidence jar. "You're right; it's not. Put it in here."

She did, and he screwed the lid on and began writing on the label.

Bambi stuck her forceps back in the sample and pulled out another fragment of the same material, but this one was greenish yellow. "Here's another one!"

Pete opened up the jar, and she stuck it in with the blue one.

I sniffed. "We need to get out of here. I smell bitter almonds."

"So what?" asked Bambi. "I don't smell anything."

"I do," Pete said. "Come on; put the lid back on that stuff, and let's go!"

We piled out of the van. Bambi slammed the doors shut. Pete opened them again. "Let it air out, or we won't be able to drive it back to the station."

We rejoined Mum and Hal at one of the picnic tables. "You guys found something, didn't you?" Hal said, looking at our faces.

"Yes, my dears, do tell," Mum said.

Pete handed the jar to Hal, who peered at it from all angles, turning it this way and that. "But what the hell *is* that?" he murmured.

I peered over his shoulder. "Looks like it might be pieces of a capsule," I said.

"Spot on, my girl!" Nigel said. "That's exactly what it is. Two halves of a capsule. One blue, the other greenish yellow. Looks like Marcus took a pill with his lemonade, eh what?"

"But he didn't," I said. "He just gulped down the lemonade. I would have seen it if he'd taken a pill."

"Maybe he took one earlier," Pete said.

"Not too much earlier," I said. "Doesn't that gel dissolve pretty fast in the stomach?"

"That doesn't look like it dissolved at all," Nigel said. "It looks like the two halves just came apart."

"I wonder what kind of pill it was," Pete said.

"I can look it up in the *PDR* when we get back to the hospital," I said. "The *Physicians' Desk Reference*, I mean," I added as I noted quizzical expressions among my audience. "But maybe it doesn't matter. Maybe what was in that capsule had nothing to do with whatever it was supposed to be."

Nigel looked at me. "Are you suggesting that the cyanide was in it?"

"Well, it's possible, isn't it?"

"Oh, yes, it's possible, but how will we know?"

"We'll test it when we get back," Pete said.

"How?" I asked. "It was in his stomach with all the cyanide. How are you going to know if it came from that capsule or was just contaminating it?"

"Hmm," said Pete. "Good point."

"We could get a clue," I said, "if we find out what the pill was and see who has a prescription for it."

"That would be a HIPAA violation," objected Hal.

I shrugged. "Get a warrant."

Bernie Kincaid joined us. "Warrant for what?"

"A warrant so that I can look people up and see who's taking whatever this pill was," I said.

"You have to be more specific," Bernie said. "You can't just get a blanket warrant to look up everybody involved in this case. No judge would issue one."

"I can at least find out what the drug is," I retorted. "Then you can ask people if they're taking it or look for it in people's houses. You can get warrants for that, can't you?"

"How are you going to find out what the drug is?" Bambi asked.

"Look it up in the *PDR* or ask the pharmacist."

"Toni," said Bernie with a sigh, "why don't you just let us do our jobs and stay out of it?"

"It's not my nature," I said demurely. "Anyway, I can help you, and you know it. I have medical knowledge that you don't."

"You might also be a suspect," Bernie said. "You obviously had reason to wish Marcus dead. You said so yourself just now."

"I didn't want to kill him! I wanted him fired, not dead. However, dead works too. He's out of my life either way, isn't he?"

"Not necessarily," Bernie said.

The look he gave me made my blood run cold.

CHAPTER 26

She knows wot's wot, she does.

—*Charles Dickens,* **The Pickwick Papers**

Pete and Bernie still had lots of people to interview, but they let us go. They probably figured none of us was a flight risk. Mum scratched her arm. "Can we go now, kitten? The mosquitoes are coming out. It's almost dark, and I don't have repellent on."

"Sure, but I want to stop by the hospital first and check on George."

"What about Marcus?" Hal asked.

"Okay, I'll check on him too."

Jodi and Elliott went home. Bambi got permission to stay with the crime van and follow the evidence to see what they did with it. She left with the crime van. But Hal, Nigel, and Mum came with me to the hospital. They stayed in my office while I went up to ICU.

Marcus hadn't made it. I really hadn't expected him to survive. But George was another matter. He hadn't ingested cyanide; he'd only inhaled it, and I didn't think he'd inhaled enough to kill him, especially if he got treated quickly, which he had been.

Russ and Dave were still in George's cubicle, and so was George's wife, Marjorie. I peeked around the curtain and asked, "How's he doing?"

George was awake and looked extraordinarily healthy and pink cheeked under his oxygen mask, even in the fluorescent overhead light, which washes everybody out. Marjorie was smiling. "He's doing great," she told me. "Look at the roses in his cheeks!"

I smiled at her and said nothing. I didn't want to rain on her parade, but I knew that cyanide was like carbon monoxide in its ability to turn the blood bright red. Carbon monoxide does it by binding to hemoglobin so that oxygen can't, and cyanide does it by blocking the enzyme cytochrome oxidase, which allows the tissues to use oxygen. In both cases, the oxygen circulates and doesn't get taken up by the tissues, so that venous blood is as red as arterial blood, no matter what else may be going on with the patient. Therefore, George's pink cheeks weren't necessarily a good sign.

But Russ and Dave were smiling too, which made me feel better.

"He's gonna be okay," Dave said. "Too bad we don't have hydroxocobalamin here. That's a better antidote than what he got in the field and doesn't cause methemoglobinemia. It binds the cyanide and makes cyanocobalamin, which you can just pee out."

"Too bad the paramedics don't have that," I said, "instead of amyl nitrite and sodium nitrite, because you can't reverse the methemoglobinemia with methylene blue in cyanide poisoning."

"Why can't you?" Marjorie asked.

"Because it releases the cyanide from the cyanmethemoglobin," I told her, "and then you're back to square one."

"Well, at least we have sodium thiosulfate," Dave said, "which makes thiocyanate, which you can pee out. And the guy at poison control told us to use both. The point is to inactivate the cyanide as quickly as possible, methemoglobin or not. It doesn't cause that much methemoglobin, only about 25 percent, according to the poison-control guy."

"Unless you've got somebody who's been in a fire and has carbon monoxide poisoning too," I said.

"Yeah, the poison-control guy said that too," Russ said. "He asked if carbon monoxide was a factor, because then you don't want to use any nitrites."

"Anyway," Dave said, "George can go home tomorrow. But he probably ought to take a couple of days off before coming back to work."

"Nonsense," growled George. "I'll be back tomorrow."

Dave and Russ both shrugged. Marjorie laughed. "He's back to normal," she said.

I agreed and left.

Downstairs, I ran into Roland Perkins, the county coroner and proprietor of Parkside Funeral Home, pushing a gurney. "Well, hello there, young lady," he greeted me in his usual sepulchral tone, which belied his jolly, fat-man persona. Rollie and I had known each other as long as I'd been here, but he always called me either "Doctor" or "young lady," never Toni, although I'd asked him to more than once. "I've come to pick up the body of your late administrator, Marcus Manning."

"Up in ICU somewhere," I told him. "And by the way, I already know about him, so you don't have to call me in the middle of the night about the autopsy, okay? I'll call *you*, tomorrow."

"Yes, ma'am," he said and disappeared into the elevator.

Hal, Mum, and Nigel had made themselves comfortable in my office and were drinking coffee. Hal had introduced them to Brenda, the tech on call, and she'd gotten the coffee from the nurses' station on the second floor. When she heard my voice, she offered to get me some too, but I was too familiar with what that coffee usually tasted like at this time of night and declined.

"Marcus didn't make it," I told them. "I just ran into Rollie coming to pick him up."

"I hope this doesn't mean he's gonna call you in the middle of the night," Hal said sourly.

"I told him he didn't need to," I said. "George is doing well. They're going to let him go home tomorrow."

"Splendid," Mum said. "Shall we go home now?"

"You guys can go anytime you want," I said, "but I'm going to look up a couple of things."

"I'd like to stay," Nigel said, "but Fiona's dead on her feet."

Hal stood up. "Okay, we'll go," he said. "You won't be long, will you?"

I assured him that I'd be right behind them, and they left. Then I took down my *PDR* and turned to the section that had pictures of all the pills. I expected to find a lot more capsules than I did. Most of the things that used to come in capsules were now in gelcaps or caplets, which couldn't be pulled apart to put anything else into. I supposed this was a reaction to the spiking of Tylenol with cyanide about twenty years ago that had killed several people and resulted in everything being sealed to the point where one had to use a tool to open practically anything anymore.

So that narrowed down the number of capsules to look at, and besides, the blue film Bambi had pulled out of the vomit was a very specific dark cobalt, almost a blue-violet color, which eliminated anything light blue or turquoise blue. I could also eliminate anything that was blue and pink or blue and red, all blue, or any combination except blue and white, yellow, or yellow green. I ended up with three candidates.

First was Trilipix, a drug used in conjunction with cholesterol-lowering statins to reduce low-density lipoproteins and triglycerides. The 135 mg capsule was blue and yellow.

Second, Vyvanse, a drug for ADHD. The 50 mg capsule was blue and white.

And finally Cymbalta, an antidepressant, widely advertised on TV. The 30 mg capsule was blue and white; the 60 mg capsule, blue and yellow green.

Almost any family could have one or more members taking one or more of those three drugs. For example, Marcus could have been taking Trilipix; LaNae, Cymbalta; and the kids, Vyvanse. Unfortunately, looking them up in the computer would be violating HIPAA, and there were ways to track who looked what up.

I'd had enough trouble with Marcus. I didn't need any more grief from his family because of a HIPAA violation.

Although the sun had set some time ago, it still wasn't quite dark when I walked home. Here in the Pacific Northwest, it stayed light until after ten in the summertime. Everybody was still up, despite the late hour, out on the back deck, with citronella candles to keep the mosquitoes away. Even so, Mum had put on a long-sleeved shirt.

Killer and Geraldine announced my presence almost before I put a foot on the front porch, by whining and scratching at the screen door. As I made my way through the house, I heard Hal say, "Maybe Toni knows."

"Knows what?" I asked through the screen door. I snagged the scotch off the bar and grabbed a glass from the cupboard.

"How anybody would get cyanide," Hal said. "I mean, you can't just go down to Walgreens and buy it off the shelf, can you?"

Now how was I supposed to know that? It boggled my mind sometimes, the kind of stuff people expected me to know just because I was a pathologist!

"I doubt it," I said. I put ice cubes in my glass and poured a generous slug of scotch over them, then joined the others on the deck, making sure to close the screen door tightly behind me. I didn't want mosquitoes in the house any more than Mum did. Besides Hal, Mum, and Nigel, Pete and Bambi were there too.

"You could ask the chemist," Nigel said, meaning the pharmacist, which made him sound like someone out of an Agatha Christie mystery.

"I'm pretty sure that drugstores don't keep dangerous chemicals around, even back in the pharmacy," I said. "You'd have to get them from a chemical company, and you'd probably have to be licensed to buy them."

"How about on the Internet?" Pete asked. "If you can find a recipe for a bomb, surely you could find cyanide."

"Well, let's just find out," I said and went inside to get my laptop. I brought it back outside, where I hoped the wireless router upstairs on my desk would still work.

It did. I fired it up, got on the Internet, and Googled "cyanide." Multiple pages of articles and websites came up. I tried to narrow it down by entering "purchase cyanide," but it didn't seem to change anything. I tried "suicide by cyanide" and "suicide pill," and several related sites came up, including the Right to Die and the Hemlock Society. I opened the Hemlock Society page and found links to chemical companies where presumably one could buy cyanide, but when I opened them and clicked on "Purchase," they asked for a company name, a purchase order number, and a license number. Without that information, the site wouldn't open at all. I opened the Right to Die site and got the same results.

Pete, Nigel, and Bambi clustered behind me, looking over my shoulder, as I went through all that. When I was done, Nigel said, "No joy there, what?" and Pete said, "Well, I guess she didn't get it that way."

"She who?" I asked.

"His wife," Pete said.

"Seriously? You've already decided LaNae poisoned her husband?"

Bambi giggled. "We thought maybe she boiled smashed-up peach pits," she said.

"We don't really know who did it," Pete said. "It's just that when somebody is murdered, the most likely suspect is always the spouse. Most people are murdered by someone close to them, you know."

"Isn't that peach-pit business just an old wives' tale?" Mum asked.

"I don't think so," Hal said. "Remember all that hoo-hah back in the seventies about cancer patients going to Mexico and getting treated with Laetrile? They said you could die of cyanide poisoning if you took too much and that the stuff it was made of came from peach pits."

"Actually," I said, "I think it was apricot pits."

"So she boiled apricot pits," said Bambi with a shrug.

"She could have," I said. "Who was I talking to who said LaNae was always canning something and that she'd gone around the neighborhood giving everybody jars of peach-apricot jam?"

"Oh, I think I know," Hal said. "Remember that night we were at John Stevenson's house and Marcus was slapping LaNae around and John called the police? I think it was John's wife who said that."

"Marcus was a wife beater?" asked Nigel, his face twisted in distaste.

"Apparently," I said. "He was a pathologist beater too." I waved my no-longer-bandaged arms.

"He was a thoroughgoing blackguard," Mum said. "He came to the house looking for Antoinette after she charged him with assault and battery and demanded to see her. Apparently he thought he could get her to drop the charges. He was exceedingly rude too. He called me a shriveled-up old bag."

"Apparently," I said, "that's Marcus's idea of sweet talk."

"Blimey," said Nigel. "I hope you slammed the door in his face."

"I did," she assured him.

Bambi changed the subject. "So is it peach pits or apricot pits?"

"Let's just ask Google," I said and got back on the Internet and Google. "Both, it seems. Peach, plum, apricot, and cherry pits; apple and pear seeds; and bitter almonds all contain amygdalin, which is a cyanogenic glycoside, it says here, and that's the main ingredient in Laetrile."

"Oh, dear," Mum said. "I love almonds. I had no idea they were dangerous."

"No, it says that the common sweet almond doesn't contain amygdalin. It's the *bitter* almond, which is what they make almond extract out of."

Mum sighed with relief. "Oh, thank God."

"'Amygdalin,'" I continued, still reading from the screen, "'taken by mouth, is potentially lethal because certain enzymes called glucosidases act on them to produce cyanide.'"

"Maybe she didn't have to go to all the trouble of mashing up apricot pits," Hal said. "Maybe she has a relative with some leftover Laetrile and borrowed some."

"After all these years?" I said with skepticism. "It didn't cure cancer. Anyone who had Laetrile back then is dead now."

"Besides," Mum said, "how would she explain what she needed it for?"

"Good point," Hal said.

"'Amygdalin,'" I said, continuing to read from the screen, "'is extracted from almond- or apricot-kernel cake by boiling in ethanol; on evaporation of the solution and the addition of diethyl ether, amygdalin is precipitated as white, minute crystals.' Hmph. I suppose she could get both of those from the hospital, but how would she know where to look?"

"Obviously somebody'd have to help her," Bambi said. "Somebody in the lab, maybe."

"One of *my* techs?" I said in mock outrage. "What would she say she needed it for?"

"Maybe she could just go buy a fifth of vodka and boil crushed apricot and peach pits in that and not bother to precipitate it," Hal said.

"She's Mormon," I said. "Would she even think of that?"

"She's no ordinary Mormon," Pete said, "if she's thinking of poisoning her husband."

"Good point," I said and continued reading, "'Sulfuric acid separates it into D-glucose, benzaldehyde, and prussic acid,' which is a fancy name for hydrocyanic acid."

"She'd have to steal that from the lab too, but it's dangerous; what if the kids got into it or spilled it?" Bambi said.

"Not to mention the smell," I said. "But we don't have those strong acids in the lab anymore. We don't have to make our own reagents; they all come in cartridges. You just plug 'em into the instrument, and Bob's your uncle."

Nigel looked startled to hear Brit-speak coming from me, but I was sure he knew where I'd gotten it from. "Here's another source," I went on. "'Sodium nitroprusside, a medication used in the treatment of hypertensive emergencies ... toxic levels of cyanide may be reached in patients who receive prolonged infusions. Treatment for three to ten hours with five to ten micrograms per kilogram per minute has resulted in fatalities.' But where would she get nitroprusside in the first place?"

"In the hospital, I'm thinking," said Hal.

"But someone would have had to help her," I said. "Show her where it is. But who? A pharmacist? A nurse? What could she say she needed it for? And besides, it's given intravenously. How's she gonna get Marcus to hold still for that? No, I think that's a nonstarter. But here's something," I said. "Potassium ferrocyanide. We've got that in histology. We use it in the iron stain, the Prussian blue reaction. It says that upon contact with strong acid, it can release toxic cyanide gas."

"Is lemonade acidic enough?" Mum asked.

"Does it say what the pH of lemonade is in there?" asked Hal.

I went back to Google and typed in "pH of lemonade." "It says from two to three, so I think so."

"The lower the pH, the more acidic, right?" asked Bambi.

"Right." Just for fun, I typed in "pH of gastric acid." "It's as acidic as gastric acid," I said. "The pH of gastric acid is from one point five to three point five."

"So what's she gonna do?" Hal asked. "Steal some from histology? How would she know where to look? Would Lucille or Natalie give it to her, especially if they knew what she was going to use it for?"

"Maybe," I said. "He did try to fire them both. But it'd be stupid. They'd be accessories to murder."

"But if LaNae put it in Marcus's lemonade and if it releases gas, wouldn't it poison her before she could get him to drink it?" Bambi asked. "Not to mention anybody else who might be hanging around. Like her kids."

"Good point," said Hal. "Maybe the safest thing would have been to crush the pits of all the fruits she'd been canning and boil them in booze and then spike the lemonade with it."

"It says here," I said, "that skin contact with cyanide salts can result in burns, which allow for enhanced absorption of cyanide through the skin. LaNae should keep the kids out of the kitchen. She should send them over to a neighbor's house."

"You realize," Nigel said, "that anyone could get this information. It doesn't have to be a medical person."

"That's a scary thought," Pete said.

"It doesn't have to be LaNae either," Mum said. "Surely there are lots of other people who'd wish Marcus dead. How about ... well, your techs, for example, or this Debra person—now, who is she exactly?"

"She's our new community-outreach person," I said. "Rumor has it that she and Marcus were having an affair ... oh my God."

"What is it, kitten?" asked Mum.

"I just remembered. Debra came to see me the week before last about doing a TV interview, and she wanted to know what all I did in the histology lab, so she'd know what questions to ask. I took her through the grossing and processing and the cutting and staining, and while I was talking, she was poking around in the cupboard and pulled out a jar of potassium ferrocyanide and freaked."

"Because of the cyanide?" Hal asked.

"Yes. She asked a lot of questions. I told her how it was used in the iron stain, but even so, she seemed really shaken up, and then she left."

"So she goes to the head of the class," Pete said.

"I really hate to say this," Hal began, "but ..."

"If you hate to say it," I said, "then don't."

"You know where I'm going with this, don't you?"

"Yes, I do," I snapped at him. "*I'm* a medical person. *I* have access to potassium ferrocyanide; therefore, theoretically, I could also have spiked the lemonade. But I couldn't have. I was standing there on the other side of the table with two beers in my hands. How would I get cyanide into Marcus's cup? I would have had to spike that whole carboy of lemonade ahead of time, and obviously I didn't, because nobody else who drank lemonade died or even got sick. Besides which, loads of people had a grudge against Marcus. He was wreaking havoc all over the hospital. You heard Jack and Charlie and Monty and Russ over there just before all this happened."

Pete held up a hand. "Everything you said makes sense, Toni, but you gotta realize that the women have a better motive if for no other reason than 'hell hath no fury ... '"

I gave him a disgusted look. "Oh, for God's sake."

Hal waved a hand. "Okay, okay, but if you eliminate all the men, it still leaves any female employees who may have had a grudge and ..."

"LaNae," I finished.

Pete wasn't finished, however. "You want to be very careful, Toni; I'm just saying. Because he not only threatened your job; he physically assaulted you and tried to fire three of your employees. Of all the people who held a grudge against Marcus, you had the biggest one of all."

I refused to back down. "Not as big as LaNae's. She had to live with him. I didn't. Neither did Debra. Besides, I was suing him, charging him with assault and battery with intent to commit grievous bodily harm. Sooner or later, he was going to prison. After that, he'd be out of my life for good."

"Yeah," Bambi said. "They certainly wouldn't give him his job back after that."

"Don't be so sure," Hal said. "Remember George Hansen?"

Hal had a point. George Hansen had been a popular Idaho congressman back in the seventies. He'd gone to Iran during the hostage crisis to try to help get the hostages home. He'd also been convicted of tax evasion and spent two years in prison, after which the good folk of Idaho had reelected him to Congress.

If a felon could be reelected to Congress, who's to say a felon couldn't get his old job back?

Idaho. Ya gotta love it.

CHAPTER 27

Don't look back. Something might be gaining on you.

—Satchel Paige

We didn't get to bed until after two in the morning. Hal didn't have a class until ten, and Mum and Nigel were on vacation, but I had to go off to work bright and early after less than four hours of sleep, and I couldn't help feeling just a trifle pissy about that.

Plus, I had an autopsy to do.

In retrospect, I probably should have asked Mike to do the autopsy, since I was a possible suspect in Marcus's death. But I didn't even think of it. Mike was on call, and I wasn't, and therefore the autopsy was my job.

I didn't have a morgue in the hospital. For fifteen years I'd done autopsies in funeral homes. For most of that time, I'd had to cart all my equipment and specimen buckets around with me as I went to funeral homes as far away as Sun Valley.

A few years ago I'd arranged to do all my autopsies at Parkside, because it was closest to the hospital, just across the city park; it had the largest, most user-friendly embalming room; and Rollie Perkins, its owner, was the county coroner. So I kept my equipment there. Maybe in the new hospital I'd have a morgue, but that was at least two years away.

Pete and Bernie were waiting for me when I got there. Rollie already had the fan going. Usually he didn't do that until I opened the bowel, which usually sent Bernie running hand-over-mouth out of the room. I guessed Rollie wanted to take no chances on cyanide fumes. I hoped the fan was strong enough to handle them. I sniffed the air experimentally. Nope, no bitter almonds, just the sweet smell of embalming fluid.

Marcus lay on the autopsy table, still in the body bag. While I got out my equipment and dug in my toolbox for the instruments I planned to use, Rollie unzipped the body bag. There lay Marcus in all his glory, all pink cheeked and healthy looking. Except that he was dead.

I watched while Pete and Bernie turned the body this way and that, looking for anything in the way of trace evidence. Personally, I thought it was a waste of time, seeing as how Marcus had gulped lemonade and died right there in front of God and everybody at the picnic. What would there be? Leaves? Grass? Dog doo? If it were me, I'd be looking for trace evidence in LaNae's house, perhaps a bit of peach pit that got away and was lurking behind the Cuisinart, or an empty Smirnoff bottle in the trash can under the sink. But I supposed they had to go by the book to be sure they wouldn't miss anything.

They'd get to LaNae's house in good time, after she'd had a chance to clean up all the evidence.

Finally they finished their examination and began to take Marcus's clothes off, bagging each item separately. His hands had already been bagged at the hospital to preserve any evidence that might be on them, after he was officially pronounced dead. We'd had to clean under his fingernails and put the material in evidence bags; then I'd had to do the rape kit, which had really seemed like a waste of time; plus it had been really disgusting. Then, with a cardiac needle, I'd drawn as much blood as I could from the heart and put it into the appropriate tubes.

Finally Marcus's body was ready for me to proceed with the autopsy. I started with the brain, seeing as we were leaving no stone unturned. Bernie clapped his hands over his ears to drown out the sound of the bone saw, but he stood his ground. I felt almost proud of him. *You've come a long way, baby.*

Once the brain had been safely lowered into a bucket of formalin, I opened the body. Wow. I'd never seen such bright colors in an autopsy.

The bright-red blood against the bright-yellow omental fat reminded me of a sunrise. I practically needed my shades. I sniffed again. No almonds.

The first thing I did was remove the colon and small bowel, to get them out of my way. I left them in a bucket in the sink, intending to run them later. Bernie wrinkled his nose and pressed his lips together at the slight fecal smell that ensued, but he still didn't leave the room. *Attaboy!*

I removed the organs one by one, weighing them, dissecting them, and placing samples from each one in another bucket of formalin.

I was using the Virchow method of doing an autopsy, as opposed to my usual technique, the Rokitansky method, wherein I would haul the entire organ block up out of the body in one piece and dissect it on the cutting board. I was reluctant to do that in case it caused a leakage of stomach contents. I wanted to tie off the stomach before removing it and then open it under the exhaust vent, which was located right over the sink, to remove the smells of embalming.

All went well until I began running the bowel. That got Bernie out of the room.

I took the tied-off stomach over to the sink and removed the esophageal tie. I tipped it upside down and began pouring its contents into a specimen cup.

I should have known better, I suppose. But I figured that (a) Marcus had vomited, (b) the paramedics had put activated charcoal down his NG tube, and (c) between the fan and the exhaust vent, any residual cyanide fumes would be sucked out and blown away.

Boy, was I wrong.

The bitter-almond smell just about knocked me over. Maybe the fan wasn't working right. Rollie, standing next to me, made a strangled noise and collapsed.

I dropped the stomach into the sink. "Everybody down!" I yelled. I did have the presence of mind to screw the lid onto the specimen container and strip off my contaminated gloves before getting down on the floor. "Pete, help me! We've gotta get Rollie out of here."

Pete crawled over to me. "Oh jeez," he said and then yelled for Bernie.

"What's going on in here?" Bernie demanded as he walked into the room.

"Get down on the floor!" I yelled.

Bernie just stood there. "Why?"

Shit, I thought, *he must be one of the 40 percent of people who can't smell bitter almonds.* "Cyanide fumes! Get down! Help us get Rollie out of here."

It couldn't have been an easy job, because Rollie wasn't exactly a small man, but Pete and Bernie each grabbed a foot and managed to drag his nearly three hundred pounds of dead weight out of the room while I held the door and then shut it securely behind us.

Once in the safety and comfort of the carpeted outer hallway, I checked Rollie's respirations and pulse. He had both, although they were a trifle fast. His skin had taken on the bright pinkness of Marcus's. Pete called 911 for an ambulance and told them to bring cyanide kits and then asked for a hazmat team to come and decontaminate the embalming room.

The ambulance arrived first. The paramedics went through the same routine they had gone through with George. Then, with help from Pete and Bernie, they managed to get Rollie on a gurney. But before they rolled him away, I stopped them. "You know, we breathed that stuff too," I told them. "Do you have some extra amyl nitrite?"

Their eyes widened. "How long were you in there?" one asked.

"A couple of minutes. Less than five anyway." I said. "And we all got down on the floor. But we had to get Rollie out first."

"Was he the closest to the source?"

"No, I was."

"So how do you feel?"

"Like crap," I said. "I have a terrible headache, and I feel dizzy, and my mouth tastes like … keys." Did I really just say that?

"A metallic taste," the other paramedic said.

"How about you two?" paramedic number one asked Pete and Bernie.

They looked at each other and shrugged. "Okay, I guess," Pete said. Then they both looked at me.

"Toni! Are you okay? Someone catch her!" I thought it was Bernie's voice, but I wasn't sure.

I opened my mouth to answer them, but the room suddenly tilted, and I drifted gently away on a wave of red that faded gradually to black. I never felt the impact of hitting the floor.

I woke up in ICU. The light stabbed my retinas painfully, causing me to squint.

"I think she's awake," a voice said. Hal's face swam into view. I focused on him with difficulty.

"Antoinette? Kitten?" That clearly was my mother. Yep, there she was, on the opposite side of the bed.

I tried to speak, but my throat and mouth were so dry I could only grunt. I thought my tongue might break off and disintegrate into dust if I tried to move it. Too bad. I had so many questions.

What happened?

Am I going to be okay?

Where's Rollie? How is he doing?

What happened at the mortuary after I passed out?

What did the hazmat guys do? What did they say?

What's going to happen to Marcus's body? Cremation? Decontamination? How do you decontaminate cyanide anyway? Spray sodium thiosulfate? Embalm with it? What?

Is that what's in my IV?

When do I get to go home?

Oh God, I've got to finish that autopsy! When am I gonna do that?

Am I gonna get out of here in time for Mum's wedding?

Arrgh!

It must have been the oxygen that was making my mouth so dry. I reached up to take the mask off, but wouldn't you know, my hands were restrained. *Damn.* The nurse, Leslie, came bustling in. "Is she awake? Oh, good, I'll call Dr. Martin." She bustled back out.

Hey, wait a minute, I need some—

But she was gone. Bernie came in and leaned over the bed rail on Mum's side. "Well, that was exciting!"

I grunted under the mask and tried to look encouraging.

"The hazmat guys came while the paramedics were trying to stabilize you, and they said the cyanide level in the embalming room was fifteen hundred parts per million. They said that level could kill a human in five minutes. Guess we weren't in there that long."

Mum gasped. "You mean—"

Bernie interrupted her. "Oh, by the way, Rollie's awake too. He's in the cubicle right next to you."

Well, that answers one question. Maybe two.

Leslie came back in. "Dr. Day, how are you feeling?" She checked my vitals while I worked my tongue around, trying to dredge up a few molecules of saliva. "Water," I finally managed to say.

"Oh, of course, you must be dry as dust with that oxygen," she said. She picked up a plastic cup that sat on my bed table, which had been shoved out of reach to make room for Hal and Mum and now Bernie. Leslie cranked up the head of my bed, removed my mask, and held the cup up so I could sip through the straw.

How do you spell relief? I spell it H_2O.

"I think we can get rid of that mask now," she said. "You can have a nasal cannula instead. I'll tell respiratory."

Dave Martin came in next. He greeted Hal and Mum. Bernie Kincaid introduced himself and then left, after telling me he'd be back later.

"So you've decided to rejoin the living," Dave said to me.

I smiled. "My headache is much better now."

"Well, you've kept us hopping," he said. "Apparently you were exposed to a lethal level of cyanide in that embalming room. Whoever poisoned Marcus probably didn't anticipate how much collateral damage he was doing."

"He? He who?" I'd been so sure a woman had poisoned Marcus that Dave's choice of words really surprised me.

"He or she. I was being generic. So let's review your case."

"Do you want us to leave?" Hal asked.

"No, no, you might as well stay," Dave said, "as long as it's okay with Toni."

"It's okay," I said.

"When you came in, your blood gases showed a metabolic acidosis, and your electrolytes showed an anion gap. I don't know if you knew this, but cyanide causes an anion-gap metabolic acidosis. Your pO_2 looks good, but as you know, that's useless in cyanide poisoning because cyanide keeps oxygen from getting to the tissues. The reason your blood looks so red is because there's the same amount of oxygen in your venous blood as there is in your arterial blood because the tissues can't get any of it."

I nodded. "I knew that."

"However," Dave continued, "serum lactate correlates pretty well with blood cyanide, and we're using that to monitor your progress. It was pretty high when you came in. It's better now. If it keeps dropping like that, you'll be out of here tomorrow."

"Good," I said.

"Why can't you just test her blood for cyanide?" Hal asked.

"It's a send-out test," I said. "We won't get it back soon enough to do me any good."

"Oh."

"That's why we have to use surrogate tests like lactate and monitor anion-gap metabolic acidosis to follow it," Dave said. "Now, we've got sodium nitrite and sodium thiosulfate running in your IV. I had to talk to the poison-control guy at the state lab in Nebraska to find out what dosage to use, and of course, we had to make sure you weren't pregnant, because we can't use nitrites in pregnant women. Something about the effect on fetal hemoglobin—I forget what exactly."

Mum asked, "What do they do, those things that she's getting?"

Dave seemed delighted to be asked these questions. He'd obviously done his homework. "There are three strategies in treatment of cyanide poisoning," he lectured. "All of them bind cyanide so it isn't toxic anymore. One is to convert a percentage of the hemoglobin to methemoglobin, which binds cyanide. That's what the sodium nitrite is doing."

"Right," said my husband, the chemistry professor. "It oxidizes the iron in hemoglobin from the ferrous to the ferric form. But that can't bind oxygen. Isn't that dangerous?"

"That's probably what it does to fetal hemoglobin too," I said.

"It would be dangerous," said Dave, "if she also was suffering from carbon monoxide poisoning. But it only converts maybe 25 or 30 percent of her hemoglobin, so she should still be fine. Anyway, cyanide binds to methemoglobin, creating ..."

"Cyanmethemoglobin," I said. "Back in the day, they used to measure hemoglobin that way."

"The other thing she's getting," Dave went on, "is sodium thiosulfate. There's an enzyme in the cells that detoxifies cyanide by changing it to thiocyanate, which gets excreted in the urine."

"What about the cyanmethemoglobin?" asked Hal. "How does she get rid of that?"

"Unfortunately, she doesn't," Dave said. "Ordinarily, we treat methemoglobinemia with methylene blue, which is a reducing agent, but in this case that would just release the cyanide, and we'd be back to square one."

"So she's just gonna have to walk around with it?" Hal said.

"For the lifetime of the affected red cells," Dave said.

"Which is a hundred and twenty days," I said. "Four months."

"I don't understand," Mum said. "If you can give her something that lets her piss out the cyanide, why bother with the other thing?"

"Because thiosulfate takes effect so slowly," Dave said. "It can take up to thirty minutes for it to do anything, and the point is to detoxify the cyanide as quickly as possible. That's why we use both."

"Oh," Mum said thoughtfully.

"The best thing to use," Dave continued, "is hydroxocobalamin. If you use that, you don't need the other two. It converts cyanide to cyanocobalamin, and she could pee that out too. But we don't have any."

"Can't you get some?" Mum asked.

"Sure. But it wouldn't get here in time to do her any good, and by the time it arrived, she'd have already gone home."

"But—" Hal began.

"We probably don't have it, because cyanide poisoning only happens once in a blue moon," Dave said. "It would expire before it could be used."

"Maybe it might not be a bad idea to have some available," I said. "I read that people who've been in a fire and are suffering from smoke inhalation usually have cyanide poisoning in addition to carbon monoxide poisoning. You can tell by doing a lactate level. But you have to do all your lab work before starting the hydroxocobalamin because it interferes with colorimetric tests and co-oximetry."

Dave wiped his forehead and sighed. "Whew. Between you and me, Toni, we've learned more about cyanide than I ever wanted to know."

"Not enough," I countered. "I still have to find out what happened when I put Marcus's tissue into formalin."

"It formed a cyanohydrin," Hal said.

"Is that good or bad?" I asked.

"It's potentially dangerous," Hal said, "because if you put it in acid, it releases cyanide gas."

"Well, then it's a good thing the formalin was buffered to a neutral pH," I said, "so it's not acidic or alkaline."

Pete and Bambi came to see me right after Mum and Hal left.

Bambi was all atwitter. "Toni, Toni, oh my God! Are you gonna be okay? It wasn't from me poking around in the vomit, was it?"

"Oh no," I assured her. "It was from the autopsy. I was trying to get a sample of the gastric contents, and it just about knocked me over."

Pete cleared his throat. "It did knock Rollie over. How's he doing, by the way?"

"Okay, I think," I said. "We both get to go home tomorrow. He's right next door, if you want to go see him."

"Maybe later," Pete said.

"So what happened after I passed out?"

"Well, the paramedics put an IV in you and gave you the same stuff they gave Rollie and put an oxygen mask on you and called for another ambulance. Then they took Rollie away, and then the other ambulance came and took you."

"What did the hazmat guys do?" I asked.

"I don't know. We didn't go back in there. They went in with their space suits and all, and then they came out and said that the cyanide level in there was enough to have killed us all in five minutes."

"What did they do with my tissues?" I demanded. "What about the sample of gastric contents? What did they do to decontaminate the spillage from the stomach?"

"They sealed off the doors and told us nobody could go in there for at least three days. That's all I know."

"So all my stuff is in there, just sitting there?"

Pete shrugged and looked defensive. "As far as I know. They didn't bring anything out with them."

Jeez.

On the other hand, nobody was going to be bugging me about the autopsy, under the circumstances. I had only one other question. "What happens to the body now?"

"How the hell should I know? That's probably up to the wife." Pete really sounded defensive now.

Bambi nudged him with her elbow. "Hey, take it easy, huh?"

"I'm sorry," I said. "I didn't mean to grill you. I just wanted to make sure that Rollie isn't going to get gassed again when he embalms Marcus or cremates him. I suppose the body is still in there too?"

Pete shrugged again. "I guess so."

Ugh. Three days at room temperature, unembalmed, decomposing. I sure didn't envy Rollie the chore of dealing with *those* remains.

Mike showed up just before suppertime, having just gotten off work.

"Hey, how're you doing?" he asked. "I heard you were back up here. What happened this time?"

"Cyanide poisoning," I said. "Rollie's here too. The last thing I did was get a sample of gastric contents, and it almost did us in. Everything was fine up till then."

"Jesus," Mike said. "I tell you what. Aren't you supposed to tie off the stomach and only open it under a fume hood?"

"I did tie it off," I said. "I tied it off and took it over to the sink where the exhaust fan is, and I didn't even open it; I just untied one of the ties and poured it into a specimen cup. That's all I did. I smelled bitter almonds, and Rollie keeled over, and the three of us got down on the floor and dragged him out of there and closed the door and called an ambulance. And then I keeled over. So they had to get a second ambulance for me."

"So what about the autopsy?"

"The hazmat guys came and sealed the room off for three days. Everything's still sitting in there, including Marcus."

"I don't suppose he's embalmed," Mike said.

"Nope."

"Is your stuff all in formalin?"

"All but the stomach."

"Boy, I don't envy Rollie. How's he doing?"

"Fine. We both get to go home tomorrow."

"Well," Mike said, "don't worry about coming back to work Friday. I can handle everything."

"Are you sure?" I asked him. "Seems like that's all you do, cover me when I'm in the hospital or just out of the hospital. I feel like I'm taking unfair advantage."

Mike patted my arm. "You did it all yourself before I showed up. I figure I can do this little bit. So just take it easy and have a good weekend."

"Oh my God," I said. "That reminds me. My mother is getting married Saturday."

"Really? Isn't that kind of sudden? Where?"

"At my house."

"Jeez. Leezie and I could help. Are we invited?"

I smiled right out loud. "Of course you are. The more the merrier."

Mum would kill me. I'd invited Bernie Kincaid and the Commander too. The "quiet little wedding" was threatening to turn into a major bash.

Dinner consisted of overcooked pork, scalloped potatoes, and overcooked broccoli, followed by lime Jell-O. The potatoes were the only thing that even remotely appealed to me, and I felt too exhausted even to eat those.

Julie, who had replaced Leslie, tried to tempt me with some

chocolate-flavored Ensure, which was really not too bad poured over ice cubes. But after that, all I wanted to do was sleep.

Alas, it was not to be. My final visitor was the last person I would have expected.

LaNae.

CHAPTER 28

All seems infected that th' infected spy,
As all looks yellow to the jaundic'd eye.

—Alexander Pope

LaNae came into my room diffidently, as if not sure of her welcome. I had to make an effort not to show my nervousness. On the one hand, I wanted to feel her out about Marcus and sympathize with her about the way he'd treated her, but on the other hand, I'd just about convinced myself that she'd killed him and wouldn't hesitate to kill me too.

And here I lay, helpless in a hospital bed with an IV line hanging out there just begging for someone to shoot a dose of cyanide into it. An absolute gift for your average poisoner.

Or perhaps she just wanted to know about the autopsy, like any bereaved wife. Maybe she hadn't killed Marcus after all. But then who did?

I arranged my face into something that I hoped looked welcoming.

She wore one of those Laura Ashley-Molly Mormon dresses in a nondescript floral. I couldn't tell the color in the dim light. She appeared to have lost weight since I'd first met her. Her eyes looked sunken with dark circles around them. Perhaps she wasn't sleeping well. Small wonder, considering whom she'd been sleeping with up till now. Her pale hair needed shampooing.

"Toni?" she said softly. "Is it all right if I talk to you? I didn't wake you up, did I?"

"No, of course not. I was just reading. Pull up a chair. What's on your mind?"

"Well, Marcus, of course," she said.

"Oh, of course," I said. "I'm sorry for your loss." I wasn't, of course, but one can't really say that, not to a grieving widow. "I know it's going to be hard for you and the kids."

"Thanks for your sympathy, but actually, we're all going to be better off now. Marcus wasn't the easiest person to live with."

"I know," I said before I could stop myself. But LaNae didn't seem offended.

"I know he assaulted you, Toni. I want to apologize to you for that. I couldn't believe he did that. He's never done *anything* like that before."

Oh yeah? I wanted to say. Could she really not know about his attack on Tom Parker's wife? What was her name? Marcie—that was it. Or maybe LaNae was in an advanced state of denial. A lawsuit, however, was kind of hard to ignore. Marcie hadn't filed charges, but the administrator had.

"Marcus was so ambitious," she said. "He wanted so badly to provide a good life for me and our children. He wanted lots of children, at least a dozen. But he ran into roadblocks everywhere he went."

Roadblocks, huh? Is that what you call them?

"He had all kinds of good ideas," she continued, "but nobody would listen."

Good ideas like firing all the women?

"So eventually, he'd just have to move on."

Always a good idea after one has been fired.

I was having difficulty keeping my mouth shut. I concentrated instead on maintaining a straight face.

"But then, at his last place before here," she said, "he had an opportunity to become CEO. The old CEO was retiring, and they were interviewing for his replacement. But they didn't choose Marcus; they chose a woman. And she had the nerve to sue him for sexual harassment! So he sued her right back, but unfortunately he lost. He was devastated."

"I can imagine," I said.

"So when Bob Allen told him about Perrine Memorial and the plans to become affiliated with Cascade, he saw an opportunity to be CEO of not only a hospital but of an entire system of hospitals! It was a dream job. So we came here, and it was all going according to plan. Marcus was going to be CEO in a year, and he could go from there to a system position. There was nothing standing in his way."

Mum was right! I thought. *She nailed it.* This explained why Marcus had felt he'd needed to remove any women who might get in his way. All three of us female docs at Perrine were possible threats. We talked back. We took no shit. He'd seen that at the first staff meeting.

"But it didn't happen," LaNae said. "He died. Somebody killed him. Who could do such a thing? Who didn't want him to be CEO bad enough to do that?" Her voice quavered, and I expected her to break down in tears, but she pressed her lips together and didn't.

"LaNae," I said as gently as I could, "I'm sorry to have to tell you this, especially under these circumstances, but nobody wanted Marcus to be CEO. You probably had no idea, and Marcus wouldn't have told you, but he demonstrated that he wasn't the kind of person we wanted to be our CEO. Manhandling me was only a small part of what he did to people."

LaNae's hand went to her mouth, and tears gathered in her eyes. "You mean he did the same thing to other people that he did to you?"

"No, I don't think he physically attacked anybody else, but he threatened people's jobs and tried to blackmail them. He fired people just to undermine the doctors they worked for. He fired my chief tech and both of my histotechs, for example. He even tried to fire Charlie, for God's sake."

"I had no idea," she murmured. "I'm surprised Debra didn't tell me."
"Debra? Carpentier?"
"Yes. She's my best friend. She should have told me."
Huh. "Yes, well, she probably didn't want to upset you," I said. "And that reminds me. There's a rumor going around that Debra was having an affair with Marcus. If she's your best friend, obviously it's not true."
"Of course not," LaNae asserted. "She wouldn't do such a thing. I'd

know if she did. In fact, she told me she'd heard that Marcus was having an affair with *you*. She said that was why he assaulted you—because you insisted that he get a divorce and marry you."

My first thought was to marvel at the unnatural calmness with which she dropped that little bomb. Most women would scream and try to tear my hair out. My second thought was that I should do the same to her, but I couldn't seem to muster up enough energy. My third thought was *Thank God Hal isn't hearing this.* So I swallowed my outrage and endeavored to match her composure. "Well, it's just a rumor, because I wasn't. Marcus assaulted me because I accused him of lying to me."

"You mean he told you he was going to divorce me, and then you found out he wasn't?"

Could this woman really be as naive as she seemed? I sighed. "No, LaNae, I accused him of lying about what went on in the executive committee meeting. I told you: I wasn't having an affair with your husband, even though he kept suggesting it."

"Marcus wouldn't do that," LaNae said primly. "You must have misunderstood him."

"Oh, no. He made it quite clear. He made the same proposition to Mitzi Okamoto too."

LaNae looked mystified. "I don't understand. Why would Debra tell me that if it wasn't true?"

"Maybe to cover up the fact that *she* was having the affair," I said before I thought.

"I told you," LaNae insisted. "Debra wouldn't lie to me. I'm her best friend. Why, she even gave me some of her antidepressants once when things were really bad at home."

Like when Marcus was beating the shit out of you and the kids? "What kind of antidepressants were they?" I asked.

"I can't remember the name, but they're those ones they advertise on TV all the time."

"Cymbalta?"

"Yes, that's it. I only took a couple of them, but they helped."

Bingo! So that's where she got it!

"Did you give back what you didn't use?"

"No, I thought I might need them again."

No shit. How many did you take before you came here? Because you're obviously drugged to the gills. I'm just saying.

"I don't remember seeing Debra at the picnic," I said, lying through my teeth in the interest of detecting.

"Oh, she was there," LaNae said. "She was passing out punch. I can't believe you didn't see her. She was standing right next to me."

"Oh yeah, now I remember. I guess sometimes I'm just not very observant," I said lightly. "Besides, Marcus was yelling at me, which was a bit distracting."

"I don't understand why Marcus acted that way," she said. "Like I said, he's never done anything like that before."

"I hate to burst your bubble, LaNae, but I've heard from some former classmates of mine who worked with him, and apparently he has."

"But that's impossible," LaNae protested. "If Marcus was so bad, why did Bob Allen recommend him to his brother?"

"Why do you think?" I asked, trying not to sound as impatient as I felt.

She worked it out. "Blackmail?" she whispered.

I merely nodded. She burst into tears.

"Oh, dear God," she sobbed. "How could I have been so stupid?"

Did she mean stupid to not have divorced Marcus or stupid to have married him in the first place? Or stupid to have murdered him?

I reached out and put a hand on her arm. "Don't put all this on yourself, LaNae," I said gently, trying to hide my impatience. "Abusers always act as if everything is your fault. They make excuses, saying that if you were a better wife, employee, friend, whatever, they wouldn't have to punish you. At least that's what Dear Abby always says. None of this is your fault. It was all Marcus. Not you. Stop blaming yourself, and start thinking about how much better your new life is going to be." *Assuming you manage to stay out of prison, that is.*

She fished around in her purse for a Kleenex and blew her nose. "Thanks, Toni," she said tearfully. "I feel much better now. I'd better go. Debra's staying with the kids." She stood up and turned to leave. At the door, she turned back. "What if I can't do it?" she asked piteously.

Oh, the work. "Some people need therapy," I said. "It's like PTSD. There's no reason to feel ashamed if you need it, any more than if you just got back from a tour in Iraq."

She lifted her head, squared her shoulders, and left. I flopped back on my pillow and stared at the ceiling.

Had I just been aiding and comforting a murderer? Or had Debra done it? Both of them had motive, and I'd just established means and opportunity. Furthermore, I'd done it without violating any laws.

Which left the thorny little matter of being considered a suspect myself. Oh sure, none of the cops had come right out and told me not to leave town, but it was only a matter of time, especially if they heard the rumor about me having an affair with Marcus. They weren't just going to take my word for it that I wasn't.

And then—oh shit, they'd be asking Hal about it. I'd better tell him before they did, or I'd really be in trouble.

CHAPTER 29

Done to death by slanderous tongues ...

—*William Shakespeare,* **Much Ado about Nothing**

By morning my serum lactate was back within the normal range, and my metabolic acidosis and anion gap were gone. So Dave discharged me, telling me not to even *think* about going back to work until Monday.

I was only too happy to comply. My labs may have been back to normal, but I wasn't. I still felt tired, and sleepy—hospitals not being the best places to get any rest in.

Besides, a quarter of my hemoglobin was tied up as cyanmethemoglobin, thanks to the sodium nitrite I'd been treated with, dropping my functioning hemoglobin to nine grams instead of the normal twelve and giving a whole new meaning to the term "tired blood." That wouldn't get back to normal for another three or four months, and I'd just have to suck it up.

Hal picked me up at noon, right after his morning class. The dogs were all over me from the moment I walked in the door, but there was no sign of Mum and Nigel.

I immediately ensconced myself on the couch with my coffee, my book, my afghan, and Geraldine and went right off to sleep.

I woke up when the dogs announced that Mum and Nigel had come back from wherever they'd been. Apparently they didn't realize

I was home, because I opened my eyes to see them kissing passionately just inside the front door. Next they'd be heading up the stairs to their bedroom, I figured. Then they'd probably be embarrassed that I'd witnessed that performance and hadn't said anything.

I stretched and yawned, and they jumped apart as if they'd been burned.

"You guys are so cute," I said.

Nigel harrumphed and pulled at his moustache. It reminded me of George Marshall.

"Antoinette, darling," Mum said, pink cheeked. "I had no idea you were home. When did you get out of hospital?"

"About noon," I said. "Where is everybody? I'd have thought there'd be people all over this place, doing last-minute wedding stuff."

Mum and Nigel looked at each other.

"What?" I asked.

Nigel harrumphed again. Mum looked embarrassed. "Didn't Hal tell you, kitten?"

I guessed he'd been too busy listening to me to tell me anything. "Tell me what?"

"We decided to postpone the wedding," Mum said.

"Postpone the wedding! Why?"

"Because of all that's going on here," Mum said. "We decided that we couldn't just run off and enjoy our honeymoon while this situation is still unresolved."

"This situation?" I echoed. "You mean while we still don't know who killed Marcus? What does that have to do with you two getting married?"

"In case you've forgotten, darling, you've been in the hospital twice in the last two weeks," Mum said. "What if we go off on a honeymoon and you end up getting killed?"

"I see," I said sarcastically. "You'd rather I end up getting killed while you're here."

"We'd rather be here to help," Nigel said, "and possibly prevent it, don't you know."

"Oh." Suddenly I felt silly. Of course they'd rather stay and help me than run off on a honeymoon. After all, it didn't really matter when they actually tied the knot. They'd been living together without benefit of clergy for some time already. What would it change if they postponed the wedding? Other than the fact that one or the other of them might die. But that could happen whether they were married or not.

"Does everybody else know?" I asked. "Jodi and Elliott? Pete and Bambi? Father Fred?"

"Yes, dear, everybody knows," Mum reassured me. "And the flight and hotel reservations have been canceled."

I sighed and suddenly realized that I was relieved. I wasn't supposed to be able to go back to work until Monday anyway, and the thought of all the wedding preparations and excitement had me worried that I wouldn't be recovered enough to get through it all without having to go lie down somewhere and get everybody all worried about me. A wedding should be all about the bride and groom, not the matron of honor and her various medical problems.

Hal pulled into the driveway right then, and moments later he came into the kitchen through the door from the garage, carrying bags of groceries. Mum and I hurried to take them from him and began putting things away. "Toni, you get back to the couch," Hal said in a tone that brooked no argument. "You need all the rest you can get if you're going to Marcus's funeral tomorrow."

"Oh, I am?" I asked in surprise. "I'm going to Marcus's funeral? Since when?"

"Since I just found out where and when it is," he said. "It's at ten o'clock at the Fifteenth Ward LDS Church, the one over on Eastland. And you're going to go early, because there's a visitation before the service, at nine."

A visitation? Was Joseph Smith himself going to arise from the dead and appear behind the altar to welcome Marcus into the celestial kingdom? Did Mormon churches even *have* altars? I didn't know. I'd never been inside one. I had no idea what to expect. "A visitation?" I asked. "From whom?"

"Don't be silly," Hal said. "They have the open casket out in the foyer—"

"Wait a minute," I interrupted. "Open casket? After lying around unembalmed for three days before the hazmat guys let anybody go back in there? No way is he in any condition to be displayed in an open casket!"

"Oh," Hal said. "You've got a point there. Maybe not in this case, but usually they do that so that everyone can go by and pay their respects before going inside. You're going to circulate and see what you can overhear. Then when you get inside, get as close to the family pew as you can."

"Okay, I get it," I said. "I'm supposed to detect. But I'm not a Mormon. Will they even let me in? I thought—"

"It's just the temple that non-Mormons can't go inside," Hal said. "It's okay at the church. Besides, people from the hospital will be there too, you know. You won't be the only non-Mormon."

"Maybe I should sit with them instead," I said.

"Whatever you think best," Hal said.

"Besides, when did you become such an authority on Mormon funerals anyway?"

"Since I ran into Rollie at the grocery store. He told me about the funeral and what to expect."

If Rollie was feeling anywhere near as wiped out as I was, what on earth was he doing at the grocery store? The very thought made me want to go lie down. *By golly,* I thought, *I'd better build up some usable hemoglobin fast.* Maybe I should get some iron tablets. "And what are *you* going to do while I'm at the funeral?"

I knew Hal wouldn't go to the funeral. He'd rather have his fingernails pulled out one by one with a pair of pliers than go to a funeral. "I volunteered to stay at their house during the funeral, in case someone tries to rob them."

Hal had done more staying-at-the-house-during-the-funeral duty than anyone I knew. Some people cased the obituaries just for that reason, to find out when the house would be empty so they could go in and rip off the family while they were at the funeral of a loved one. The whole idea made me mad. Talk about adding insult to injury! "What a clever idea! So you can find the Cymbalta and the leftover peach pits. Want my digital camera so you can take pictures? You can't take anything out of the house, or it won't be admissible in court."

"Isn't that only if it's illegal search and seizure? I have permission to be there. There's nothing illegal about that."

I wasn't so sure. I thought the police had to find the evidence in situ, as it were, and have a warrant to be there doing that. "Maybe you'd better check with Pete about that," I said. Suddenly I was so tired I could hardly stay upright. "I think I'll go lie down now."

Hal followed me into the living room. "Rollie told me that Marcus is going to be cremated right after the service. He also said that your specimens have been taken over to your lab."

That was a relief too. I'd been worried about how I was going to complete the autopsy without them. "What about the blood and urine and gastric contents?"

"The police have them. Oh, and guess what else I found out."

I couldn't possibly. Guessing was way too much work. "What?"

"You were wondering what they were going to use to neutralize the spilt gastric contents."

Well, yes, I had been. "So tell me already," I said wearily.

"Sodium hypochlorite," he said. "Just plain old bleach."

I closed my eyes. "Well, ain't that just a kick in the head," I murmured sleepily. I wondered if they'd bleached Marcus's body as well.

I think that was the last thought I had at that point.

I completely forgot to tell Hal what LaNae had told me.

CHAPTER 30

Man proposes, but God disposes.
And when he is out of sight, quickly also is he out of mind.
Of two evils, the less is always to be chosen.

—Thomas à Kempis

The foyer of the Fifteenth Ward LDS Church was packed when I got there. I was surprised at how many people I recognized. I hadn't known so many of them were Mormon either, but then I realized that people from the hospital were there too and not necessarily Mormons.

A line had formed that led out the door and down the steps. I saw Monty and his wife in line just outside the door and several of the doctors in line ahead of me.

Someone touched my arm, and I turned around to see Debra Carpentier in line behind me. After greeting each other, she said sotto voce, "I wonder how many people are here just to make sure the son of a bitch is really dead."

"Jesus, Debra," I said in astonishment. "Why don't you tell me how you *really* feel?"

"Sorry," she said. "I guess maybe I should think before I speak."
Ya think?

"I mean, I know he's dead," she continued. "I saw him die."

"Like everybody else who was at the picnic," I said. "Including LaNae, poor thing."

"Don't feel too sorry for *her*," Debra murmured. "You know, the only reason she put up with Marcus all this time was to help him get ahead, so that she could enjoy the good life. But it didn't take her long to realize that life with Marcus was never going to be good. She was planning to divorce him and take him to the cleaners, but somebody saved her the trouble."

"Any ideas who?" I murmured back. "Who else was he having an affair with?"

Too late I realized what I'd said. Debra jumped on it with both feet. "Who else besides who?" she demanded. "If you mean me, you're way off base. And what about *you*?"

"What about me?" I returned. "I wasn't having an affair with Marcus. Not that he didn't suggest it more than once."

"Well, I heard you were."

"Who told you that?"

"Charlie—who else?"

Good old Charlie. Why hadn't he told me? "Who told him?"

"How the hell should I know?" Debra asked irritably. "For that matter, who told you *I* was?"

For a minute, I couldn't remember. It seemed like weeks ago. Maybe it was. "Mike, I think. The first time I was in the hospital, with my arms."

"Who told him?" she demanded.

I shook my head. "I have no idea."

"Probably Charlie," Debra said. "Honestly, that man! Puts us girls to shame."

"So you weren't having an affair with him either," I said.

"No way."

"Good," I said. "It's just rumor. I'm glad it's not true."

"It's not for lack of trying," she said. "He kept asking, and I kept saying no. I wouldn't do that. LaNae is my best friend."

"That's what she told me."

Debra looked startled. "She did? When?"

"She visited me in the hospital."

"Oh. I didn't know."

"She told me you gave her some of your antidepressants," I said.

"Yeah, I gave her some of my Cymbalta," Debra said. "I thought they might help get her through the divorce."

"So she was planning to divorce him that soon?"

"She'd already filed. Marcus didn't know yet."

By this time we'd reached the coffin, and it was closed. I sniffed the air experimentally. Apparently Rollie'd done a good job of dealing with the smell. He must have sealed Marcus up in plastic and sealed the coffin as well. I couldn't smell anything except flowers. There were certainly a lot of them. I admired them and endeavored to dredge up some good thoughts, but I couldn't manage it, so I just walked on by.

Inside the church, I found that I couldn't get anywhere near the family pew, so I contented myself by sitting a few rows back with Elliott. Debra, on the other hand, continued forward to the front pew and sat down next to LaNae. The two women embraced each other briefly and then sat talking quietly, their blonde heads together. The kids were freakishly quiet. No talking. No crying. No fidgeting. It was creepy. Had Marcus beaten the childishness right out of them?

Well, if he had, I could certainly understand why they weren't crying. On the other hand, actually jumping up and down and shrieking with glee might be somewhat inappropriate in a church setting.

LaNae wasn't crying either. Neither was Debra.

I looked around. Most people sat quietly, their faces stony. Across the aisle in the front row sat a middle-aged couple who wiped their eyes from time to time, and that was the closest thing to grief that I saw in the entire congregation. Were they Marcus's parents or LaNae's?

As if in answer to my question, another middle-aged couple came in and sat next to Debra in the front row. The woman reached over and touched LaNae's arm. The man sat ramrod straight. I recognized him as the severe-looking man who'd sat next to LaNae in the courtroom. Obviously these were LaNae's parents, and they weren't crying either. The only signs of grief came from the other couple across the center aisle, who must, by the process of elimination, be Marcus's parents.

I could hardly wait to hear the eulogies. This would be a very interesting funeral.

The church was nearly full. LaNae's father rose, stepped to the podium, and asked the congregation to stand. We did so, and the pallbearers brought in the casket.

It was a very personal funeral. There was no service as such. Several people spoke, most of them relatives. Marcus's brothers, who spookily resembled him, told stories about how mischievous Marcus had been as a child. Nobody mentioned torturing small animals or pulling the wings off flies, but then one wouldn't expect them to under the circumstances.

A couple of teachers talked about his high school years. Apparently Marcus had played football in high school. He'd been quarterback and homecoming king. LaNae had been homecoming queen. Had that been the beginning of their relationship? I wondered. If Marcus had had abusive tendencies in high school, nobody mentioned it.

A teenage girl sang a hymn that I didn't recognize, accompanied on the piano by an older woman who was probably her mother. A small boy recited a poem. An older girl played the violin. A quartet of black-suited young men sang a popular song in four-part harmony without accompaniment.

This sort of thing went on for about an hour, and then it was over, and we all filed out of the church. People gathered outside in little groups, talking. I wandered around, hoping to catch a clue in the conversations around me, but no luck—not until I turned away and headed for the parking lot.

Raised voices emanating from the same general area as my car caught my attention. I slowed and stepped toward them on tiptoe, as much to be able to hear what they were saying as to sneak up on them.

"How dare you!" cried an angry female voice. "He wouldn't do that to me. How can you suggest such a thing?"

Her companion laughed coarsely. "Why wouldn't he? He beat you up just for the fun of it. What would stop him from cheating on you as well?"

"He did not beat me up! He didn't cheat on me either."

"Come on, LaNae. Get real. You think we were all born yesterday? It was obvious. That hairdo and those long sleeves aren't fooling anybody."

"Shut up, Brent! Stop saying that!"

"I know my brother," the male voice said. "He told me all about it. And with your best friend too. Some friend!"

"No!" LaNae cried. "Not Debra! She wouldn't do that!"

"She would and did," said Brent cruelly. "Maybe if you'd put out once in a while, he wouldn't have had to go elsewhere. He told me that Debra is a real tiger in the sack."

I heard the crack of a hand slapping a face, a short scuffle, and then a scream.

"You goddamn bitch," said Brent. "Where do you get off hitting me? Why, I ought to …"

At that moment I reached my car. Brent had LaNae pushed up against it, holding both her wrists. His face was as purple as Marcus's would get whenever he talked to me.

"Excuse me," I said, and he let go of LaNae as quickly as if he'd received an electric shock.

"LaNae, do you need any help?" I asked.

She said nothing, but her eyes beseeched me.

"This is none of your business, lady," said Brent rudely.

"But it is my car," I pointed out. "If you want to beat up your sister-in-law, please do it up against your own car, while I call 911." I pulled my cell phone out of my purse.

"I know who you are," Brent said. "You're that bitch doctor that gave him so much trouble. He said he was fucking you too, by the way. For all I know, *you* probably killed him."

I restrained myself with difficulty. I held up my cell phone. "Want to get away from my car now, or shall I use this?" I asked.

I heard footsteps behind me and turned to see Debra coming toward me. "Toni? What's going on here? Do you need help?"

At that point Brent knocked the cell phone out of my hand, sending it flying. It landed several feet away, breaking apart on impact. The battery fell out. A car turned into the aisle. Quickly, I went after the pieces of my phone, before they could be turned into cell pizza. As I dropped them into my purse, I heard Debra say, "LaNae, honey? What's going on here?" I turned in time to witness a whole new drama.

The look Brent turned on Debra could have curdled milk, but it was nothing compared to LaNae's reaction. She wrenched herself out of Brent's grasp and launched herself at Debra, fingernails rampant. "You fucking bitch!" she screeched. "I'm gonna kill you! I'm gonna tear your hair out! I'm gonna …"

She continued hurling incoherent threats at Debra as Brent grabbed her from behind and forcibly turned her away from us. "LaNae, cut it out!" I heard him say. "And be careful what you say. That bitch'll probably go tell the cops as it is!"

I decided to forgo asking him which bitch he was referring to. It could have been either or both of us. Debra gazed at me in bewilderment. "What the hell was that all about?" she asked.

"You're busted," I said. "So am I. Marcus's brother told her all about the respective affairs that we were supposedly having."

"What affair?" Debra said, throwing up her hands in frustration. "There wasn't any affair. I keep telling you. Marcus kept coming on to me, but I just said no thanks."

"Then why would his brother tell LaNae that there was one?"

Debra shrugged. "I have no idea. Look, can we get out of here? I don't want all these people overhearing us, and frankly, I could use a stiff drink."

I thought that was a dandy idea. The number of people milling about the parking lot had increased; it was hot, and frankly, I could use a stiff drink too. So we agreed to meet at the Cove, a rustic-looking bar in the industrial part of town that was so dark and smoky inside that we were unlikely to be seen, let alone recognized. No Mormon would ever venture there. The usual clientele consisted of guys with beer bellies and seed caps, and girls with teased hair, tight jeans, and cowboy boots. The country-western music blasting from the speakers and the loud conversation would guarantee that we wouldn't be overheard.

Not too many people were there, though. The lunch hour was over, and it was too early for happy hour. Debra and I sat in the booth in the back. I ordered my usual scotch on the rocks, and she ordered a martini, extra dry, extra olives.

"I'm betting," I said, "that Marcus told his brother he was having affairs with us, just because he could."

"The man was a stone liar," Debra said. "He could have told anybody anything he wanted to."

Whoa. That sounded like Debra knew Marcus a lot better than I thought. I decided maybe I'd better Google *her* when I got home.

"Did he ever do anything more than just talk about it?" I asked. "Did he touch you inappropriately or assault you?"

"No," she said. "Never. He'd just compliment me on my appearance and ask me out."

"Did anybody ever overhear him?"

"I suppose so. There were always people around."

"Anybody in particular?"

Debra shifted uneasily in her seat. "Like who? I can't think of anybody in particular. Toni, why are you asking me all these questions? I feel like I'm being interrogated or something."

"Because it might be important," I said. "If nobody overheard him, it becomes a he-said–she-said thing, and people might think you're the one who's lying to cover your ass."

Debra put her drink down so hard it sloshed. "People like who? Marcus is the one who's lying, not me."

"But he's dead," I said. "There's no way to get the truth out of him now. His brother and his wife and God knows who else think he was having an affair with you, and you deny it. Why should anybody believe you? You could be the woman scorned. You could have a motive for killing him!"

Debra's cheeks flushed red. "Lots of people could have motives. What about you? He harassed you, he threatened your job, and he assaulted you. Now it turns out you had an affair with him too. Why couldn't you have killed him? You were standing right there."

"You're right," I said, resisting the compulsion to again deny that I'd had an affair with Marcus. "I was standing right there, with a beer in each hand, arguing with him. People were standing around listening. I had no opportunity to put anything in Marcus's lemonade, because my hands were full, and I have witnesses."

"What are you saying, Toni? That if you didn't do it and I didn't do it, LaNae must have done it? Or do you still think I did it?"

"Debra, I don't know who did it. You and LaNae were both right there, pouring drinks, while everyone stood around watching me and Marcus fight and paying absolutely no attention to either one of you. I have witnesses out the wazoo. You don't."

Debra put her face in her hands and leaned her elbows on the table.

"Find some witnesses, Debra," I urged. "It's your only chance. Otherwise you're as big a suspect as LaNae is."

"That was a hell of a long funeral," Hal complained when I got home.

"Oh, I wasn't at the funeral all that time," I said.

"No shit. LaNae got home two hours ago, all weepy and talking about how you and Debra both had affairs with Marcus."

Damn. I'd forgotten to forewarn him.

"Oh."

"Yes, 'oh,'" he mimicked. "Where were you?" He wasn't smiling. He sounded mad. Was there more to his anger than just my failure to call and let him know where I was? He couldn't really think … could he?

"One thing I *wasn't* doing was fooling around with Marcus!"

"Toni …"

"That sounded pretty accusatory, sweetie."

"Accusatory, my ass!" he shouted. "There's a murderer out there! Where the fuck were you, goddamn it?"

Okay, now I got it. He'd been worried about me. "At the Cove, having a drink with Debra."

Hal threw his hands up and shouted at the ceiling, "*Oy gevalt!*"

Mum and Nigel came downstairs in time to witness this phenomenon. "Hal, dear, please calm down," Mum said. "You'll do yourself a mischief."

Hal's hands dropped, and his shoulders slumped. "Sorry," he said. "But there *is* a murderer out there. It's got to be either LaNae or Debra.

They're the only ones with a motive. Toni, she's a fucking suspect," he continued. "She could have slipped something in your drink."

"But she didn't," I said. "I had hold of my glass the whole time. I always do. You know that."

Hal should know. I typically kept my glass on the table right in front of me, with both hands wrapped around it, as I leaned over it to talk. One would be hard pressed to slip anything into it without my knowing about it.

"How did you happen to go for a drink with Debra in the first place?" Hal asked in a more civil tone.

I told him about our confrontation with Marcus's brother.

"So that's how she found out," Hal said.

"Funny thing about that," I said. "When she came to see me in the hospital, she swore up and down that Debra was her best friend and would never do such a thing, but when Brent said Marcus had told him she was, LaNae was all ready to rip her face off."

Hal looked startled. "LaNae came to see you in the hospital? When?"

Shit, now he was going to be pissed off about that too. "The night before I came home. I forgot to tell you," I said.

"Did she try to rip your face off too?"

"She didn't get a chance," I said. "Brent grabbed her and hauled her off."

"So what you're saying is that Marcus told his brother that you and Debra were both having affairs with him," Hal said.

"Apparently," I said. "He must have told others too. The other night LaNae told me she'd heard that I was having an affair with Marcus from Debra. Debra claimed she'd heard it from Charlie. I don't know who Charlie heard it from."

"Shit," Hal said. "If Charlie knows about it, everybody knows."

Mum changed the subject. "What did you find at LaNae's house, Hal, dear? Cymbalta? Peach pits?"

"Either that woman is the most phenomenal housekeeper I've ever met, or she uses one hell of a cleaning service," he said. "I searched the kitchen. I checked every appliance she had, on the counters, and in the drawers. I checked the cupboards. I checked the pantry. I got down on the floor and looked under the stove and the refrigerator. Not a crumb. Not even a dust kitty did I find."

"Well, you didn't stop there, did you?" I said, thankful to be off the subject of affairs.

"What do you think I am?" he said scornfully. "Of course I didn't stop there. I went out into her garage. She's got a cabinet out there just stuffed with food. I think they call it a Mormon closet. She had boxes and boxes of cereal, bags of flour and sugar, cases of canned food, jars and jars of stuff she's canned, and a fifty-pound bag of dog food."

"Dog food? There was a dog?"

"Two," Hal said. "A black Lab and a little dust mop–type thing. Yappy and annoying. They were outside. I left them there."

"I didn't notice any dogs the night we were at Russ and Trish's house," I said. "Where'd they come from?"

Hal shrugged. "Maybe they're dog-sitting somebody else's dogs," he said.

"How does she manage to keep it so clean with six kids and two dogs?" I asked. We couldn't keep our house clean with *no* kids and two dogs. And a cat. That must have been it. LaNae didn't have a cat.

"I don't know," Hal said. "Like I said, she must have a hell of a cleaning service. Maybe she got ServiceMaster in there after Marcus died."

To remove all traces of Marcus, perhaps. I couldn't blame her for that. Those were the guys who cleaned up after things like floods from sewer backups and broken pipes. Maybe they cleaned up crime scenes too. Why not detritus from toxic marriages?

"Anyway, I looked around with a flashlight. I moved things and looked under them."

"What about the tool bench?" I asked. "Maybe she used a hammer to smash up pits and forgot to clean it or something."

"I did look there," he said. "I thought of that too. But none of the hammers had anything on them. And before you ask, I checked the sledgehammer too."

"Did you check the trash?" I asked.

"There wasn't any. It had just been picked up."

"Well, that was handy. Was there anything stuck to the bottom of the trash cans?" There was always stuff stuck to the bottom of ours.

"No," Hal said, "not a thing. It was as if they'd been washed out."

"Who washes out trash cans?" I wondered aloud.

Hal shrugged. "Someone trying to hide something?"

"Or a superwife."

"Or both," Mum said.

CHAPTER 31

Where the streame runneth smoothest, the water is deepest.

—John Lyly

The weekend passed more or less peacefully, if one discounted the fact that Hal had barely spoken to me for two days. Luckily I had Mum and Nigel to keep me company.

"Let him be, kitten," Mum advised me. "You've been through this before. He'll get over it. He always does. Remember Bernie Kincaid?"

A couple of years ago, Hal had thought I was having an affair with Bernie Kincaid, but I hadn't been, and I really didn't want a repeat of trying to convince him I wasn't. Eventually he'd gotten over it, but I thought it highly unfair to be given the silent treatment for something I hadn't done, damn it. How my own husband could believe I'd fool around with the likes of Marcus Manning was mind-boggling, not to mention highly insulting, and this time I resolved to let him stew in his own juice.

Thus it was that I went off to work Monday morning in a state of high dudgeon, when I should have been celebrating the long-awaited absence of our late COO. I also was not pleased with Charlie for spreading my nonexistent peccadilloes around the hospital. Nothing remained a secret for long with Charlie about, and the juicier the better. I could literally *feel* people looking at me askance, including my own partner. If Mike could doubt me, then so could Dave, George, and Russ, who had previously been my champions. If they could doubt me, how much easier would it be for Monty and, God help me, Jack? And, oh God, what about Mitzi and Jeannie and my own techs?

I needed to nip this whole thing in the bud fast—as if there weren't already enough work to do—starting with my partner.

I shoved my purse into its usual drawer and stuck my head into Mike's office. He was sitting at his desk, his back to the door. "I'm back," I said.

"Good," he said, not turning around. "How do you feel?"

"I'd feel better if you'd look me in the eye," I said.

Startled, he looked up at me. "What's wrong, Toni?"

"I went to Marcus's funeral Friday," I said, "and afterward I had a drink at the Cove with Debra Carpentier. In between, I had the misfortune of meeting Marcus's brother Brent. Apparently rudeness runs in that family."

"What happened?" Mike was at attention now and had no trouble looking me in the eye.

"I found out that Marcus went around telling everybody he was having an affair with Debra."

"I knew that," Mike said, puzzled.

"And with me," I said.

I had his attention now, by golly. "You've got to be kidding," he said. "Who'd believe that after what he did to you?"

"He supposedly did that because I confronted him about divorcing his wife and marrying me."

Mike burst into laughter. "Who the hell would believe that?"

"LaNae, for one."

"How ... when did she say that?" he spluttered.

"She came to see me in the hospital," I said. "She wanted to apologize for Marcus assaulting me. She couldn't understand it, because he'd 'never done anything like that before.'"

"Somehow I doubt that," Mike said.

"It's not true," I said. "I talked to a former classmate of mine who worked with Marcus. His wife left him for Marcus, but when she confronted Marcus about divorcing LaNae, he beat her up and dumped her on her husband's doorstep. So he has, at least once before, done exactly that."

Mike took off his glasses and wiped them on his shirt. "Jesus, that's cold, I tell you what."

"LaNae apparently took everything Marcus said as gospel, and now she's in such an advanced state of denial, I wonder how she's going to make it in the real world," I said. "When she came to see me in the hospital, she wouldn't believe Debra would have an affair with Marcus, but then when she heard it from Marcus's brother, she practically attacked Debra."

"Wow. Good thing she didn't know about you."

"Well, she did. She heard it from Debra, who heard it from Charlie. She heard it again from Brent, but he restrained her and took her away before she had a chance to do any damage."

"So she might come after you next," Mike said.

Oh. I hadn't thought of actually being in danger, wrapped up as I was in Hal's silent treatment.

"Well, so she might," I acknowledged after a beat. "What I mainly came in here to tell you is that I wasn't having an affair with Marcus, no matter what Charlie says."

Mike got up and gave me a hug. "Hell, I knew that. I told Charlie there was no way."

"Thanks," I said. "I wish it was as easy to convince my husband."

Mike frowned. "Hal? You're kidding, right?"

I shook my head. "Oh, it's not that he came right out and accused me or anything. He just heard the rumors like everybody else. LaNae told him, after the funeral. He was staying at the house during the funeral so nobody would break in and rob it."

"The bastard put you in the hospital, or has Hal already forgotten that?"

"Remember my classmate's wife? Marcus put her in the hospital too, and Hal knows about that."

Mike put up a hand. "Wait a minute, Toni—you mean he thinks ..."

"No, no, I don't think he thinks that at all. He's just so uncomfortable with the whole idea that he's withdrawn into himself. Mum says he'll get over it in a day or two. He did last time."

"Last time?"

"Yeah, with Bernie Kincaid."

"You had an affair with Bernie Kincaid?"

"Now see, there you go, thinking the worst. No, I *didn't* have an affair with Bernie Kincaid. But Hal thought I did."

"Jeez, Toni," Mike said. "When you tie all that together, it all makes some kind of crazy sense. I can see what Hal is thinking."

Now *that* was scary. "Seriously? What's Hal thinking, Mikey? That I'm the femme fatale of all time and a stone liar besides and he's better off without me?"

Mike put his hands on my shoulders. "Listen to me, Toni. Once, I thought Leezie was having an affair. She wasn't—I knew perfectly well she wasn't—but it scared me so badly to think that she might and that I might lose her someday that all I wanted to do was curl up in a little ball and hide. It made my stomach hurt. I withdrew from her just because looking at her made me hurt."

"You think that's what Hal is doing?"

"I'd bet money on it."

"Doesn't he *realize*," I said, unleashing all my pent-up frustration, "that he's just pushing me away and that he might just conceivably push me into doing the very thing he fears?"

Mike looked startled. "Do you think Leezie felt like that?" he asked me.

"I'd bet money on it."

I was relieved to get back into my own office after that supercharged aha moment that left me feeling emotionally exhausted. A conversation like that between me and Jodi, say, might have ended in the catharsis of tears, followed by a couple of drinks and chocolate. With my partner, no such catharsis was possible, and it was back to business as usual, which in my case, right then, was the business of debunking the rumor that I'd been having an affair with Marcus.

It dawned on me that Marcus could have gone around bragging that he'd had affairs with countless women without their actually knowing anything about it and been believed implicitly by all the other men. Meanwhile, the women would have to fight their way through all that emotional baggage to get a grudging acceptance that maybe Marcus had been exaggerating a teeny bit. But so what? "Boys will be boys" after all, as if that forgave everything. This realization royally pissed me off. That was the frame of mind in which I decided to tackle Jack next.

Perhaps luckily for Jack, he was doing yet another bronchoscopy. I left a message with his nurse to call me when he was done. I wondered if he actually would.

Mike tapped on my door and came in with a lab report in his hand. "I wondered if you'd seen this," he said, putting it down in front of me on my desk. "It's your blood cyanide level."

It was a report from the reference lab we usually used. The usual reference range was replaced by a note that informed me that "blood cyanide levels of 0.5 to 1 mg/L correlate with tachycardia/flushing, 1 to 2.5 mg/L with obtundation, 2.5 to 3 mg/L with coma, and greater than 3 mg/L with death."

My blood cyanide level had been 1.5 mg/L. I'd been lucky.

"What was Rollie's?" I asked.

"Hang on," Mike said. "I wrote 'em all down." He fetched a slip of paper from his own desk and handed it to me.

"Toni 1.5, Rollie 1.8, George 1.75, Marcus 3.5," it said.

We'd all been lucky, except for Marcus.

A frozen section arrived, a sentinel node from a breast cancer patient. Mike handed it to me. "Think you remember how to do this?" he teased.

"Like riding a bike," I assured him, and to my delight, cranking the cryostat caused me only minor discomfort.

There were actually two lymph nodes in the specimen, and the surgeon sent two more while I was still working on the first, so it took about half an hour before I could assure him that all the sentinel nodes were negative, which made him very happy, because that meant he didn't need to do an axillary lymph node dissection. Times had sure changed since my residency, when every patient automatically got a mastectomy and axillary node dissection. Now most of them kept their breasts. The downside of that was that they also had to have chemotherapy and radiation, whereas those who had mastectomies sometimes didn't. Sometimes.

Everything's a trade-off.

Jack called shortly thereafter. "Toni? You wanted to see me?"

"I'll be right down," I told him.

Jack was in his street clothes and shrugging on a lab coat when I got to his office, which I took to mean he wouldn't be rushing off to do another bronchoscopy anytime soon.

"I suppose you want to talk about Marcus," he said. "Before you start, let me just say that you were right all along, and we should have listened to you in the first place."

Whatever I might have expected to hear from Jack, this certainly wasn't it. Jack Allen admitting that he was wrong and I was right? What next? Would I hear celestial trumpets announcing the rising of the dead?

I opened my mouth to reply, but Jack raised a hand. His face was red, either from sunburn or embarrassment. "I made a major mistake, not going through the usual channels for finding an administrator. My brother pushed me pretty hard to hire the guy. And before you ask why Bob would recommend such a sleazeball, let me just say that Marcus was blackmailing him. Don't ask me what about, because I won't tell you."

Aha! I knew it!

"My goodness," I heard myself saying.

"We all owe you an apology because of what he did to you," Jack continued, "and we plan to cover all your medical expenses from that attack."

I should hope so. "What about the cyanide poisoning from the autopsy?"

"That too."

Well, isn't that nice. Jack had turned away from me and begun to mess with some papers on his desk, which I took to mean he was done with me, but I wasn't done with him. "That's all very well, Jack, but it isn't what I came to talk to you about."

"What, Toni?"

"There's a rumor going around that I had an affair with Marcus. I want it stopped."

Jack burst out laughing. "You must be kidding."

"Kidding? About the rumor? Are you telling me there isn't one? Because I've been hearing about it all weekend."

"Oh, there's a rumor all right. Marcus started it himself. He told me he'd gotten both you and Mitzi to put out and was working on Jeannie. He told me, he told Monty, and he told Charlie. That's all he needed to do, as you know. No, what I was laughing at was your demand that I stop it."

"Has he put it on Facebook yet?"

Jack went white. He seemed to have trouble catching his breath. "F-Facebook?"

"Yes, Facebook." I told him briefly, without names, about Patti and Syd. Jack put his hand over his face and leaned his elbow on his desk. "I never thought of that. How can we stop that?"

"We can't," I said. "Any more than you can stop a rumor. Something like this could go viral."

Jack groaned. "This is worse than anything I could have anticipated."

"Oh, I don't know," I said. "There could be something on YouTube."

"YouTube?" Jack appeared to have assumed the demeanor of a drowning man.

"Yes. All my confrontations with Marcus got recorded on cell phones. Someone could have put it on YouTube." I was beginning to enjoy Jack's discomfiture.

"How do we stop that?"

"We don't," I said. "We wait until some well-meaning person e-mails somebody the link. Then it'll get around, and you'll hear about it."

"Isn't there something in our hospital policy that prohibits employees from spreading private hospital matters around outside the hospital?" Jack asked. "There's got to be something to prevent this sort of thing."

"If you don't know, Mr. Chief of Staff," I said, "I sure don't. And it might not be an employee, you know. It could be a friend or a relative of an employee or somebody with no ties to the hospital at all."

"Christ." Jack had both hands over his face now and appeared to be slowly sinking in the west. "We gotta have a meeting. Or something."

Bernie Kincaid was waiting in my office when I got back, sitting in my visitor's chair, head back, eyes closed. I stood there for a few seconds, waiting to see if he would snore. But he didn't; he opened his eyes with a start and demanded, "How long have you been standing there?"

"How long have you been sitting there?" I countered.

"Not long," he said. "Got a minute?"

We'd come a long way from the days when Detective Lieutenant Kincaid would demand my presence at the police station and threaten to arrest me if I couldn't come right away, frozen section or no frozen section.

I sank into my desk chair with a sigh. "Sure. What's up?"

"You do realize, don't you, that you're a suspect in the death of Marcus Manning?" he began.

"I suppose so, but I shouldn't be," I said.

"How so?"

"Haven't you interviewed enough people from the picnic to know that I had a beer in each hand and there was no way I could have slipped anything into Marcus's lemonade?"

"We have talked to several people who said the same thing. But you have as big a motive as all the other women who were having affairs with the man," he said.

I looked at him narrowly. It wasn't so long ago that Bernie himself had been urging me to have an affair with him. Was he thinking about that? Wondering what Marcus had had that he didn't?

"You've been talking to Charlie," I said.

"Well, yes, among others," he said.

"It isn't true, you know."

"Really? Your husband didn't seem quite sure."

Oy gevalt! I threw my hands up in the air in frustration. "I don't know what Hal's problem is," I said, "but it isn't true. I would no more have an affair with the likes of Marcus Manning than grow an extra boob. The man threatened my job and damn near twisted my arms off."

"Well, you realize, that's a motive too."

"I suppose so, but I was charging him with grievous bodily harm, and he was going to end up in prison. What would I need to kill him for? I just wanted him out of my life, and he would have been." Then I had a thought. "Have you talked to Dr. Allen?"

"No, not yet. Why?"

"Because at the picnic he was talking to both Monty and Charlie, and it sounded to me like they were considering firing Marcus. They told Hal and me that Debra Carpentier had given her notice and that two of the new physicians had said they weren't going to stay if Marcus became CEO."

Bernie hauled out his notebook. "Which physicians?"

I told him the names, and he jotted them down.

"Jack also told me that the reason he was so quick to hire Marcus was because Marcus was blackmailing his brother. You might want to ask him about that too."

"I will," he said. "And we'll be talking to Debra Carpentier. But don't think you're off the hook yet." Here his voice grew noticeably less friendly. "You're still a suspect, so don't go anywhere."

The Bernie Kincaid of old was back—the one who wanted to throw me in the slammer and throw away the key. I shivered.

As soon as he left, I called Pete.

"What's up, Toni?" he greeted me.

"Bernie was just here," I said, feeling like a tattletale, but no matter. "He told me not to leave town."

"Well, that's Bernie for you," Pete said flippantly. "Why use one threat when two will do?"

"So am I really a serious suspect or not?"

"Well, here's the thing," Pete said. "We narrowed the suspects down to those with motive, which so far includes you, Debra Carpentier, LaNae Manning, Mitzi Okamoto, Jeanne Tracy, Charlie Nelson, and Dr. Jack Allen. But since Marcus was poisoned at the picnic, we have to consider opportunity, and that eliminates everybody except you, Debra, and LaNae. Soon as we figure out where the cyanide came from, we might narrow it down further."

"But Pete," I said, "my hands were full. Even Bernie said he'd talked to several people who would testify to that."

"True," he said, "but you have a source for cyanide right there in your lab. You said so yourself, the other night."

"I know. Potassium ferrocyanide. But how the hell did I get it into Marcus's lemonade?"

"Well, there we run into a slight problem. You would have had to sneak around in back of LaNae and Debra at the drinks table, and several people have already said you didn't. Or you could have poisoned the entire carboy of lemonade, but since lots of people drank that lemonade with no ill effects, that's not a viable option either. Third, you could have given the cyanide to someone else to put into Marcus's drink. But the same people who didn't see you go around in back of the table didn't see anyone else do that either. You would have had to be in cahoots with either Debra or LaNae."

"I wasn't," I said.

"Well, we'd have to take your word for that, because you yourself told us that you practically showed Debra where the potassium ferrocyanide was and what it was used for."

"Pete, for God's sake," I said. "I showed her the cupboard where all the reagents are kept. She picked up the potassium ferrocyanide herself and asked me all these questions about it. What was it used for? Was it poisonous? Would it turn into cyanide if taken by mouth? Stuff like that."

"And you answered them, didn't you?"

"Well, of course I answered them—why would I not?"

"And how did Debra act when you did?"

"She seemed … upset."

"Are you sure? Could she have been excited?"

"I don't know!" I said in frustration. "Maybe. She was agitated and couldn't seem to get out of there fast enough. That's all I know. What are you getting at?"

"Perhaps she couldn't wait to tell LaNae how she could get rid of her husband."

"You think they were in cahoots with each other?" I asked in disbelief. "Whatever for? Why would they both want to kill Marcus?"

"I don't know. LaNae because Marcus abused her and played around on her; Debra because she was having an affair with him and he wouldn't divorce LaNae and marry her?"

"I don't see it," I argued. "LaNae had filed for divorce, and Debra claims she wasn't having an affair with Marcus. If she's telling the truth, neither one of them needed to kill Marcus."

"But you don't know that Debra's telling the truth," Pete argued back, "and maybe Marcus wouldn't give LaNae a divorce. Maybe getting sealed in the temple doesn't allow for divorce."

That stopped me, but just for a moment. "That can't be right. I know several divorced women who are LDS."

"Well, maybe they weren't sealed," Pete said.

"Maybe LaNae wasn't either," I said.

"This is getting us nowhere," Pete said. "There's too much we don't know."

I agreed, and we said our goodbyes and hung up. Then I called Monty.

"What can I do for you, Doctor?" he asked, a trifle warily, I thought.

"I've got another Mormon question for you," I said.

"I'll answer it if I can," he said.

"If a married couple is sealed in the temple, can they get a divorce?"

I wasn't sure, but I thought I heard a sigh of relief. "Of course they can. Any Mormon can get a civil divorce, but to break the seal requires a temple divorce."

"Oh. How difficult is that?"

"No more difficult than a civil divorce," he replied.

"Do you know if Marcus Manning and his wife were sealed?"

"I don't," Monty said, somewhat stiffly, and I sensed that I was trespassing on his bishop's sense of propriety again. "And I fail to see what business that is of yours, Doctor."

"Because she's a suspect in her husband's death," I said, "and I heard that she had already filed for divorce, so I was wondering how difficult that would have been for her, because if it wouldn't have been too difficult, then she doesn't have as much of a motive, do you see?"

"I see," he said. "Is that all, Doctor?"

"Yes," I said, and then something else occurred to me. "No, wait. Do you know Debra Carpentier's husband's name?"

"Brent, I think."

Brent? Really? You don't suppose ... "Brent what?"

"Carpentier, I presume."

"Where was she before she came here?"

"Somewhere in California, I think. I'd have to look at her file."

"Can I look at her file?"

"Really, Doctor, I don't see—"

"Because she's a suspect too," I said.

"It's my understanding that you are also a suspect, Doctor," Monty said.

"Yes, I am, but I know something about myself that I don't know about them."

"And what's that?"

"That I didn't do it."

Monty coughed. I suspected he was covering up a laugh, but maybe not. "Very well, Doctor. As a member of the medical staff, you have the right to look at any employee's file."

"Thank you."

"You're welcome."

Next I called Kay Osterhout and asked for Debra's file. But it was out, and Kay didn't have any idea who had it.

Shit.

Shouldn't she be keeping track? Why in hell hadn't these things been digitized? Talk about dragging ourselves into the twenty-first century! Oh well. I could always Google Debra.

But not until I got some work done.

I didn't get a chance to Google Debra until I got home from work.

Nigel took Mum out to dinner again, possibly to escape the tense atmosphere in the house as Hal continued to ignore me. I went to

McDonald's and got myself a Big Mac and Hal a Quarter Pounder with cheese, along with fries and chocolate shakes for both of us. I left Hal's on the kitchen table and took mine upstairs to the office, where I fired up the computer.

To my severe surprise, I could not find a single Debra Carpentier. I found a couple of Deborah Carpentiers and countless Debra Carpenters and Deborah Carpenters and Deb Carpenters and Debbie Carpenters. But no Debra Carpentier.

On a hunch, I typed in "Brent Carpentier." I found several, but they were all on the East Coast. The search also turned up many Brents with other last names, including Brent Manning. Could that possibly be our Brent Manning? I clicked on him. Nope. That Brent Manning was located in Southern California, in Orange County—Costa Mesa, to be exact. Gosh. Costa Mesa was pretty close to Newport Beach, as I recalled. Hmmm.

Maybe if I typed in "Brent Manning" from the get-go, I'd come up with a different page with more information. So I tried it. Brent Alexander Manning, CPA, born in … oh my God … Twin Falls, Idaho. College: Brigham Young University. MBA: University of Utah. Last position, a large accounting firm in Costa Mesa, California, and the address, phone number, and website were provided. I wrote them down.

Then I accessed the website. Profiles of all the partners were provided, complete with photographs. There was our Brent, all right. Wife: Debra. Children: Spencer, age twelve, and Kimball, age eight.

No wonder I couldn't find Debra Carpentier. She was Debra Manning.

Only she was divorcing her husband; hence the name change. Back to her maiden name, which was presumably Carpentier. So why couldn't I find her under that name?

Could it be an assumed name? An alias? What would she need an alias for? Why does anyone need an alias?

I could only think of two reasons: being a criminal or trying to escape something.

What kind of criminal activity would Debra Carpentier be involved in? What would she be trying to escape?

Was she in witness protection, perhaps? Would they let her keep her first name?

Maybe she was trying to escape an abusive husband. Marcus had been abusive. It wasn't beyond the realm of possibility that his brother was too. He certainly had been in the parking lot of the Fifteenth Ward LDS Church.

Whatever. Brent knew where she was now, since he had seen her at the funeral. No wonder he'd given her such a vitriolic look when he'd seen her. Maybe the only reason he hadn't attacked her right then and there was because he'd been so busy restraining LaNae.

Did that mean he would attack her later? Was Debra in danger?

I had to know.

I shut down the computer and ran downstairs. Hal was in his recliner, watching TV. I ignored him. I grabbed my purse and opened the door to the garage.

"Where do you think you're going?"

I spun around, clutching my chest in mock surprise. "You spoke! My goodness! What's the occasion?"

"I just wondered where you were going."

"Why do you care?"

He cranked his recliner to a sitting position, got up, and came over to me. "Damn it, Toni. I care because I love you."

I put my hands on my hips and cocked my head to the side. "You don't say. So what was with the silent treatment for the last three days?"

"What was with you ignoring me all that time?"

"Why shouldn't I ignore you? You were ignoring me!"

"Well, I got tired of it."

"I've gotten tired of it every time you've done it. Did that make any difference to you? Hell no."

"So what was different this time?"

"Mum and Nigel are here. I had someone to talk to besides you."

"I didn't like it, being ignored. Usually you pester me to talk to you, and I kind of like that."

"Well, I don't. So how about you quit doing it, huh?"

"I didn't really think you were having an affair with Marcus Manning."

"So you were giving me the silent treatment just for fun?"

"I told you: it wasn't fun."

I threw my hands up. "Then stop doing it!"

Hal threw his hands up too. "Fine. I'll stop. Now, where are you going?"

"To Debra Carpentier's."

"Why?"

"Because I think she may be in danger. Did you know that she was married to Brent Manning?"

"She was?" He seemed genuinely surprised. "How do you know that?"

"Google," I said tersely. "I think her ex-husband may be trying to hurt her. Or kill her. I need to warn her."

Hal put his hands on his hips. "Why can't you just call her? Why do you need to go to her house?"

I put my purse down. "Fine. I'll call her." I stomped over to the kitchen phone and dialed Information. "Debra Carpentier," I snapped when someone answered. "On Canyon Rim Drive."

I wrote down the number, disconnected, and dialed.

Nobody answered.

"See?" I said. "She's not answering. She's probably already dead for all we know. I need to go!"

Hal grabbed me by the shoulders. "Toni. Think. If she's not answering, she's probably not home."

I shook myself loose. "Or she's already dead."

"Then call 911 and let *them* go to her house. What if you went there and found her dead? What would you do?"

I had to admit that he had a point. "Call 911, I guess."

"Then do that. Please don't go rushing off into God knows what kind of danger. I don't want to lose you."

"It scared me so badly to think that I might lose her someday that all I wanted to do was curl up in a little ball and hide." Mike's words echoed in my head. "Is that what this was all about?"

"All what?"

"All this silent treatment. Was that because you thought you might lose me?"

For an answer, Hal put his arms around me and held me so tight that I could hardly breathe. I felt his breath hitch in his chest, and when he finally loosened his hold, I saw that his eyes were wet. "Toni, my dearest love, I couldn't stand the thought of you with that guy."

I pulled back so that I could see his face better. "I'm a little insulted that you could think for a nanosecond that I'd mess with someone like that asshole."

Hal let go of me. "The rumor I heard was that Marcus assaulted you because you'd been involved with him and wanted him to divorce his wife and marry you. I heard that he beat up another woman for that reason, so it made sense."

I clutched my head and turned away from him. "Oh, for heaven's sake, Hal! *I* told you about that. It was my classmate Tom Parker whose wife was having an affair with Marcus. Marcus beat her up and left her on Tom's doorstep. Don't you remember?"

"Oh yeah. Now that you mention it."

"So are we okay now?"

He hugged me again and kissed me with feeling. "Please don't leave me, Toni. I love you so much."

I pulled back and cupped his face in my palms. "I won't leave you, if you don't leave me."

He put his hands over mine. "I *didn't* leave you."

"Yes you did," I insisted. "Not physically, but emotionally, you were out of here. It was worse than if you'd actually left the house, to have you still here but unreachable. If Mum and Nigel hadn't been here …"

"They weren't here much," he said.

"Can you blame them? You could have cut the tension in here with a knife. It couldn't have been pleasant for them either."

"Okay. Point taken," he said. "Now call 911."

I called Pete instead.

"What's up, Toni?"

I told him what I'd found out about Debra. "I'm worried about her.

I think she might be in danger, and she's not answering her phone. I wanted to go check on her, but Hal insisted I call 911 instead."

"Hal's right," Pete said. "If she's in danger, you might run right into it yourself. Tell you what—I'll run over there and check on her myself."

"Can I go with you?"

Behind me Hal said, "*Oy gevalt!*"

"I don't think that's a good idea, Toni," Pete said. "If there really is a situation, I don't want you in the middle of it. Neither does Hal, by the sounds of it."

"I'll stay in the car. I promise. Please?"

Pete sighed. "Okay. As long as you stay in the car. I'll swing by in a few."

Hal grabbed the phone away from me. "No, you won't. She's not going!"

But Pete had already hung up. Hal turned to me. "You're not going."

"Come on, Hal. I told Pete I'd stay in the car. I'll be perfectly safe."

Hal snorted. "Yeah, right. You'll stay in the car. What are the chances?"

Oh, he knew me so well. "I'll be with a cop. What could be safer?"

"Not if you don't stay in the car," Hal pointed out.

"I told you already, I'll stay in the car."

"I don't believe you. I know you. You never stay where you're told. I can't let you go."

At that point, Pete's squad car pulled up. I grabbed my purse and ran out the front door before Hal could stop me.

CHAPTER 32

Lord, Lord! methought, what pain it was to drown!

—*William Shakespeare,* **King Richard III**

Lights were on at Debra's house, and at LaNae's, when we drove up Canyon Rim Drive, even though it was still light. The sun was just setting and reflected off the windows in a peach-colored glow.

Pete had a pass that he swiped at the gate to allow us in. I guessed there would have to be a way for police to get into these gated communities, to say nothing of the fire department. He drove past both houses to a point where the road widened. Then he made a U-turn and parked just beyond LaNae's house, where the trees shielded the squad car from view. "You stay here," he said as he opened the door and got out.

"I will," I promised.

Just then a door slammed and a garage door went up. Pete got back into the car, started it up, and blocked Debra's driveway. He jumped out and ran up the drive to intercept the car backing out.

Well, I was damned if I was going to stay in a car that was about to be broadsided, so I got out too, grabbed my purse, and hid behind a tree to watch. Pete had his gun out, but the occupants of the car were too fast for him. They burst out of the car on both sides, Debra from the passenger side and a tall blond man from the driver's side. Pete had his gun trained on the driver, who turned toward us enough for me to identify him as Marcus's brother Brent. But it was Debra who got off the first shot. Pete fell to the ground and lay ominously still.

Oh, no. No. Not Pete. But Debra wasn't through. She aimed the gun at Brent. "Get going!" she ordered, gesturing toward LaNae's house. "Unless you want to join the cop."

Together they ran across the road and disappeared into the trees around LaNae's property. As quietly as I could, I ran up the driveway to where Pete lay so still and squatted down by his head. To my astonishment, he was breathing, and there was no blood. Gingerly, I stuck a finger through the hole in his shirt and felt some hard, unyielding substance. Of course! He was wearing a Kevlar vest! He was just knocked out. He wasn't dead. But he wasn't in any condition to chase a killer either. And neither was I. I wasn't wearing a vest, for one thing. Nor did I have a gun.

But Pete wasn't using his. I pried it out of his hands and put it in my shorts pocket—after making sure the safety was on. I did know how to shoot. Back in the day, Hal and I had gotten interested in skeet shooting, and I had done quite well at it. Trouble was, those had been shotguns, not handguns, and it had been years ago. But one had to make do in times of trouble, and this sure looked like trouble to me.

I ran over to the car, keeping low and hoping that it blocked any view of me from Debra and Brent, and picked up the radio mic. I pressed what looked like a switch. "Hello? Is anybody there?" I said in a hoarse whisper and let go of the switch.

The radio crackled, and a male voice said, "Identify yourself. Over."

I pressed the switch. "This is Toni Day," I said. "I'm with Pete Vincent, and he's been shot. Over."

"State your location," the voice said. "Over."

I gave him Debra's address on Canyon Rim Drive.

"What's the situation? Over."

"Debra Carpentier has a gun, and she shot Pete," I said. "I think she's holding her ex-husband hostage, and they ran across the road to LaNae Manning's house." I gave that address too.

"Did you say hostage? Over."

"Yes," I said.

"You need to say over, please. Over."

"Oh, sorry," I said. "Over."

"Help is on the way," the voice said, sounding slightly more human. "You stay where you are. Over."

"Okay," I said. "Over and out."

"Toni," said the voice reproachfully, "that was my line. Over and out."

Smiling, I hung up the mic. Of course I had no intention of staying with the car. I couldn't see or hear a thing. The only problem was that if I ran into trouble, I wouldn't have access to the radio. Too bad my cell phone was ... Wait. I dug into my purse and located the pieces of my phone. To my relief, there were only three—the phone, the battery, and the battery cover. I slotted the battery into its space and snapped the cover over it. I turned it on and discovered I had service and three bars of battery power left. I put it on vibrate, stashed it in my other shorts pocket, and stuffed my purse under the front seat.

Then I ran across the road and hid in the trees, trying to see something—anything. There were no lights showing in LaNae's house now. Not a good sign. Stealthily, I made my way through the trees around to the back of the house, which faced the canyon. The sun had set by now, but the pink glow remained, reflected off the river. I crept up to the house, staying below the level of any windows, until I reached the floor-to-ceiling ones facing the river. Only a snake could have stayed below those. I crouched there, trying to hear something.

What I heard did not fill me with joy.

"What are you going to do now, Debra?" I heard Brent say. "First you killed my brother, and now you've killed a cop. If they catch you now, they'll throw the book at you. Cop killers don't do well in the court system. You might not even make it to court. They'll probably just shoot you—accidentally, of course. They'll call it suicide by cop. You just don't think things through. You never did."

Oh my God. So it was Debra, not LaNae, who had put the cyanide in Marcus's lemonade. I wasn't just stalking a kidnapper but a murderer. If she didn't manage to kill me, Hal most certainly would.

"You shut up," Debra said furiously. "I'm through taking shit from you. I'm the one with the gun, or have you forgotten?"

"You won't shoot me," Brent said. "You haven't got the guts."

"You want to take that chance, asshole?"

I didn't hear Brent's reply, because I was losing my balance and needed to move my foot in order not to fall over. It didn't work. I fell over anyway and hastily scrambled back around the side of the house.

"What was that?" I heard Brent say.

"What was what?"

"Didn't you hear that?"

"I didn't hear anything. You're just trying to distract me so you can get my gun away from me. Well, it won't work."

"I'm telling you, there's somebody out there."

"Okay, you go look. I'll be right behind you."

The sliding door swished open, and I held my breath. They stepped out on the stone patio and looked around. They must not have seen me, because they went back inside. But they didn't close the door.

"See?" Debra said with undisguised sarcasm. "There's nobody out there. Your little scheme didn't work. Don't try it again."

"Or you'll do what?" Brent taunted her. "Shoot me? You wouldn't dare. My family won't pay you one red cent for my dead body."

Oh my God, I thought. *This isn't just a hostage situation. It's a kidnapping for ransom. That's why Debra hasn't already shot him.* I wondered what the ransom was.

"You aren't worth a red cent," Debra returned. "Or a plugged nickel either. Not to me. Let's hope your family thinks otherwise."

"They're not stupid," Brent said. "They're not going to play by your rules. They're going to send the police after you, and they're certainly not going to pay you ten million dollars."

"They will if they ever want to see you alive again," Debra replied.

"What are you going to do with ten million dollars? Gamble it all away like you did before?"

"No way," Debra said in a smug tone. "I don't have to depend on your paltry salary at Scrooge and Marley's countinghouse anymore." I supposed she was referring to the accounting firm Brent worked for in California. "I was trying to make your money work for me."

"Right," he mimicked. "And you fucked that up, as usual. You never could do anything right. You finally had a decent job, and now that's gone too."

"With ten million dollars, I'll never have to work again. So you can just stuff it, dickweed."

My cell phone vibrated. Shit! I couldn't answer it; they'd hear me. I crept toward the trees at the edge of the property. Of course, by the time I reached a suitable spot out of sight of the house, and hopefully out of earshot, it had stopped ringing. I flipped it open. *Missed call. Hal.* I pressed Send to call him back. "Where the hell are you?" he hissed. "Bernie Kincaid just called here looking for you. I told him you were with Pete at Debra Carpentier's house, but he said Pete had been shot and his gun was missing and you were nowhere to be seen. So where are you?"

"I'm at LaNae's house," I whispered. "Hiding in the trees. Debra is holding Brent Manning hostage inside the house and asking for ten million dollars."

"Shit! Where's LaNae? What about the kids? And the dogs?"

"There's nobody else here," I said.

"You get out of there right now!" he insisted, but at that moment I heard angry voices.

"I told you there was someone out here," Brent said.

"You don't have to keep on about it, asshole. I heard it too. Over here in the trees."

I flipped the cell phone closed and flattened myself.

"I don't see anything," Brent said.

I felt a sneeze coming on, and despite pinching my nostrils shut, I couldn't prevent it.

"There you are! Hey you! Show yourself!"

Well, that would have been a stupid thing to do, what with a deranged madwoman brandishing a gun at me. Of course, if she was aiming that thing at me, she wasn't aiming it at Brent, who took the opportunity to bolt.

In a lightning-fast motion, Debra had the gun back on him and away from me, and I took the opportunity to bolt too. But just as fast, she swung the gun back to me and fired. I dove over the side of the canyon, and the shot missed me.

But once over the side, I couldn't stop rolling. Debra, standing at the edge, continued to fire at me. I tried to roll in a zigzag path, and it seemed to work; either that or she was a lousy shot. And there were entirely too many rocks on this slope. I fetched up against a boulder in plain sight of Debra, who loosed off another shot. I dove behind the boulder and the shot ricocheted off it, sending down a cloud of dust that made me sneeze again. My eyes itched, and my nasal passages had slammed shut in the course of my precarious path down the canyon wall. I was now about twenty feet above the river, with only a gnarled tree branch extending out over the water to stop me from falling the rest of the way, and in the throes of a major allergy attack.

I heard another shot and a scream from Brent. "You fucking bitch!" he yelled. Apparently she had overcome her initial reluctance to shoot him, but he clearly wasn't dead, because he continued to hurl invective at her from the patio.

Debra started making her way down the side of the canyon toward me. She was doing a much better job than I had, managing to keep her feet under her. "Now I've got you," she called to me. "I know exactly where you are, and you've got nowhere to go but into the river!"

She was right about that. Of course, the tree branch would break my fall, but then I'd be more of a sitting duck than I was now.

Debra made her way inexorably down the steep slope toward my boulder. Once she got around where she could get off a clear shot, I'd be dead. I had to get out from behind this boulder. I looked around for a safer way down, but there was no other way but to grab the tree branch, hope it would hold me, and swing myself down into the water.

So that was what I did. I landed in the water and fell on my butt, which of course drowned my cell phone and rendered it useless. I hoped it hadn't done the same to Pete's gun. The water only came up to my shoulders as I sat there on my butt, and if there'd been a beach, I could easily have crawled out of the water. But as it was, there was nowhere to go except upstream or downstream. Downstream would be easier, but it would also be in plain sight. So I made my way upstream until I came to another large boulder. I hid behind it and waited.

Debra had to have heard the splash, and I was sure she had heard me making my way upstream as well. I heard no sound from her. What I heard was a much more welcome sound. Sirens.

Well, it's about fucking time, I thought. What had they been doing all this time? They'd had time to finish their dinners and watch a couple of TV sitcoms by now.

But when I looked at my watch, I saw that barely fifteen minutes had passed since Pete and I had arrived at Debra's house.

No matter. Debra was lying in wait somewhere on the other side of this boulder, and they were still out on the road in their cruisers. How long would it take them to get their butts down this hill and rescue me?

A hell of a lot longer than it would take Debra to find me and finish me off—that was for sure. So what was I going to do, just stay here and wait? Like a rabbit that thinks if it stays very still nobody will see it? Maybe a rabbit could get away with it, being brown, but I was wearing bright-blue shorts and a turquoise top, in contrast to the green-and-brown brush around me behind this gray rock. Any minute she'd see me and blow my head off. All I had to do was … *Oh God, no, here comes another one …*

Debra stepped around my boulder, aimed her gun, and fired … just as I sneezed. The shot parted my hair but did no obvious damage. She fired again. Click. She was out of ammunition. I pulled Pete's gun out of my pocket and aimed it at her. With her face twisted in hate, she sprang at me.

I turned and dove into the river. I swam out and let the current carry me downstream, well out of her reach. I could have shot her. It would have been self-defense. Why hadn't I? People would ask. What would I say?

It was getting dark. The sunset's colors had faded. But I could still see Debra in her bright-yellow top, walking into the river and starting to swim in my direction. Holy crap, but she was a good swimmer. Fast, too. Much faster than I was. She'd be catching up to me any minute now. I still had the gun in my hand, which slowed down my crawl stroke—none too good to begin with. I sidestroked away from her, keeping her in sight. Any minute now ...

Suddenly she dove under the water. I could no longer see her, but I felt her. She had grabbed my feet and was pulling me down. I took a deep breath and put my head under. Now I could see her. I aimed the gun in the general direction of the yellow top and fired.

She let go of me. Blood blossomed from the yellow top. She wasn't moving. She began to sink. Soon she'd be out of sight. They'd have to drag the river, and God knew where she'd be by then.

I stuck my head above the water, took another breath, and dived down to grab her by the hair. The current was getting stronger now, and I stroked hard with the hand that still held the gun, kicking as hard as I could to get both our heads above water. I managed to get her on her back and hold her head up on my chest as we both floated farther downstream. Where would we end up? I wondered. Would anyone see us, now that it was nearly full dark? Would I be able to get us onto the shore somewhere accessible? Centennial Park? Kanaka Rapids? Hagerman?

Not that I'd be able to see where we were in the dark.

Suddenly my feet touched bottom, and I found myself lying on a rocky surface with Debra's inert body on top of me.

I looked up and saw tall columns of red rock jutting out of the water. Now I knew exactly where we were. Pillar Falls.

This was good news and bad news. The good news was we were on dry land. The bad news was this bit of dry land was accessible only by boat. Heaven knew how long that would take.

In the spring, when the water was high from the snowmelt, Pillar Falls was completely underwater. Water from upstream cascaded over it, and it really *was* a falls. Only the pillars were visible, and boats could get around them. But in July when the water was low, the rocky bottom was completely out of the water, and boaters had to portage across it.

If this had happened in April, we'd be well on our way to the Columbia by now, and from there out to sea; and we'd probably die of hypothermia in the process.

I maneuvered Debra's body off me and onto a flat, rocky surface, pulling her until her feet were out of the water. I felt for a pulse. To my astonishment, she had one. Suddenly she drew a shaky breath, and blood bubbled out of her mouth.

She was alive, but for how much longer? Evidently, I'd shot her in a lung. And now that my cell phone was permanently out of service, I had no way of telling anyone where we were.

So I sat next to Debra's unconscious form and listened to her wet, gurgling attempts to breathe, which were getting less and less frequent. Eventually they stopped altogether. I felt for a pulse. She no longer had one. She was dead.

Could I have done something? I wondered. But as a physician, I knew that there was nothing I could have done. She would've had to have been right next door to a hospital where she could have been rushed into surgery and had a thoracotomy to repair the hole in her lung.

I had killed her. Sure, it had been self-defense. She'd been trying to drown me. She'd fired several shots at me. I could have shot her at point-blank range right at the water's edge, but instead I'd dived into the water to get away from her. I'd fled rather than shoot her. I'd only shot her when she'd grabbed my feet and pulled me under the water.

A gripping tale, to be sure. I could have made the whole thing up. There were no witnesses. No living ones, at any rate.

When Brent Manning found out that I'd killed his ex-wife—or maybe she was still his wife, I didn't really know—he'd want me charged with murder. Bernie Kincaid would be only too happy to cooperate.

But she was trying to kill me, I'd protest, and he'd ask me if anyone could corroborate that.

Well, no. She's dead.

Well, there you are. He said, she said.

I had just worked myself up into a nice little panic when I heard a sound. It got louder. I'd just identified it as an outboard motor when I saw lights from downstream shining on the canyon walls. I jumped up and climbed across the rocks until I could see the lights bobbing on the water, whereupon I began jumping up and down and waving, totally forgetting that they couldn't get past us if they tried.

As the boat got closer, I saw that it was a police launch, and I could make out faces. There was Bernie Kincaid and, oh my God, Pete! There were also a couple of paramedics whose faces looked familiar. The bow eventually drifted gently up onto the rocks, and Pete jumped out and wrapped the bowline around a handy rock. He grabbed me and wrapped his arms around me. "Thank God you're okay," he said fervently. "Hal was a basket case."

"Thank God you're okay too," I said. "I thought you were dead, but when I checked you, I saw that you were wearing a vest."

"Yeah. It just knocked the wind out of me for a bit, and my chest is gonna be sore for a few days, but I'm fine. How's she?" he asked, gesturing toward Debra.

I looked and saw the paramedics scrambling over the rocks with a stretcher. "She's dead," I said. "I killed her, Pete. With your gun. Here," I said, pulling it out of my waistband where I'd stuck it. "Take it. It's evidence."

He took it, turning it over in his hand. "Jesus, Toni, don't you know to keep the safety on? You could have shot yourself in the belly!"

Uh-oh. "I guess I forgot," I said. "I had a few other things on my mind. Like being a murderer, for instance."

"Surely it was self-defense," he said. "Wasn't she trying to kill you?"

"Yes, she was, but there's nobody who saw it."

"I wouldn't worry," he said. "I can testify that she tried to kill *me*, and I've got the bruise and the hole in my shirt to prove it. She was a killer, Toni, and nobody will have any trouble believing you. We'll find the slugs where she shot at you. And by the way, there *was* a witness, at least for some of it."

"There was? Who?"

"Brent Manning. He saw the whole thing, at least until you both jumped into the water and drifted out of sight."

"I thought she shot him," I said.

"She shot him in the kneecap. So he couldn't walk, but he managed to drag himself over to the edge of the patio and watch everything over the retaining wall there. He'll be only too happy to testify on your behalf."

I wasn't so sure. "Really? I killed his wife. And you think he's going to testify in my defense?"

"He said so," Pete said. "He mentioned it before anyone asked him about it. He said she was the one who poisoned Marcus. Apparently she was a real piece of work. He's well rid of her. Anyone in the Manning family will agree, he said. They've all had to deal with her at one time or another."

An ambulance was waiting at the dock in Centennial Park when we arrived. Rollie's hearse stood next to it. "Who's that for?" I asked Pete, gesturing to the ambulance as we all clambered out of the police launch onto the dock.

"It's for you," he said.

"I don't need an ambulance," I protested. "I'm fine."

He looked me up and down speculatively. "Have you taken a good look at yourself?" he asked. "Because you look like hell."

I looked down at myself. My turquoise top was soaked in blood. My legs were a road map of cuts, scrapes, and bruises. A flap of skin hung from my right knee. It would bleed like stink once I warmed up. My arms didn't look much better. Well. Clearly that knee flap needed attention. The rest would heal by itself. "Okay," I said.

One of the paramedics opened the back door to the ambulance so that I could climb inside, but before I could, Hal materialized beside me and picked me up in his arms. That was when I realized that there was a huge abrasion on my back where I'd been pushed up on the rocks of Pillar Falls by the current. My turquoise top must have been hanging on by shreds. "Hey!" I said. "Take it easy."

Hal passed me to the paramedic inside. "Don't bitch at me," he said. "I didn't want you to go, but off you went anyway. You're lucky you got away with just scrapes and bruises."

The back doors closed behind me while the paramedic carefully arranged me on a gurney and immobilized my head. "I don't need that," I objected. "I walked here under my own power, after all."

"You've got a head injury," he told me. "We can't take any chances."

"Head injury?" I asked. I didn't remember hitting my head on anything.

"You've got a six-inch laceration on the top of your head," he said. "It looks deep. I'm surprised you're not bleeding more."

Oh. I would have reached up and felt it, but the paramedic had thoughtfully restrained my hands. "That must have been the bullet," I said.

"Bullet?"

"Yeah. Debra shot at me. She would have hit me too if I hadn't sneezed. It went right over my head."

I was pretty sure I heard a muffled *"Oy gevalt!"* from Hal in the front seat.

"Well, it didn't go *over* your head," the paramedic said. "It plowed a furrow right down the middle of your scalp. Doesn't it hurt?"

"Not so far."

He stuck the tip of a digital thermometer in my mouth, and when it beeped, he removed it. "You're hypothermic. Your temperature is ninety-four. That's why you're not bleeding and nothing hurts yet. Just wait."

I didn't have to wait long. It took only a few minutes to reach the hospital from Centennial Park. At that time of night, there wasn't much traffic. By the time the paramedics whisked me into the emergency room, I could feel the blood running down the back of my head, and the bandage that the paramedic had wrapped around my knee flap was already soaked through with blood. All the scrapes I could see on my arms and legs looked much gorier than they had in the light of police flashlights. And everything was beginning to hurt. A lot.

Soon I was ensconced in a cubicle with Hal by my side and a nurse who took my vital signs and asked for my insurance card.

"I don't have it," I said.

"Where is it?" Hal asked.

"In my purse, which as far as I know is still stuffed under the front seat of Pete's squad car," I said.

"That's all right, Doctor. You can get it later," she said, putting the clipboard aside and setting to work on my injuries. She put a pad on my scalp laceration, a new bandage on my knee, and applied antibiotic ointment and bandages to the more superficial abrasions. But when she got to my back, she shook her head. "That one's nasty. It's gonna have to be debrided. It's got *rocks* embedded in it."

Jeez. No wonder it hurt so much. Thank God it hadn't been hurting this much in the ambulance when I'd been strapped down on my back.

But my suffering wasn't over. Next stop was radiology—sorry, diagnostic imaging—for a neck x-ray and a CT scan of my head, which required me to lie on my back.

When I got back to my cubicle, Mum, Nigel, and Pete were keeping Hal company there. Pete had brought my purse. "Thought you might need this," he said.

"Antoinette!" exclaimed my mother. "What is the meaning of running off and deliberately putting yourself in danger? Do you have any idea what you've put your poor husband through? I ought to tan your backside!"

Hal looked smug. I gave him a dirty look through slitted eyes, still puffy from my allergy attack. "I rather think that's been done," I told her. "Wait till you *see* my back."

She opened her mouth for another blast, but Dave Martin came in and effectively shortcut any further outbursts. "Toni. This is getting old."

"No shit, Sherlock," I said rudely, whereupon my mother came in with her usual "Antoinette, *really*, your language!"

"Okay," Dave said. "Lie back and let me examine you."

"No, please don't make me lie on my back. It really hurts. Can't you examine me sitting up?"

"I suppose so," he said. "Let me see your back."

Obligingly, I turned so he could see it, and at that angle, so could Mum and Hal. Mum gasped. Hal put a hand over his mouth. Nigel harrumphed and pulled at his moustache.

"Okay," Dave said. "I want all of you out of this room. First I'm going to sew up her scalp laceration, then the knee, and then debride her back. After that, she's going to spend the night in the hospital on IV antibiotics. Heaven knows what she might have gotten into in the river. You can wait outside, or you can go home. This is going to take a while."

Pete said, "I need to interview her. Can I do that while you're patching her up?"

"It's okay with me if it's okay with Toni," Dave said.

And so while Dave stitched and stitched and picked rocks, I told Pete everything that had happened between Debra's bullet putting him down for the count and me being rescued by the police launch.

"You know, if I read this in a book, I wouldn't believe it," Dave remarked.

"Believe it," I said. "I'm living proof."

"And Debra isn't," Pete said. "Are you gonna have to do the autopsy? Because—"

"No, thank God," I said, silently giving thanks for my partner. "Mike can do it."

CHAPTER 33

Revenge, at first though sweet,
Bitter ere long back on itself recoils.

—*John Milton*, **Paradise Lost**

With IV pain medication on board, I slept like a baby. In the morning, however, I awoke feeling three hundred years old. But everything hurt. Even places I didn't know were injured hurt. Every muscle in my body hurt. I could barely move.

On a bright note, the puffiness from my allergy attack had subsided. That allergy attack had saved my life.

Nonetheless, I got discharged with oral pain meds and oral antibiotics and strict orders not to get anything wet for ten days.

"Ten days!" I objected. "My hair's full of blood. And it's July. I'll stink so bad Hal's going to make me sleep out on the porch."

But they were adamant.

"Come on, sweetie," Hal said. "We'll manage."

And we did. When we got home, he helped me sponge bathe and wash the blood out of my hair. Mum fixed me lunch. Nigel offered me the use of his smoking jacket, which I politely declined on the basis of extreme summer heat. Here in southern Idaho, in late July and early August, temperatures typically topped one hundred degrees, and this year was no exception.

So I lay on the couch in the blessed air-conditioning, in clean shorts and a tank top—the old ones having been deemed unsalvageable—with a drink, a book, and Geraldine curled up on my stomach like a furry little heating pad. I welcomed her body heat on my sore muscles but wondered how I was going to teach her not to walk on my legs for the next couple of weeks. Then I fell asleep.

Several people called. I vaguely recalled Mum answering the phone, thanking someone for their concern, and telling them I was sleeping and she would pass on the message when I awoke.

My first visitor, late in the afternoon, was Mike.

"Whew! Hot enough to fry an egg out there, I tell you what" was his first comment as he sank into my recliner with a gusty sigh. The dogs got right up close and personal, and Geraldine, fickle female that she is, jumped into his lap.

"I know," I said. "It was hot enough when I got home from the hospital this morning."

"Well," he said, getting right down to business, "I just finished Debra's autopsy. Bullet went right through her. Tore a hell of a hole in her lung, and did you happen to see the exit wound?"

I hadn't.

"Well, it was impressive, I tell you what," he said. "What the hell did you shoot her with? A cannon?"

"I don't know," I said. "It was Pete's gun."

"How the hell did you get Pete's gun?" he demanded.

So I told him the whole gory story, and he seemed suitably impressed. So did Mum, and I realized that this was the first time she'd actually heard the whole thing. She put her hands over her face, and Nigel came and put his arms around her, stroking her hair as she clung to him. How lucky she was to have found such a caring man after being alone for so long with nobody but a daughter who kept trying to get herself killed—a fact that Nigel pointed out to me with some asperity when he joined us, lowering himself into Hal's recliner.

"Are you purposely trying to shorten your mother's life?" he demanded. "Because you scare her out of ten years' growth every time you get into these situations. I just found her, and I'm not ready to lose her yet, thank you very much."

"Nigel, please," Mum said, perching on the arm of the recliner. "I taught Antoinette to be on the side of right and not to back away from a fight. She's just doing what she was brought up to do."

He put his arm around her and harrumphed. "You're right, Fiona, as usual, and I wouldn't have reacted like that if I didn't love you so much. Bit hair-raising, that story, eh what? Come; let's let these young folks get back to business. Care for a libation?"

That was one of the things I loved about my new stepfather-to-be.

They went into the kitchen, and I said to Mike, "That sounds like a good idea. What can I get you?"

"A nice cold beer, if you've got it," he said.

Hal came into the kitchen through the connecting door from the garage, bearing groceries. "That sounds like a good idea," he said. "Scotch on the rocks for you, Toni, or will it fight with your pain meds?"

"It might put me to sleep, but since I'm already lying down, I don't really care. Bring it on."

"What I want to know," Mike said, "is why the hell you didn't shoot Debra when she shot at you and ran out of ammo. You could have saved yourself all that trauma in the river."

"I don't know," I said. "Maybe because I was looking her in the eyes. Maybe I didn't want to see her die because of me. All I know is that when she sprang at me, my first instinct was to get away from her."

"Good thing you held on to the gun," he said, "or you'd have drowned."

At this point Hal brought us our drinks. "Keep your voice down," he cautioned. "I don't want Fiona to hear that."

"Do you suppose this has anything to do with Marcus's death?" Mike asked.

"Definitely," I said. "I heard Marcus's brother Brent say that she was the poisoner. She didn't deny it."

"Funny thing happened the other day, now that you mention it," he said. "I wanted to get an iron stain, and Lucille said she couldn't find the potassium ferrocyanide; it wasn't in the cupboard. She was going to order some more, but this morning I saw it, right back where it belongs. I pointed it out to Lucille, and she swore that it was gone the day I'd wanted that iron stain."

"That makes sense. Timewise, it fits."

"Are you gonna be able to come to work tomorrow?"

"I think so."

"Okay." He drained his beer. "I'll see you in the morning."

Hal saw Mike out and then sat in his recliner, sipping his beer. "Did you hear all that?" I asked him.

"Yeah. How about you tell me what happened last night? I still haven't heard the whole story."

I obliged. Mum and Nigel joined us, Mum having recovered from the shock of the first telling. Perhaps it softened with the retelling, like sharp edges being worn smooth with repeated use. Perhaps she had already mentally filed it under Antoinette's Little Misadventures, saving it up to tell it to her friends in Long Beach. Maybe it was easier to think about it that way, rather than harping on how close I'd come to dying. I, on the other hand, couldn't deny the reality of it, having actually been there. I would probably be waking in a cold sweat from time to time, from reliving it in my nightmares, just as I had with my other little misadventures.

Pete and Bambi came over after supper. They had both been busy all day, Pete doing interviews and taking statements from members of the Manning family, and Bambi getting extra credit in her college classes by hanging out at the crime lab and helping to analyze evidence.

"Speaking of which," I said, "where were LaNae and the kids last night?"

"They're all with the grandparents," Pete said. "Marcus's parents."

"Debra's kids too?"

"Yes. They were scared to let any of the kids out of their sight, in case Debra had any ideas about kidnapping them too, and LaNae thought they'd be safer there."

"Did those poor people have a prayer of coming up with ten million dollars?" Mum asked.

"They thought they could," Pete said, "if they all chipped in. There are three more brothers, you know, and they're all doing well at whatever it is that they do."

"Except Marcus," I said.

"Well, yes, they did refer to him more than once as the black sheep," Pete said. "He was the youngest and had grown up spoiled and feeling entitled."

"How did they talk about Debra?" I asked.

"Well, that's a story in itself," Pete said. "Apparently she had serious mental problems. Bipolar, at the very least. Borderline personality disorder. She could be charming, as long as she stayed on her meds. Trouble is, she didn't, and then she'd get into trouble. She'd pick up men in bars, steal cars and go on joyrides, crash parties, get high on street drugs, disturb the peace. She's got quite a rap sheet, our Debra, down in California."

"No wonder Brent called her a piece of work," I said. "So were they divorced or not?"

"They were. Brent divorced her. Said she'd cost him enough. And also, he corroborated your story in every detail, so you don't need to worry about being charged with murder, like I said last night."

"Good heavens!" Mum exclaimed. "I never even thought of that."

"In that case," Nigel said comfortably, "no need to think of it now, eh what?"

Bambi hadn't said much, which was unusual for her, considering how enthusiastic she usually was about her studies, especially now that she'd gotten her chance to be involved in one of "my" cases.

After they left, Hal commented on it. "Bambi looked like she didn't feel good."

"She said she was just tired," I said. "Maybe she just needs some sleep." But as I said that, I reflected that Bambi hadn't just looked tired; she'd looked sick. She'd been pale, almost green …

"Oh my God," I said. "Do you suppose she's pregnant?"

Hal looked surprised. "I suppose it's possible," he said.

"Oh, how wonderful," Mum said. "You'll be grandparents."

"Now, Fiona," Nigel cautioned, "don't go putting the cart before the horse."

"No, dear," Mum said, her lips curved in a little secret smile.

Mothers always know.

I wondered about Hal, though. How did he feel about being a grandfather? He'd only had two years to get used to being a father, and Bambi had been married to Pete for most of that time. But when I turned to look at him, he was smiling too.

However, before I allowed myself to get carried away by visions of grandmotherhood, I needed to clear some things up. So I hauled out my laptop, got on the Internet, and Googled Debra Manning.

"What are you doing?" Hal asked.

"Looking up Debra, now that I know what her last name really is. Hey, here she is. Last known position, public relations coordinator at Hoag Memorial Hospital in Newport Beach, California. And she was there at the same time as Marcus. She already knew him when she came here."

"She would have known him anyway, being married to his brother," Hal pointed out. "Do you suppose they were having an affair down there, and it continued when she followed him up here?"

"Maybe. Who knows?" I said, and then I had an idea. "I bet I know who'd really know about that."

I called my former fellow resident Patti, who was happy to hear from me again so soon and all too ready to dish the dirt about the biggest scandal to hit Hoag since the one about herself and Syd.

"Everybody was talking about it," she told me. "She'd been having an affair with him; heaven knows how long it'd been going on. It turned out she was married to his brother, of all things, and he didn't even know."

"A family affair," I said.

"You could call it that. Anyway, the shit hit the fan when she got impatient and started bugging him about divorcing his wife and marrying her. He beat her up and dumped her on her husband's doorstep; then he rang the doorbell and left."

"That sounds familiar," I said.

"You mean he did that up there too?"

"No, here he beat *me* up, so to speak. No, he did something like that at John Wayne."

"Oh yeah. There was something in the papers about that. Something about sexual harassment."

"That was him."

"So how are your arms?"

"Fine." I didn't want to interrupt her story by telling her how my arms really were, not to mention the rest of me. "So then what happened?"

"Well, her husband divorced her, and then she left."

"Were the police involved at all?"

"Not that I know of. What I heard was that her husband took her to the emergency room, the police came, and she wouldn't press charges."

"That old story."

"Yeah, wouldn't you think they'd learn?"

"You'd think."

"Why did you want to know all this, Toni?"

I told her about everything from Marcus's death to the happenings of the previous night.

"Oh my God. You mean they're both dead?"

"As doornails."

"And you actually *shot* her?"

"Well, it was either that or be drowned," I said.

"Do you suppose she followed Marcus up there to get revenge?"

Ya think? "Definitely. Then she tried to get revenge on her ex-husband too. And the whole family."

"Wow. What a story. I can't wait to tell Syd."

We said our goodbyes and hung up. I could just see Patti, rubbing her hands together and giggling fiendishly at the prospect of telling her partner all about it.

"So what did you find out, kitten?" Mum asked.

I told her.

"My goodness," she remarked. "What a mess. There was more to it than sexual harassment at work, then. This took a bit of premeditation."

"They do say that revenge is a dish best served cold," I agreed.

"Blimey," said Nigel, "I'd say the blighter got what was coming to him, eh what?"

"If they put it on the telly," Mum said, giggling, "nobody'd believe it."

"They also say that truth is stranger than fiction," Hal said. "Now, do you suppose we can settle down long enough to have a wedding?"

EPILOGUE

Mum and Nigel were married in my backyard on Saturday, August 1. Father Fred did a lovely service.

Hal was the best man; I was the matron of honor. Bambi and Jodi were the bridesmaids; Pete and Elliott were the groomsmen. Five-year-old Emily Maynard, whom Jodi and Elliott had adopted two years ago, served as both flower girl and ring bearer. I watched in trepidation lest she throw the rings and hold on to the flowers, but she didn't. Renee Maynard, Jodi and Elliott's daughter and Bambi's best friend, took pictures.

Mum wore a cool green floral muumuu that complemented her red hair and green eyes. Nigel wore white slacks and a Hawaiian shirt, as did all the groomsmen. The bridesmaids wore muumuus too. Everyone wore leis. The weather was lovely; it was sunny, with the temperature topping out at 105. Which was why we had the reception indoors, with the doors closed and the air-conditioning running full blast. Then we all went to the country club for dinner.

The bride and groom left for their honeymoon in Hawaii the next day. Hal and I were on our own again. That is, until the arrival of our grandchild.

Bambi definitely was pregnant. Far from looking sick, she looked radiantly happy. Lucky for her, the morning sickness was short-lived.

It was Elliott who tied up the last loose ends of the mystery for us. These lawyers all know each other.

Brent Manning went back to California, leaving his kids with his sister-in-law, LaNae, the superwife. And of course, every superwife needs a husband.

So LaNae married her divorce lawyer, with whom she'd been having an affair.

Oy gevalt!

THE END

ACKNOWLEDGMENTS

The inspiration for this novel, as with my previous ones, came from thirty-plus years as a pathologist in a small rural town. This is a work of fiction. All the characters in it are figments of my imagination, and any resemblance to any real persons is coincidental. Any anachronisms, medical misstatements, or other errors are entirely mine.

Some of the places in the book are real, such as the Snake River Canyon, the Perrine Bridge, Pillar Falls, and Centennial Park; however, Perrine Memorial Hospital and Southern Idaho Community College are fictitious.

My heartfelt thanks go to my dear friend Dr. Semih Erhan, who would not let me give up. Without his incessant encouragement, my first novel would have never seen the light of day.

Thanks are in order for many other people as well:

Thank you to Janet Reid of FinePrint Literary Management, whose advice has been invaluable. She read several versions of my first novel, and although she ultimately rejected it, without her input Toni Day wouldn't be the kick-ass character she is.

Thank you to Dennis Chambers, formerly of the Twin Falls Police Department, formerly county coroner, for information on police procedure and for introducing me to the police lab. I'm still using the book he gave me twenty years ago.

Thank you to my good friend Marilyn Paul, Twin Falls County public defender, for getting me into the courtroom and giving me essential information on courtroom procedure.

Thank you to my dear friend Teala Percin, who answered all my Mormon questions.

Thank you to my BFF, Rhonda Wong, who reads my drafts and points out all my egregious errors, lets me bounce ideas off her ad nauseam, and comes up with ideas of her own that she lets me use.

Finally, to all the folks at iUniverse, without whom this book would not exist.

Fans of medical drama and mysteries will be sure to love this fast-paced and fact-laced romp through the world of pathology.

—US Review of Books

I was not at all surprised to see that the author is a pathologist. It is to her credit that she is able to write a mystery with so much technical detailing involved and makes it so very interesting—not at all like a classroom lecture.

—Caryn St. Clair for Booksellersworld.com

I found myself thinking of Miss Marple in the Agatha Christie novels or Hercule Poirot since it reads very much like a classic whodunit. Told very effectively in the first person, the story moves along at a good pace as Toni slowly peels back the murder mystery like the layers of an onion and I look forward to the next Toni Day mystery. Five stars for Jane Bennett Munro and *Death by Autopsy*.

—Terry Rollins, Amazon top reviewer

PRAISE FOR *THE BODY ON THE LIDO DECK*

An entertaining murder mystery to cruise through.

—Kirkus Reviews

The Body on the Lido Deck will keep readers guessing until the action-packed end. And when it's all over, the story's satisfying solution will leave them eager to explore Toni Day's other adventures.

—BlueInk Reviews

This book offers believable dialogue, a breakneck pace, and a unique story that breathes new life into the literary murder-comedy genre. It's Jessica Fletcher meets *CSI*, with the usual crime-scene gore and droning medical jargon now wrapped up in a charming, entertaining package.

—Clarion Reviews

The mystery's nomadic setting—on a cruise ship still on course for its vacation destinations—and the protagonist's go-getter attitude make for an enthralling beach read.

—US Review of Books

Printed in the United States
By Bookmasters